The Potential of Heartbreak

A Novel

EMMA WAGNER

I want to dedicate this book to the boys who broke my heart or left scars that only I could see. Thank you for teaching me that I deserve better.

But even more than that, I want to dedicate this book to the people who helped piece me back together, with the perspective I didn't have, into a stronger and more beautiful mosaic.

But most of all, I want to thank my mama who has been the biggest support for me throughout this process. You are everything to me.

I love you.

PART I

Chapter 1

"What are you looking at, weirdo?" Her eyes shoot up to catch him staring.

"Nothing!" A warm rush washes over him as he averts his eyes. *Everything*. He chances another glance at her, admiring the little details that make him smile, like the way her hair falls in golden waves over her shoulders, how her freckles have darkened in just the first week of summer, the chipped polish on her fingernails (his favorite color), and especially the way she sticks out her tongue when she tries to concentrate. She's done that her whole life, yet it makes him smile every time he notices it.

"Done!" He jolts back, startled.

"Done what?" he asks, trying to look uninterested.

"Give me your hand." She reaches for him.

"Why?"

"Just give it to me!" She grabs his hand. Her fingers are warm against his sweating palm. "Here." She places a meticulously crafted bracelet of varying blues in his hand.

The sun shifts through the open window, igniting his amber eyes to pools of honey. Her stomach flutters when he looks at her that way with his crooked smile. "I love it." Their eyes finally connect, the blue waves of hers melting into the amber glow of his. Maybe those eyes inspired his love of the color. "Will you put it on?"

She nods, tucking a loose strand of hair behind her unpierced ear. “It’s so you don’t forget me when you’re gone.” A breeze drifts through the window, the tree house groans with age, and her hair shifts back into her face.

In a gentle movement he guides the hair back, lingering against her skin. Her fingers fumble tying the knot, but she can feel the pulse in his wrist thrum faster, which puts her at ease.

“There.” It’s nearly a whisper. Her face burns where his hand rests by her ear. She can feel him smiling at her but her eyes remain lowered.

“We have all summer.” She leans into his palm, now warm and comforting. “Look at me, Lele.” Her eyes flick up to rest in his. “I could never forget you.”

At once they shift, entangling in each other’s arms for a familiar embrace.

“Everly, Jackson,” her mother calls from the back porch. “Come in for dinner.”

The butterflies of youthful souls mingle in a delicate dance as their cheeks mirror the glow of young hearts ignited for one another.

⁕

“Don’t you dare, Jax!” Everly shrieks, dodging the water balloon. Her mouth gapes open as it bursts against the tree behind her.

But where he thrives in speed, she thrives in accuracy. Hiding behind the swingset, she jumps out to fling a water balloon in his direction. It explodes against his bare back, dousing him with water as he runs for the tree house ladder. Her squeals of victory ring through the neighborhood.

Jackson climbs up, taking cover. He chances a look through the cutout window and falls backwards as a yellow balloon flies straight for him, raining water across the floor as it ruptures against the wall. “Hey!” he shouts out to her.

"Come out and face me," she taunts. "Scaredy-cat!" She knows exactly how to get under his skin. Jackson never turns down a challenge.

In a second, he's on the ground racing for her, her legs propelling her as fast as they can. But it's not enough. They collide hard, sliding on the wet grass until coming to a stop. Everly cradles her stomach as it aches from laughing, and Jackson props himself up on his forearms above her.

I love that dimple. He looks at her as she finally settles down. "Oh!" He reaches for her temple where a single trickle of blood runs over a few freckles and disappears into a golden maze of hair. "Lele, I'm so sorry."

She touches the cut, flinching harshly. A smile beams across her face as she watches his concern grow. "I'm just kidding!" She pokes him in the ribs. "It doesn't hurt." Jackson supports himself on one arm as he examines her injury further. "Really, Jax. I'm okay."

He runs his fingers through her hair in search of any other injuries. Confident that he hasn't hurt her too badly, he looks back at her face. Those beautiful eyes staring up at him. He falls. Not physically, but hopelessly into those pools of blue that trace along his lips.

Still holding himself above her, he's close enough for their breath to mingle. A summer breeze kisses his skin and shifts his dark hair across his temples. The sound of the trees is barely audible over their heartbeats pounding in sync.

Everly looks into his shadowed eyes, her lips parting slightly. Jackson shifts on his arms, his eyes studying her features when a rush of water pours over him as she pops a water balloon. Everly throws her head back cackling, and Jackson pulls her to his lips. A warm wave surges through both of them as their lips learn to move together. Their first kiss.

At once they pull apart, cheeks red and smiles beaming in a way they never have before.

❊

“Don’t you dare, Jax.” It hurts to speak. It’s like her throat’s a chimney guiding the flames of a raging fire. “Don’t say it,” she begs.

“Lele…” He pauses. “Come lie with me.” Everly sits with her back to him by the windowsill, arms crossed and eyes low. He taps on the glass, three gentle knocks. Just like always. “Please.”

The moon reflects silver in her eyes. The window opens quietly, and her bare feet move to rest on the rough tiles of the roof.

Every night. Every summer night Jackson races down the street, climbs up the gutter, moves along the slanted tiles until he reaches her window. Three taps. Three taps for their past, present, and future. And every night, she leaves the window unlocked, knowing he’ll come.

Settling against the warm tiles, they lie beside each other gazing at the stars. He rests patiently next to her, waiting. He’d always wait for her.

“You can’t leave,” she pleads, reaching out for his hand. She’s trembling as he intertwines their fingers. “For the rest of my life, I’ll leave my windows open, hoping that one day you’ll come back to me.”

“I will.” He presses her hand to his lips, and a warm tear trickles between their fingers. “I promise.”

Chapter 2

It's been two weeks since Jax moved away and I can't breathe. He left me a letter but I haven't read it yet. I don't want to read any "goodbyes" or "I'll miss yous." I feel utterly lost without him, like I don't know who I am without him beside me.

Tomorrow is the first day of high school and I don't know how I'm going to do it without him. We've done everything together. I can't remember the last time I went more than two days without seeing him. We grew up together, learned to walk together, celebrated holidays together. Now he's gone and I don't know when I'll see him next.

He's my everything. My best friend. My first kiss. My partner in crime.

My soulmate...

⁕

"Welcome, everyone. My name is Mrs. Anderson. Let's start off by going around class and introducing ourselves. Please state your name and a nickname you'd like to be called if you have one, your favorite memory over the summer, and what you're looking forward to this school year." The class mumbles in anticipatory preparation to their neighbors. "Would you like to start," she asks, gesturing to a boy in the back corner.

Everly's stomach sympathetically drops as he stares at the teacher wide-eyed. "Uh. Hi, I'm Thomas."

"Hello, Thomas. Please stand up to introduce yourself," she adds.

He slides out of the stationary seat, his high cheekbones reddening. He's taller than she thought, almost six feet already. "He was held back," the girl beside her whispers, obviously noticing the shock on her face.

"I just go by Thomas. Uh, I guess my favorite memory from this summer was going to the beach with my family and learning to surf." He flops down in his seat, fidgeting with his pen.

"And what are you looking forward to this school year, Thomas?"

He looks up through the brown curls hanging in his eyes, "I don't know."

"That's all right," she continues. "We'll come back to you." She turns on her thick-heeled shoe to pick another reluctant soul to introduce themselves.

"And you," she gestures towards Everly, who's hopelessly zoned out, staring at the teacher's cankles. Clearing her throat, Everly looks up to see her standing over her, a ruler in hand. "And you," she repeats more sternly.

Everly shifts from behind her desk to face the class, tucking a lock of hair behind her ear. "Hi, my name's Everly. Sometimes I go by Lele." She pauses, thinking about what the name signifies, *who* it signifies. "Actually, you can call me Ev." Taking a deep breath, she composes her thoughts, shuffling through summer moments and trying to find one without Jackson's perfectly crooked smile in it.

"Your favorite memory this summer?" Mrs. Anderson's patience is wearing thin.

"My favorite memory from this summer was laying on my roof at night watching the stars." Her mind clouds with the feeling of Jax beside her. Blinking away the thought, she continues. "This year I'm most looking forward to playing for a new soccer team."

"Yeah," someone calls from the back of the classroom. "Same." Mrs. Anderson's eyes narrow on the slouching, long-limbed figure who spoke. She nods silently, stepping close to the girl seated beside Everly who anxiously taps her foot. "Great. And you?"

The bell sounds and the shuffling of feet and book bags drowns out the teacher's instructions. "Whoa, whoa, whoa," she calls over the chaos. "*I* dismiss you, *not* the bell." There's an collective groan in response. "Everyone take your seats." She stands, her arms crossed over her large bosom, her heeled foot tapping. Once everyone is seated, she scans the room staring into each set of eyes then announces, "All right, you are dismissed."

Piling through the doorway, the students rush to their lockers before heading to their next class. Everly passes through and her backpack strap catches on the door handle. *For god's sake*, she exhales frustratedly.

"Here." A firm hand shifts her backpack and releases her from capture. She turns to say thanks when she's shoved from the back and pressed up against his torso. She can feel his abdomen contracting as he laughs.

"Sorry." She steps back, craning her neck to look him in the eyes. He looks down at her smiling, his teeth perfectly straight after two years in braces.

"It's all good. I'm Thomas," he introduces himself.

"I know." She freezes, embarrassed by her response. "I mean, from class. You told everyone your name and stuff." *Idiot.*

He chuckles and she thinks about how the muscles of his stomach felt against her. "And you're Lele, right?"

She forces herself to look him in the eyes. "You can call me Ev."

"Ev it is," he smiles.

⁕

The ball glides across the freshly cut grass. She sticks out her foot, taking control of it and dribbling down the field, weaving expertly out of reach of her opponents. One last push and she drives her foot so hard into the ball it shoots through the goalie's grasp and into the back of the net.

Yes! She cheers for herself silently, jogging back. "Well done, Everly," the coach announces. "All right, bring it in everyone." Coach Daniels waits as all the players gradually collect on the sideline. "Now that everyone has arrived, I'd like to go over a few things. First off, look around. This is your new team." Everly's eyes pass over her new teammates, noticing how some girls wear makeup and perfect braids and how some of the boys puff out their chests and try to stand taller. "Everyone here has a right to be here. I have a zero tolerance policy for any bullying, discrimination, or sexist remarks. Got that?" He scans to the boys smirking at the end of the bench. "We're here to learn, grow, win, and play the sport we all love." A mumble of agreement emanates through the group. Bounding footsteps approach from behind them. “How nice of you to join us.” Coach Daniels looks at his watch. “Twenty minutes late.” He looks back to the long-legged boy as he stops behind the bench. “What’s your name, son?”

Brushing the hair from his eyes he scans the backs of his teammates on the bench, his eyes settling on the blonde ponytail in front of him. “I’m Thomas.”

Everly’s stomach drops. *Oh shit.*

Chapter 3

Two months.

It's been two months without a single text from Jax. He hasn't responded to any messages I've sent.

What if he's forgotten about me already? Am I so unremarkable that I'm not worth remembering?

⁕

"Hey," a call rings out through the crowded hallways. "Ev, wait up!" Everly stops dead in her tracks as the other students continue past her. A fish caught on a hook waiting to be reeled in as the river continues to rush past. Thomas knocks her shoulder with his elbow. "Hey," he says again, smiling down at her.

"Hey," she replies, eyes forward.

"What's up? You look like a zombie," he teases.

"Just having a rough day. Not a big deal." Walking side by side they make their way to Mrs. Anderson's class.

"Can I do anything to help?" She shakes her head.

Before she can walk into the classroom he throws his long arm across the doorway, blocking her entry. She looks up at him, annoyed. "All right, this is what's gonna happen. I'm going to pick you up for our soccer game tonight. You're going to use whatever's bothering you to kick ass and win the game. Then afterwards I'm buying you ice cream." She opens her mouth to respond or argue, she hasn't decided, but before she can make a sound, he's already walking to his seat.

The horn honks twice and Everly skips down the stairs of two at a time. "Ev," her dad calls out as she opens the door. "Are you sure you don't want us to come watch your game?"

"No, it's fine," she shouts as the door slams behind her.

Bounding across the lawn, she smiles as Thomas rolls down the window. "Throw your bag in the back and hop in." He leans over to shove the door open for her. She has to pull herself up into the lifted Jeep, making her feel smaller than usual. Looking over at her, he cranks up the volume, the bass rattling her brain. He smiles mischievously, and the tires screech on the pavement as they speed away.

"Good game. Good game." Everyone jogs down the field shaking hands with the opposing team. Thomas catches up to Everly, clapping her on both shoulders.

"I don't know what the hell got you so fired up, but that was the best I've ever seen you play." Everly laughs, slapping his hands away.

"Had some pent-up anger I needed to get out, I guess."

"You guess? You just scored a hat trick on one of the toughest teams!" His fingers run through his sweat-drenched hair. "That deserves the biggest ice cream sundae they have. Let's go." He pulls her bag over his shoulder, not waiting for a response as he heads to his car.

"What do you want?" he asks, scanning the menu for himself.

"I'll just have a small vanilla cone dipped in chocolate." She smiles, thinking back on how many times she's ordered that exact cone growing up.

Thomas looks at her and rolls his eyes. "I have a better idea."

He walks up to the window, and an older woman with a name tag that says *Sally* smiles up at him. "Hello, what can I get for you today?"

He straightens up and displays his most charming smile. Leaning forward he whispers, still loud enough for Everly to catch his words. "Hi, Sally, it's my friend's birthday today. Could we get her something special?"

Sally leans in too. "Of course, sweetie." After a minute, Sally comes back with an ice cream sundae the size of her head. "Happy birthday, sweetheart. It's on the house." She smiles so broadly her eyes squint, and her wrinkles display the story of her life. Before Everly can correct her, Thomas ushers her away.

"Thank you, Sally!" he calls back to her as he opens the car door for Everly.

"What was that about?" She glares, settling into the passenger seat.

"Oh, come on," he smirks. "It was a little harmless fun." Before she can respond, he coats her nose in chocolate fudge. Her eyes widen, and she retaliates swiftly, throwing whipped cream at his cheek. It shifts with his smile as he tries to lick it off. "You missed a little." He reaches over, his hand caressing her cheek as his thumb swipes across her nose. He looks at her as he licks his thumb clean. Turning the key he revs the engine loudly. "I want to show you something." And they're off.

The car comes to a stop at the edge of a lookout. The sunset's golden rays reflect in the lake below. At the same time, the moon shifts higher above the pines, silencing the world around them. It's so peaceful.

He looks over at her, watching her eyes scan the horizon, admiring each wave and smiling as the birds rush to settle in for the night. "It's beautiful," she whispers. She tries batting her lashes to fight off the impending tears.

Thomas leans over, pulling her chin up. "What's wrong? Talk to me, Ev." She shakes her head, casting her eyes down. "What's going on?" He invites her to confide in him. "I want to help."

Finally looking up at him, she shakes a tear loose. "It's stupid, really. It's just that my best friend moved away before school started, and I haven't heard from him since." He rests a comforting hand on her back, pulling her into him across the center console. She leans into it, nuzzling into his arms.

"That's not stupid at all. I'd be really upset too if my friend just *abandoned* me like that." She nods against his chest. "He must be a real idiot to let you go. You're incredible." Everly wipes her tears away, gazing up at him.

Their eyes connect in a perfect moment just as the sun melts into the horizon, inviting the stars to explore the sky. The only noise is the gentle lapping of waves against the shore and a breeze welcoming the first hints of fall.

And then they're kissing. Slowly. Meaningfully. Deeply.

Chapter 4

I thought about Jax for the first time in months today. The roof to the tree house finally caved in. The rain destroyed the books we used to read to each other and birds stole the string I used to craft with.

I stopped trying to reach out. He never replies anyway.

My mind tells me to give up but my heart is still holding on.

For a while I was worried something might have happened but every once in a while his mom reaches out to mine. I think that hurts the most, knowing everything is fine but he's choosing to ignore me.

I should be happy though. Jax leaving led me to Thomas.

⁕

"Where the heck are we going?" Everly complains. New buds and anticipatory blooms of spring paint the trail with color and tickle her nose with the airborne pollen.

"Just hang on," Thomas replies, leading her further on the trail. "Okay, close your eyes."

"What?" she protests.

"Just do it." He smiles, waving his hand in front of her face to make sure they're closed all the way. She clings to his bicep as he guides her forward. "Okay. And… open."

Everly opens her eyes to find Thomas standing in front of a hammock, holding a bouquet of flowers and a huge poster that reads EV, I'D LOVE TO *HANG* WITH YOU AT HOMECOMING.

She stands there wide-eyed and stunned. He walks over to her, placing the bouquet in her arms. "A little early to be asking, isn't it?" She giggles.

"Wanted to make sure no one had the chance to steal you away from me." He looks down at her, tucking a strand of golden hair behind her ear. "So, is that a yes?" She reaches forward, pulling his shirt until their lips collide. His hands grab around her waist, pulling her onto her tiptoes.

Settling down on flat feet again, she looks at him and breathes out her response. "Yes."

⁎

Thomas guides Everly into the house. "Phones, everyone." Everly looks to Thomas, and he gives her a nod. Dropping the hem of her long dress, she searches through her purse for her phone, placing it in the collective bowl. "Come on in." He gestures for them to enter the humongous house. Everly recognizes him as the varsity football captain, Peter.

Holding on to her hand, Thomas leads her down the stairs, swaying a bit as he goes, after nursing his flask all night. Rounding the corner, they see the cheerleaders dressed in tight sequins squealing at the beer pong table, stoners lighting up by the windows, and a dozen other high schoolers playing spin the bottle on the sectional.

Thomas releases her hand, making his way to stand beside the cheerleaders who continue shooting for the opposing cups in vain. "Celeb shot," Thomas announces, launching a ball. It hits the rim of one cup and splashes into another.

"That's two cups!" one of the girls squeals, grabbing onto his bicep. He wraps his long arms around their shoulders as the girls across the table chug their cups. Everly takes a deep breath, passing by them to settle on the couch.

The bottle spins forcefully, its label a blur of color as it goes around and around until pointing directly at her. The group turns to face the newcomer. Everly stares wide-eyed at the crowd of people. "I, uh…" she stutters. "I'm not playing."

"You sit in the strike zone, you're in it, babes," the girl in the burgundy dress announces as she takes another swig from the handle of vodka being passed around. Everly fidgets with her necklace, looking around the circle of drunk and eager participants. Finally, the bottle spinner rises, approaching Everly in an instant.

Their lips press together unrelentingly. She pulls back, her eyes lingering for a second on the redheaded girl staring back at her. The next second, she turns to find Thomas looking at her intently.

Oh god.

Pulling her along by the wrist, Thomas leads her to an office off the basement, closing the door behind them.

"I'm so sorry," she exclaims. "I had no idea what was going on. It just happened so fast, I couldn't…"

"Stop!" he interrupts. Everly steps back a few paces, looking up at his dark eyes. He closes the gap between them until he towers over her. "That…" he starts, "...was so fucking hot." He pulls her against him in an instant. Pressing her body against his and without wasting any time, he reaches for the zipper of her dress, kissing her neck as he does. It glides down her back in a fluid motion. She gasps at the movement, but he silences her with a kiss. His lips taste like sour smoke and vodka.

"Wait, wait." She pulls back from him, holding her dress up.

"What? What's wrong?" His eyes rake over her.

"I… There's just," she stutters. "There's just a lot of people here."

He stares at her. "Yeah. And?" he spits out.

"I don't know. I'm just uncomfortable doing this while half the school is on the other side of the door." Thomas shoots to his feet, brushing the hair from his eyes.

"All right, prude," he spits. He strides past her without a glance and walks through the door, leaving it gaping open for the partygoers to glimpse Everly's unzipped dress. She pulls at the zipper frantically, but it snags on the fabric. Her throat burns and her cheeks flush a deep red. The door swings open and slams shut on the laughing onlookers.

"Let me help you." A smooth voice greets her, and cool hands untangle the caught material and pull the zipper up. Everly stands still, fighting to hold on to any semblance of control. The voice behind her is warm and comforting. "My name's Sadie. What's your name?"

Demanding control of her emotions, she turns to the kind soul before her. Everly's stunned by the dark makeup, bright lips, and green satin clinging to full curves but meets empathetic hazel eyes. Smiling shyly, she exhales, “Hi. I’m Everly.”

“Nice to meet you, Everly. Let’s get you a drink. You’re too sober to be dealing with this kind of BS.” She ushers Everly up the stairs, distracting her enough to ignore the mass of people staring. “What’s your poison?” Sadie slides around the island countertop, shuffling around bottles. “You look like a hard-lemonade-type girly.”

“Not tonight.” Everly reaches over the counter, grasping the raspberry vodka. Sadie smiles, cheersing an identical bottle, gulping down one too many times.

The rest of the night is a blur of flashing lights, spinning bottles, smoky rooms, and lips she doesn’t recognize.

Chapter 5

"Hey, it's me. Can we talk?" Pause. "Just call me back when you get this." Everly throws her phone against her bed, pulling the comforter over her head.

Buzz... Buzz... Buzz... Everly groans, bringing the phone to her ear. "What."

"I'm outside. Can we *please* talk?" She throws the sheets off, making her way to the window. He's looking up at her, phone to his ear and a slight smile on his face. "Nice bedhead."

"Oh, shut up," she huffs. "Give me a minute."

Walking across the lawn barefoot, she leans against the Jeep door with her face in the window. "You gonna get in?" He smiles.

"That depends. Are we going to fight or make up?"

He reaches over, grabbing the door handle and pushing it open lightly. "Get in and find out," he smirks. Everly rolls her eyes and hops in the car.

A light breeze welcomes them as they pull up to their spot above the lake. "I'm sorry. I was drunk and shouldn't have made you uncomfortable or walked away."

Looking out over the water, Everly takes a deep breath. "It's okay."

Thomas leans over, pulling her to his lips by the chin. "Good." He looks into her eyes before settling back in his seat. "We both ended up doing dumb shit, anyway." He grins. "Let's just forget about it all."

Everly searches the blurry memories. None clear enough to recall anything specific. "Done."

⁕

"Are you kidding? You don't remember what happened?" Sadie stares wide-eyed at her new friend.

"Not really. But we agreed to just move on from it anyway, so it's not a big deal."

"Okay. Then I won't tell you."

"Wait, tell me what?"

"Nothing."

"Sadie!"

"Do you actually want to know?"

Everly lays back into her pillows as Sadie analyzes the sentimental knickknacks on her shelves. "You know what, don't tell me."

Sadie puts down the ballerina figurine. "Okay."

"Good."

"Great."

Everly racks her brain trying to piece together what could have happened. Giving up, she sits up straight. "I'm starving. Wanna grab some food?"

"Yes! I know this pizza place not too far that has slices the size of your face."

"Let's go."

⁕

The days hold onto sunlight longer, and the light breathes life into young hearts, inviting them to explore and thrive in the warmth of lazy days.

Sadie's denim shorts cling tightly to her thick curves as she pedals, and her tank top dips low enough to see her new tan lines. Everly propels her bike forward, her sundress flowing to the side as they go. "Take the dirt trail on the right," Everly calls up to Sadie, who nearly wipes out on the turn.

As they get closer, they can hear the cheers and splashing up ahead. The quarry has always been a rebel's favorite summer spot. Sadie comes to a stop in front of the tall fence topped with barbed wire. "Now what?"

"Thomas!" Everly calls out, and soon enough he jogs over, tan skin glistening with water droplets and sweat.

"Hey, babe." He leans into the fence, kissing her through the wire. "What's up, Sadie." He says it as a greeting rather than a question. She simply inclines her head in response. "All right, go put your bikes behind the dumpster, and then walk down this way." They do as he says, following him along the fence, crouching and tiptoeing among the prickers. He pulls back the fencing where they used bolt cutters. "You're lucky you're small," he says as she passes through with ease. Sadie's tank top snags on the jagged wire. "Come on, Sadie."

"I'm stuck, dipshit."

"Hang on. I got you," Everly says, unhooking the fabric.

"Thanks," Sadie responds, passing through and rolling her eyes at Thomas.

"All right, ladies," he smirks. "Right this way." He gestures forward, and they follow the sound of skin smacking water.

Ooooooh, the crowd reacts to the back flop. "Oh shit." Thomas laughs. "Who was that?"

A blond girl responds, "I don't know. A couple kids from East just got here. Think she's with them." Thomas looks past her to see another group of high schoolers sending people off the cliff. Everly watches as he calls over to them. She pulls at his long fingers, trying to stop his impulsive shouts. "Yo, douchebags!"

"Thomas, stop," she begs, pulling his hand harder. He jerks his hand away, smiling as the group turns to face them.

A group of guys, none as tall as Thomas, approaches them. Close up, they look like upperclassmen, with intimidatingly toned muscles. "Sorry," one of them starts, pretending to get water out of his ear. "I don't think I heard you right. Wanna say that again?"

Everly inches forward. "Thomas, please."

He clears his throat and smirks down at him. "Sorry, I'll speak up for you old man." He begins shouting and annunciating each word, "I. Want. To. Know. Why. You're. At. Our. Quarry."

The guy grins. "Well, I don't see your name on it, stretch." He looks past him, his judging glance scanning over Everly and their friends. "Why don't you just go back to playing with your little sluts and leave us the hell alone," he says, turning to walk away.

Everly's stomach drops as Thomas spins him around by the shoulder with one hand as the other connects across his jaw. Shrieks ring out, fists start flying, and soon enough sirens race in their direction. "Oh shit." Thomas turns to run with everyone else. "Come on, Ev!" The cops always patrol the quarry for trespassers during the summer, so they made sure to hang on the far side.

The sirens close in as they climb through the fence, everyone racing through the trees and away from the trails. Sadie huffs alongside Everly who pulls at her wrist, urging her forward. Everyone crouches behind the graffitied boulders at the base of the hill, panting. "Thomas," Everly whispers. He glows with the rush of adrenaline, that devious smile plastered across his face. "My bike."

"It'll be fine. Don't worry."

Staring out the window she watches as two police cars park in front of her house, one with a yellow cruiser bike in the back. *Her* yellow cruiser. *Oh shit.*

"Pick up, pick up," she urges as the phone continues to ring.

"Hey, babe," Thomas answers.

"The cops are here. They found my bike. What do I do?"

"Whoa, calm down. First of all, how'd they know it was your bike?"

"My mom puts our phone number on them in case we get kidnapped or something, I don't freaking know." Three firm knocks hit the front door. "What do I do?" she asks again.

"Everly, get down here." Her father's voice pierces right through her heart.

"Oh god. I have to go."

"Ev," Thomas urges from the phone. "Please don't mention my name. You know I have football tryouts today, and I can't jeopardize making the team."

I think I'm going to be sick.

"You know how important this is to me," he pleads as the line cuts out.

"Everly." Her dad opens the door further as she descends the staircase. "These nice police officers would like to talk to you."

"May we come in?" The officer waits until he gestures for them to enter the living room. "Thank you."

"Please, take a seat," her father offers.

She raises a hand. "This shouldn't take long." Everly can hardly hear over the pounding in her ears. "Hi, Everly, I'm officer Diaz, and this is my partner, Officer Solace. We'd like to ask you a couple questions. Is that all right?" Everly settles into the living room chair and nods. "All right. So, we found your bike out by the quarry. Now, I know you're a smart girl, so you're aware that going beyond the fence into the restricted area is considered trespassing. Also, tampering with or damaging that fence to get inside is breaking and entering. So, here's the issue, Everly. We found your bike and another bike hidden behind the dumpster, which wasn't far from an area of the fence that had been cut and pried open." All of her words flow through one ear and out the other as Everly sits paralyzed before her. "So, were you the one who cut the fence to get into the quarry?"

Silence.

"Ev!" her father snaps.

"No! No, I didn't cut the fence. I swear."

"Was it your friend with the other bike?"

"It wasn't us."

"Then who cut the fence?" She shakes her head, refusing to answer.

"Everly Dianne!"

"I don't know!" It's not *technically* a lie. Thomas could have showed up after it was already cut.

"Okay, well, here's what is going to happen. Unless you can provide us with names of those who vandalized that property and trespassed, then you're going to take the brunt of the punishment." Silence. "Alrighty then. Now, I ran your record. Happy to see you don't have one. Also, nice to see that you're an outstanding citizen in our community, and because of that, this won't go on your record, but you'll be required to complete forty hours of community service." Everly looks up at the woman before her. "Understood?" She nods her head over and over until she turns away. The breath she's been holding escapes her in a shaky release.

"Are you kidding, Ev?" Sadie yells into the phone.

"It's not that bad. It's only forty hours of community service. I practically do that anyway. But I'll probably be grounded for the rest of the summer," she laughs without humor.

"You should've just blamed the East kids," she snickers. "But really, Thomas shouldn't have asked you to take the fall."

"He didn't really."

"Ev," she cuts in. "He told you not to mention his name. What else could you have possibly done?"

She sits against her window in silence. "All I'm saying is he better worship the ground you walk on after covering for him."

Ring... Ring... Ring... Ring... Ri— "Hey, babe!" He finally picks up. "What happened?"

Everly settles into the pillows along her window seat, pressing her forehead to the glass pane. She relays the story to him, the fear she felt, the way she thought she'd be sick all over the officer's shoes. "They ended up giving me forty hours of community service."

"Oh, that's nothing! I thought it was gonna be so much worse," he exhales happily into the phone. "So anyway, I had football tryouts, and I killed it. Didn't drop a single pass, dusted half of the team, and wrecked one of the upperclassmen in a showdown. You should've seen it, babe."

"Mhmm," "Nice," and "Good for you, babe," are the only responses she can muster.

"Are you even listening to me?" he asks pointedly.

"Were you listening to *me?"* she fires back. "I just took the fall for all your friends and got my ass handed to me by my parents, who will probably hold this over my head for the rest of my life, and you want to talk about how tryouts went? Are you kidding me, Thomas? You didn't even say thank you!"

Silence.

"I'm sorry. I didn't mean to yell. It's just a lot." She sinks into the pillows behind her, curling in on herself.

"It's okay. I was just trying to avoid the topic so you wouldn't have to think about it for a while."

"Thank you," she breathes out the tension in her shoulders.

"You're welcome, babe."

Chapter 6

"DE-fense! DE-fense! DE-fense!" The crowd stomps in time on the bleachers. "The ball is snapped and the defensive line breaks through, the ball is fumbled, and is picked up by number sixty-four! He's running it back! To the thirty! The twenty! The ten! TOUCHDOWN!" the announcer screams into the microphone. The student section erupts in thunderous cheers, and the cheerleaders launch their flyers into the air.

Thomas runs back from the endzone, chest bumping and high fiving his teammates before hopping the fence and racing to the stands. Everly rushes down the metal stairs until she's leaning over the railing. Thomas propels himself up, grabbing onto the fence and pulling Everly into a passionate kiss. The cheers around them meld into a low buzzing until they pull away. "That was amazing!" she yells over the crowd.

"That one was for you, baby!" He kisses her on the forehead before hopping down and racing back towards the field, hugging and high-fiving the cheerleaders as he goes.

After the successful field goal and punt return, the offensive team takes the field, Thomas finding his position among them. The center snaps the ball back, and without warning the quarterback is brutally tackled to the ground. He lets out an agonizing cry, cradling his arm. Whistles sound, and the play stops. Everyone on the field takes a knee, waiting for the medical team to get to him. Except for one player who walks over to the boy writhing in pain and spits on him. His team members shoot up in seconds. Fists fly, whistles blow, and savage cheers ring out from around the field.

Both sidelines clear as everyone charges the field to defend their brothers in a mosh pit of flying limbs and brutal cries.

Most of the players spend the weekend icing their faces or getting fitted for slings. Thomas spends it celebrating—getting completely hammered after the game and retelling the details of his first career touchdown.

"Did you hear about what happened after the game?" Sadie leans forward. "Christian just told me."

"What do you mean?" Everly sits back in her desk chair, craning her neck to hear over the teacher's voice.

"What Thomas did."

"At the party? I was there, Sadie."

"Yeah." She pauses. "But something happened."

"What was it?" *Shhh,* the teacher urges. Everly turns to face forward and whispers, "Just tell me after class."

The bell rings, releasing the students from their assigned seats. A group of guys in the back of the class mumble and point at Everly as she makes to leave. She catches a glimpse of them and turns. "What?" she asks, wiping at her face in case that's the issue.

"Come with me." Sadie grabs her elbow, leading her out of the room and into the bathroom.

"What is going on?"

"Do you want the real truth or the soft truth?"

Everly rolls her eyes. "Just tell me."

"Okay, Christian told me he saw Thomas hooking up with one of the cheerleaders at the party right after you left." Resting against the cold concrete wall, Everly stares up at the fluorescent lights shaking her head. "I'm sorry, Ev." Sadie moves a hand toward her shoulder to console her, but she pulls away.

After a minute of silence, she breaks it. "Was it the same girl?"

Sadie stands back to look at her. "What?"

Raising her voice, she says again, "Was it the same girl?"

"No."

"Okay… Then he's not in love with anyone else." Sadie moves in front of her, trying to read the look on her face.

"Are you kidding, Ev? You knew Thomas cheated on you, and you stayed with him, and now he did it again, and who knows how many times before, and you're just going to stay with him because he's 'not in love' with anyone else?" She rakes her fingers through her hair in frustration. "Come on, Ev. I knew you were a sucker for him, but you're not an idiot."

Everly pushes off the wall, shoving her against the stall. "He's all I have!" They stare at each other, equally wide-eyed and surprised. "He's all I have, Sadie," she nearly whispers.

"Ev." Sadie shifts forward, holding onto her shoulders. "You have *me* now." Lifting her chin up she waits for their eyes to meet. "Okay?"

Everly's lip quivers as she fights to regain control of her emotions. Her face is a mask of calm while a single tear lingers on her lashes. "It's not the same."

Just before the final bell, the principal's dry voice comes over the PA system.

"The aggressive and violent acts displayed this past Friday are inexcusable and as such need to be addressed. Although our football team is the pride and joy of our school, we need to hold our students accountable for their actions. Therefore, the members of our football team will be suspended until further notice."

"Hey." Thomas smiles as Everly walks down the hallway. She passes his locker without a glance. "Hey!" he calls after her. "What's going on?" He reaches out for her wrist, and she wrenches it away, continuing down the hallway. "Jeez, come find me when you stop your little tantrum," he shouts.

"What was that about?" one of his friends asks, leaning back against the row of lockers.

"I don't know, man. Just seems a little bitchier than usual, I guess." They laugh collectively before slamming their lockers.

"Ev, wait up!" He jogs along the sidewalk, catching up with ease. She continues her swift pace, ignoring his presence. Thomas grabs her shoulder, spinning her around, but she pushes against his chest, sending him to the ground. He looks up at her bewildered.

Her cheeks redden as she looks down at his now bloody hand. "Thomas, I'm so sorry." She lifts his hand to analyze it.

"What the hell, Ev!" he spits.

"I didn't mean to. I'm sorry." She reaches out to help him up.

"What is going on with you today?"

She looks at him, his bloodied hand littered with gravel and grass. "I thought you loved me," she whispers under her breath.

"What?"

"I thought you were my person. That this could be a forever kind of thing."

"Ev, what are you talking about?"

"You cheated, Thomas." He stiffens.

"Can we talk about this? Just let me grab my car, and we can go somewhere to talk this out okay?" Everly avoids his eyes. "Please, give me a chance to explain?" he asks again.

Everly doesn't respond but waits while he runs to bring his car around.

They pull up to their spot above the lake, the gravel popping under the tires. The engine calms and quiets as he removes the keys and takes a deep breath. "Ev." Her eyes watch the ripples on the water's surface move in steady waves. "It all just happened so quick, you know—" He cuts himself off. "Ev, please look at me." She turns to face him, and his thumb collects the loose tears on her cheeks. "I love you." He leans forward with a smile. "I love you so much it drives me insane. I love you so much that I got drunk that night because I was upset that you left early. I wouldn't have gotten that drunk if you just stayed. I don't even remember what happened after that." Her eyes narrow on him as his face contorts in sadness but remains dry. "We *are* a forever type of thing, Ev. You're my forever, and I'm yours. Okay?"

She looks past him at the pine trees swaying in the wind. He pulls her into his embrace.

"Okay?" He asks again. His arms are warm and safe, his voice familiar and lovely, his scent comforting. *He's mine and I'm his.* "Okay," she replies, allowing her body to melt into his.

Chapter 7

Sitting up in the back of the Jeep, Everly pulls the blanket up with her as she traces her finger along the fogged-up window. Thomas watches as goosebumps spread across her bare skin before pulling the blanket tighter around her.

T + E

She shifts enough to show him her work and beams when he smiles up at her. "Come here," he urges, holding his arms out to embrace her. "Quit hogging all the blankets," he teases, spreading them out over his exposed skin. She nuzzles into his arms, his shoulder like a comforting pillow against her cheek. Her hand travels across his chest, exploring the now familiar texture and warmth. "I love you." His lips press to her forehead, mumbling the words with a smile.

Shifting in his grip, she looks in his dark honey eyes, studying their depth. "I love you more." Their lips gently press together, their breath intermingling. A chilling breeze wafts along the tree tops, rattling loose leaves from their branches to drift through the twilight.

"Impossible," he says, shutting her up with another kiss before she can counter. Lying back in peaceful bliss, their trains of thought chug along on different tracks.

"How many kids would you want?"

"Why?" He shoots up instantly, "Did the condom break?"

"No, no," she says. "Jeez. I was just thinking about our future and stuff. Relax."

"Jesus, Ev. Don't scare me like that." He rests back again. She can hear his heart pounding against his chest now. Thomas is silent for a long while before deciding to answer. "I guess growing up an only child, I've always wanted a big family of my own." Pausing again, he considers this further. "I think I'd like four or five kids when I'm older." Everly's eyes widen slightly, her head still resting on his chest. "What about you?"

A wishful grin expands across her cheeks thinking about it. "I'd love it if we had two kids. Maybe three."

"Yeah, I guess it depends."

"On what?"

"A bunch of stuff."

"Like what?" she insists.

"When I have kids, who I end up with, what kind of job I have."

"Wait, what?"

"The type of job you have makes a big difference in how many kids you want."

She shakes her head. "No. What do you mean, 'who you end up with'?"

He rolls his eyes at her. "I just mean, that you never know what could happen in the future, Ev. Of course, I want it to be us. I want to love you forever, but life doesn't always work out the way we want it to." Taking the blanket, she moves to rest against the car's interior wall, as far from him as possible. "Ev, come on. You know what I mean."

"Do I? Because it sounds like *maybe* you'd want to end up with one of the cheerleaders you've been getting so close with."

"Don't start this bullshit with me right now. You know I love you. We've been together over a year now. I'm just being realistic, okay? Don't get mad at me for something you're insecure about." Everly just shakes her head, her throat threatening to burn from the inside out. "Ev, I'm sorry. I love you. I didn't mean anything by that." She turns aways from him. His long fingers firmly grip her chin, turning her face to him. "I love you. Just forget what I said, all right? It's just me and you till the end, babe." He smiles his most charming and dreamy smile at her until her body forces her to smile back, against her better judgment. Pulling her chin to him, he plants a soft, juicy kiss on her lips, then attacks her with kisses across her face in rapid succession. Her cheeks, eyes, nose, jaw, forehead, temples, and finally finishing with a deep kiss on her lips, silencing her giddy squeals. "I love you," he breathes against her neck.

The words catch for a moment in her throat before flowing past her lips. "I love you, too."

❊

The envelope stares at her, its red seal burning as she stares back, branding its design in her mind. "On three?" Sadie's shaky hand pulls her identical envelope towards her. Everly nods.

"One. Two. Three!" Tearing into the envelopes, they flip open the letters, searching the page for an invitation.

"Oh my god, I got in!" Sadie bursts from her chair, pressing her letter against her chest like an imaginary dance partner as she prances around the room.

Everly lowers her letter until it rests on her thighs. Sadie looks back at her, rushing over when she sees her face. "Oh, Ev. I'm so sorry." She embraces her friend, their arms wrapping perfectly around one another until Everly whispers in her ear. "*We* got in…"

"You sneaky bitch!" Sadie explodes backwards. "I knew it, too! There's no way they'd let my sorry ass in and not your goody-two-shoes self."

Everly laughs until it hurts, moving to flop down onto the couch beside her friend. "Wait, I have to tell Thomas!" Sadie rolls her eyes, nuzzling happily into the couch as Everly grabs her bag and dials his number as she skips out the door.

Buzz... Buzz... Buzz... "Jeez, what is it!" He leans forward just as the phone stops ringing. "Of course," he complains, reclining again. The doorbell chimes. Once. Twice. Thomas shifts forward, taking two steps towards the door when it opens. "For fuck's sake," he curses under his breath.

Everly comes bounding towards the couch, launching herself into the wide cushions beside him, her face radiating happiness. She gazes up at him until his eyes move to meet her and she can no longer contain herself. "I got in!" she squeals giddily as she sits up, shaking him by the bicep. "I can't believe it! I mean, all things considered, I figured I'd get in. But it's so different knowing I actually got into my dream school! *Our* dream school." She leans into him, resting her head against his shoulder. Realizing he's yet to say a word, she looks up at his dull expression. "What's wrong?" As she asks the question, she spots it. The torn letter below the coffee table. "Oh, Thomas." She moves to console him. "I'm so sorry, I should've asked you before ranting like an idiot. Are you okay?"

He shoots to his feet, grabbing his water glass, and sulks towards the kitchen. "It's not even a big deal. We both got into our second choice, so everything will work out fine." Everly's heart sinks into the deepest crevasse of her body. "That's what second choices are for, anyway." He smiles weakly at her.

"Thomas…" she starts.

"It'll be great, Ev. Just think about how much fun we're going to have together." A smile finally breaks through his flat expression.

"Thomas," she says again.

He turns from filling his glass, "Yeah?"

"I…" She takes a deep breath in, composing herself. "I can't pass up this opportunity."

Turning to face her, he leans onto the countertop. "What do you mean?"

Just breathe. "I mean, this is my dream school. You know how hard I've worked to get my GPA up and do extracurriculars and keep my record clean."

"Oh, wow. Low blow, Ev. Here we go again! Always bringing up how 'I forced you to take the fall' for *voluntarily* trespassing. You know what? Grow the fuck up, Ev. It's been three years! You can't hold that over my head for the rest of our lives." He turns away, raking his hands through his hair. "And what about *our* dreams? Hmm? Just going to abandon those like they mean nothing to you?"

Everly stands there in silence, eyes on the rippling water in the glass. She's learned to endure the tirade until he's calmed down.

"Is my love really worth nothing to you?"

Silence.

"I can't do this right now." His hand slaps the glass off the counter, sending it to the ground in a shattering mess. "I need some air," he growls under his breath as his shoes crunch over the broken glass.

Everly grabs a dish towel for the water and the dust pan under the sink for the glass shards. Being here, at Thomas' home, has become second nature. A home away from home, with a family she's come to love.

What am I doing? How can I choose between the person I love and the future I want? Why can't I have both?

Chapter 8

"For someone as smart as you, you're a real dumbass," Sadie shoots at her. "I mean, come on, Ev. I've been as supportive as I can be of this dysfunctional relationship, but it's been over a month since we accepted the offer to our dream school. How much longer do you think you'll be able to keep it from him?" Sadie fixes her makeup in the mirror. "Oh, but once you tell him I'm sure he'll be so super excited for you, and you'll live happily ever after." Everly scowls as her friend finishes her sardonic statement.

"Are you done?"

Sadie spins gracefully around to face her, walking slowly towards her. "Not quite. And then," she exaggerates. "You'll go off to separate schools, states apart. But don't worry, he'll be loyal. I mean he's messed up in the past…on multiple occasions…but he's learned now, I'm sure! Just like he's learned to pleasure you right—oh, wait."

Everly clutches at her stomach, laughing so hard she slides down the wall into a puddle on the floor. "Shut up, Sadie," she gasps.

Finally calming down enough to speak, she looks over at her friend who's taken a seat beside her. "Ev, he's just not good enough for you. He never has been, and I don't understand why you've stayed with him this long. Please see that you deserve better before it's too late."

Everly's eyes blur with tears as she contemplates what to do next.

"There you are." Thomas grabs Everly's hips from behind. "Where have you been?" He shifts her to the side as they walk through the hallway.

"I—"

"Anyway, we only have two more weeks to mail in our acceptance. Figured we could do that this weekend and then go out to celebrate. What do you think? Come over tomorrow and we can do that?"

"Um…can we talk about this after class?"

"Yeah, that's fine. Everything okay?"

"Mhmm, just thinking about the quiz we have."

"Oh shit," he exhales sharply. "I totally forgot. But hey—" He nudges her shoulder. "We already got into college. I can fail all the tests I want now." He walks through the classroom door ahead of her, chuckling.

⁕

Everly knocks on the door before walking into the foyer. "Come on in, Ev," Thomas' mom calls. She shakes off her shoes and follows the fluffy gray tail of Beans the cat into the kitchen. "Will you be staying for dinner tonight?" Mary asks as she chops vegetables.

"Not tonight, but thank you." Everly crouches down, her slim flingers filtering through Beans' lengthy coat. His purrs vibrate against her knees comfortingly.

"All right, sweetie. Well, we miss you around here. It's been a while since you've stayed."

"Yeah," she keeps her eyes on Beans. "I've just had a lot going on."

"Oh, I'm sure! With graduation coming up soon and all the things to get done for college, I can't imagine you have much free time these days." Everly just nods. "Thomas!" Mary calls up the stairs.

"What!" he shouts back.

"Everly is here!"

"Ev, come upstairs!" She smiles back at Mary before heading up the carpeted staircase, turning the corner to enter his dark blue room. "Hey, babe." He reclines in his chair, his headset on and eyes focused on the screen. "I'll be done in a second." Everly nods, resting on his bed, waiting.

Half an hour goes by, and Everly still lies beside Beans on the bed listening to Thomas curse and scream into the mic. "Dinner!" his mom calls upstairs.

"Hang on!" Thomas shouts back. Everly sits forward on the bed, displacing Beans who walks away annoyed at the inconvenience. "I gotta sign off, guys. I'll be back on in an hour."

"Didn't you want to talk today?" Everly asks as he throws his headset onto the desk.

"Yeah," he says, walking out the door. "How long will that take?" His legs skip down the stairs two at a time.

"Uh…" She rushes to keep up. "I don't know. But it's pretty important."

"Okay." He roams the countertop, picking up a piece of bread and taking a big bite. "So, like half an hour?"

"Thomas, could you grab your father's glass, please?" He rolls his eyes but reaches into the high cabinets for the pint glass. "Are you sure you can't stay for dinner tonight, Ev?"

She shifts in the doorway. "I wish I could, but I have to help my mom with something."

"Another time then." She smiles at her, her brown and gray-streaked hair brushing forward and into her face. Everly nods.

"Wait, don't you wanna talk about something?" Thomas turns to her, another handful of bread in his mouth.

"We can talk about it another time." He nods, taking his seat at the table.

Everly waves silently then walks to the doorway, puts on her shoes, pets Beans a few more times, and makes her way home.

It's starting to feel heavier. The weight on my chest. It physically hurts now.

❊

The deciduous trees shed their vibrant leaves into a cool breeze, a rainbow of foliage collecting along the lake's edge. Everly leans into the wind's movement allowing it to soothe her nerves. *I can do this.*

She takes a deep breath, eyes closed, to feel the world around her in silent bliss when she hears footsteps approaching. Opening her eyes, she turns to see Thomas sauntering over in his typical flannel and jeans. He smiles when she turns to him. "Hey, babe."

"Hey." She forces a smile.

"What's going on? You were being weird on the phone."

"Yeah, sorry. Just some stuff I've been wanting to talk to you about."

"Oh god," he laughs. "Nothing good ever comes from that sentence." He nudges her jokingly. Everly takes a deep breath. "Oh shit. So, like *real* stuff?" he enunciates.

Everly blurts everything out in one continuous sentence. "I already accepted the offer to my dream school, and I didn't tell you because I knew you'd be upset, but I think that if we wanted to, we could make this work even with the distance. I just really want you to understand that I had to prioritize this for myself, and if you really love me you'll see that this is the best thing, and I just really don't want to fight right now. I'm sorry I lied to you, but you don't make it easy to tell you the truth sometimes." She stares at his blank face, waiting for him to process what she's just said.

He sits back against the bench, looking out at the water where a fisherman drifts lazily by on the relaxed current. His hands rake back the dark curls that linger just above his eyes. The cruel calmness of his words drives deeper into her soul than any amount of shouting has before. "Are you *fucking* kidding me, Ev? I knew you were selfish, but I didn't think you were a coward, too." The words suffocate her. "You just decided to throw our whole future away for a stupid school and didn't have the courage to tell me about it for months." He turns to stare her dead in the eyes. "And don't give me that 'if you really loved me' bullshit. Because if *you* really loved *me*, you wouldn't have thrown this all away for a school." Thomas turns away from her, the veins in his neck bulging as he whispers under his breath, "Selfish bitch."

Those words sting like a knife pressed to her throat, but she closes her eyes, breathes, and shoots to her feet pulling him by the chin to look in her furious eyes. "No." Her voice is a stern slap in the face. "You don't get to call me that. You don't have the right to curse at me or guilt trip me or say that I ruined this for us because it's you. It's you who's cheated and lied and yelled at me these past years."

"I—"

"I am not done!" she shouts in his face. "You do not get to control or dictate what I do anymore because I'm done. I'm done with your games, your insistent manipulative bullshit, and most of all I am done with you." Everly looks down on him with a triumphant smirk before walking away, her words ringing in his ears.

Chapter 9

"Congratulations, Miss Everly." She smiles up at the principal, her fingers trembling slightly as she receives her diploma. Cheers ring out as her name echoes through the auditorium.

The room quiets as the final names are announced and each new graduate takes their seat amongst their peers. A woman in her early thirties approaches the podium. Her dark skin and burgundy dress glow in the spotlight.

"Congratulations, new graduates, on this momentous accomplishment. For many of you this has been a difficult journey of long nights studying, a balancing act of extracurriculars and homework, and trying to figure out who you are along the way. I believe I speak for most people when I say I'd never want to live out my high school experience again." A collective chuckle from parents livens the room, their nods affirming her statement.

"Many of you are looking forward to what's to come. Maybe that's college or finding a career or traveling the world. Whatever you intend to pursue next, I'd like you to think about this at each new crossroad: You are capable of whatever you set your mind to. I'm not saying that if you want something bad enough you'll obtain it. I am telling you that if you follow what ignites your soul and work hard towards that goal in some way each day, you can make it happen.

"You can dream as much as you like about being rich or famous or adventurous, but until you take real action in pursuit of that life, you will never make progress." She pauses, looking out into the sea of teenagers. Her eyes land on the few who stare at her intently, absorbing her wisdom.

"One of the biggest roadblocks for anyone to overcome is the expectations and opinions of others. *You* are in charge of your life, no one else. The only person who should be responsible for your success, failure, or happiness is you.

"I'd like to leave you with this incredibly impactful poem by Brian A. 'Drew' Chalker entitled *Reason, Season and a Lifetime.* Stick with me through this —it could change your life." She takes a moment to look into the crowd, smiling at the youthful faces anticipating her next words.

Clearing her throat, she begins to read, "'People always come into your life for a reason, a season, or a lifetime. When you figure out which it is, you know exactly what to do.

When someone is in your life for a REASON,
It is usually to meet a need you have expressed outwardly or inwardly.
They have come to assist you through a difficulty,
Or to provide you with guidance and support,
To aid you physically, emotionally, or even spiritually.
They may seem like a godsend to you, and they are.
They are there for a reason,
You need them to be.
Then, without any wrongdoing on your part
Or at an inconvenient time,
This person will say or do something to bring the relationship to an end.
Sometimes they die,
Sometimes they just walk away.
Sometimes they act up or out and force you to take a stand.
What we must realize is that our need has been met, our desire fulfilled; their work is done.
The prayer you sent up has been answered and it is now time to move on.'

"Now, 'When people come into your life for a SEASON,
It is because your turn has come to share, grow, or learn.
They may bring you an experience of peace or make you laugh.
They may teach you something you have never done.
They usually give you an unbelievable amount of joy.

Believe it! It is real!

But, only for a season.

And like Spring turns to Summer and Summer to Fall,

The season eventually ends.'

"Finally, 'LIFETIME relationships teach you a lifetime of lessons;

Those things you must build upon in order to have a solid emotional foundation.

Your job is to accept the lesson,

Love the person or people anyway;

And put what you have learned to use in all other relationships and areas in your life.

It is said that love is blind but friendship is clairvoyant.'

"So," she pauses, catching Everly's gaze. "Go out into this world with clear eyes, ambitious hearts, and open minds to live a life you'll be proud of. Thank you." Applause thunders through the room at her final words. Everly shoots up from her seat, her heart beating rapidly as a single tear escapes her lashes to touch each freckle on its path down her cheek.

Wow, she thinks to herself as the room quiets once again and she settles back into her seat. *Wow.*

Chapter 10

Day 1:

I'm leaving today for a solo road trip. I don't really know what I'm doing. All I know is that I need to get away for a while.

My truck is all packed up and ready to go. I just have to say some goodbyes and then I'll head to my first camping spot tonight.

"Okay. Okay! Mom you're gonna suffocate me," she giggles, wiggling out of her mother's tight embrace.

"Be safe kiddo, go enjoy this new adventure." Everly settles into the familiar warmth of her father's arms. His scruffy beard pokes at her forehead as he presses a light kiss to his not-so-little girl's head.

"Love you guys." Descending the stairs she looks back over her shoulder to see her parents waving their goodbyes as she sets out on her summer adventure.

"Are you sure you don't want to just fly down with us?" Sadie leans through the open window of Everly's rusting truck. "Three weeks alone is a long time, Ev."

"I know," she smiles. "It'll be good for me. And I'll just meet you guys in Nashville."

"Okay…" she exaggerates. "Have fun, don't get lost, and I'll see you in three weeks!" She jumps through the passenger side window, her legs kicking at the air behind her, to hug Everly. Their giddy squeals accompany the chirping birds and kids playing down the street. "Love you, Ev. Be safe."

"Love you, too."

The rattling engine of the truck sputters as she makes her way down the road, Sadie watching as the car continues out of sight.

Day 1: Continued...

I just finished setting up camp for the night. I didn't realize how hard putting up a tent by yourself could be. It's almost dark and I can't start a fire, so pop tarts for dinner it is.

I spent the first half of the car ride crying and the second half wishing I picked a closer place to camp. Now, I'm lying here in my tent thinking. Thinking about everyone who told me I'm too inexperienced to do this on my own or that it's really dangerous to be traveling alone.

Maybe they're right.

It's only night one and I don't have a fire, couldn't cook food, drove around for an extra 40 minutes trying to find my camp spot. I don't know what I'm doing.

But for the first time in months, I feel like I can breathe again. Maybe it's the mountain air or the twinkling stars above me, but I have a feeling everything will be okay.

Day 3:

It's day three and I am the happiest I've been in a long time. I have a full belly, a happy heart, and a clear mind for once. This morning I decided to go for a hike. There was a trail that led to a waterfall, so I packed up my backpack, filled up my water, brought some snacks, and set off.

It was nearly straight up the whole way, but it was so worth it. I could hear the waterfall before I could see it. Moving past some humongous boulders I stopped dead in my tracks. It was the most beautiful thing I'd ever seen. The water was a pristine and intense blue. The pool was so clear you could see all the way to the bottom of it.

I scrambled down some steep rocks to set up a little picnic for myself by the water's edge, and the mist of the waterfall cooled me as I laid in the sunshine.

After a while, a family came over the rocks where I had started. I hadn't seen anyone else on the trail all morning. I invited them to join me on the small boulders by the water.

Max and Kathleen were their names and they brought their three-year-old, Ozzy, and their one-year-old, Hunter, who was in a carrier on Kathleen's back. I thought I wanted to be alone, to experience the waterfall and natural bliss by myself, but they made me smile and laugh and enjoy the experience so much more.

Ozzy and I decided to walk into the water together. It was so much colder than we both expected so she squealed and climbed up on me. We ended up hiking out together and they invited me over to their campsite for dinner. I told Max I was struggling to make a fire, so he taught me what to do and showed me how to make a full dinner.

Ozzy sat on my lap as we sat around the fire eating stir fry and watched the sunset over the hills.

I'm leaving in the morning and wish I had said a proper thank you to them. I'm going to write a note and leave it on their windshield before heading out.

I feel like sometimes life knows exactly what you need and puts it in your path. Maybe that's God or maybe it's chance. Either way, I'm happy to have experienced their kindness.

Day 6:

My AC decided to stop working two hours into my drive today but I embraced the warm breeze as I drove to the NC coast. I found a campsite along the beach and after setting up I went for a quick dip to cool off. This humidity is crazy. I'll be spending a lot of time in the water it seems.

Day 10:

Today was incredible.

I set up my hammock between two trees and watched people ride the waves in. At one point, I was amazed to see a group of women, probably all nearly 60, walk by with surfboards.

I watched as they took off down the beach without a care and hopped right into the water. I stared at them completely mesmerized. They were incredible, beating out young kids for the best waves and making it look easy.

One of the women came in to take a break and sat in the shade nearby. She looked over at me and we started talking.

Everly swings on the edge of her hammock, mouth agape, watching as one of the women walks along her board to touch the nose with her foot before racing back to carve into the wave.

"Have you ever been surfing before?" a voice, soft as silk, asks her. Everly turns to see a beautifully tanned and freckled woman sitting in the tree's shade, smiling. Everly shakes her head. "It's incredible, feeling connected and challenged by nature. It takes some practice, but it's worth all the struggles. And sand in your hair," she giggles. She looks out at the other women wading in the water, bobbing on their boards with the waves. "What's your name?"

"I'm Everly."

"Hi, Everly. I'm Jean."

"It's nice to meet you, Jean." She looks back out to see another woman, curvier than the rest, ride the wave all the way into the sand. "You're all so impressive."

"Well, we had to find some way to pass the time. Hey, Addy," she calls past Everly. The curvaceous woman turns to her, walking along the sand with her board in tow. "Addy, this is Everly. We're going to teach her to surf today."

Everly whirls to face her. "Oh, lovely! I'm Adeline, but you can call me Addy." She reaches out a dripping hand.

"I…" Everly stutters. "I don't think I can. And I don't want to interfere with your day."

"Nonsense," Jean smiles. "It'll be fun, I promise." Everly takes her outstretched hand hesitantly then stands up to make her way to the water's edge between the two women.

"Hey, ladies!" Addy projects her voice over the crashing waves, grabbing their attention. "We have a new recruit." The women clap and cheer, moving closer in to meet her.

I thought that first wave was going to kill me but Christine made sure I didn't nose dive. After a while, I started to get the hang of it. They were all cheering and clapping, I was overwhelmed by their support.

After a while I finally got up and rode a wave all the way in. I don't know why, but I started to cry. All of them came in to congratulate me and take a break.

I asked them how they all got so good at this and they told me they'd been trying to learn different skills each year for the past 6 years. Last year's skill was surfing and they decided to stick with it.

"How did all of you meet? You seem really close." Everly smiles at the women around the picnic table.

Looking around at each other, LeeAnn breaks the silence to answer. "We're all widows. We met in a support group nearly a decade ago now."

Everly shifts uncomfortably in her seat. "Oh, I'm so sorry."

"Don't be," Christine blurts out. "That group gave me them, and they are the greatest thing to ever happen to me."

"I can see the question on your face, sweetheart. The support group was for the wives of terminally ill cancer patients," Ida explains.

"That must have been really hard," Everly whispers.

"It was, but not nearly as hard as it would have been alone. These women saved my life and gave me purpose again." Addy clasps Jean's hand in hers. "For every tragedy in life, there is good to come of it. I know this for sure." Her smile beams, inviting those around her to do the same.

"I don't know what I would do if something like that happened to me." Everly stares out at the crashing waves.

"It's not what you *do* that matters. It's what you *believe.*" Christine nudges Everly. "It may be the hardest thing you do in life, but when life brings terrible challenges or heartache your way, know that there is potential for good and healing on the other side of that pain. That little bit of hope will change your life." Everly nods and accepts the hugs they offer her.

Day 14:

Today was the worst.

I was heading south, hoping to make it to my campsite in Georgia tonight. I was three hours in when my tire nearly blew up. I pulled over on a back road to check it out.

Have I ever fixed a flat tire? No. Did I think I could figure it out? Absolutely.

After about an hour and a half of cursing and sweating in the damn humidity, I gave up and called a local tow company to come help me. They fixed the tire in no time, but I knew I wouldn't make it to the campsite before dark, so I grabbed some food, found a good parking spot, and now I'm eating french fries in my back seat for the night.

I'll head out bright and early in the morning.

Day 15:

My anxiety was through the roof last night. Every car alarm, barking dog or siren sent me into a panic.

I'm never sleeping in my car again.

Day 20:

The Smoky Mountains. Wow.

I've been backpacking through the Smoky Mountains the past few days and I've never been more exhausted or awestruck. Each night, setting up camp then disassembling it and hiking each morning is humbling to say the least.

I hike out tomorrow to finally shower, pack up my truck, and head into Nashville to see Sadie and her friends. I can't wait.

Day 21:

After spending the last three weeks living out of my car, dealing with some unforeseen circumstances, and meeting incredible people, I've decided to reflect on my experience before heading into Nashville this evening.

Here's what I've learned on my solo adventure:

1. *Always engage with people. Most people are really nice and helpful and even make the trip more fun.*
2. *Don't leave the keys turned in the ignition without the engine on. You'll have to find a nice person to jumpstart your car.*
3. *Journaling is a really helpful and healthy way to work through your problems or thoughts.*

4. *Don't trust the weather forecast. Always bring a tarp for your tent.*
5. *You are more capable than you think.*
6. *Plan out how much food to buy between grocery stores so you're not stuck making instant coffee and eating pop tarts for three days straight.*
7. *If you have overwhelming emotions—anger, sadness, frustration, confusion, etc.—go be in nature. It has a way of calming you and putting your feelings into perspective.*
8. *Learning to be by yourself is an incredible skill.*

Chapter 11

The setting sun paints the sky in hues of pink and orange but the neon lights ignite glares of blues and reds along the streets. Everly breathes in the Tennessee air, a mix of fried foods, cigarettes on street corners, and humid summer air. Music swings through open doorways as she inches her way down the congested street, her brakes squeaking with each pause.

Finally she arrives outside the house Sadie and her friends have rented. The sound of her car door shutting is like the starter pistol at a track meet as the back door flies open and a horde of drunken teenagers race toward her.

"Everly **hiccup** oh my god, Everly!" Sadie collides into Everly's outstretched arms, which soon welcome six other steaming bodies.

"I see you've already started the pregame," she laughs, pulling her head back from their liquor-soaked breath.

"You're gonna love it here! We have to get you caught up! Come on!" Without a chance to respond she's being dragged, pushed, and corralled into the house. It's a slap in the face when she crosses the threshold. Visibly chaotic and so aromatically repulsive her eyes start to water.

Empty handles of liquor and bottles of sweet drinks litter the floor, painting a clear picture of the activities that've been going on the past few days. The living room houses an array of pillows and piles of blankets indicating the uncomfortable sleeping arrangements they've made. *Sadie better share her bed with me,* she thinks to herself as she walks further in. Her shoe sticks to the ground. Some green liquid has dried on the hardwood and taken a liking to her sole.

"I love what you've done with the place," she jokes, shaking her head. Settling down at what she can only assume is a dining table that has now been deemed an elevated twister mat, she stares at the large light fixture hanging from the ceiling which displays half a dozen lace panties. "That might be my favorite." She throws her head back, laughing.

"Oh god," Sadie covers her face as she cackles hysterically. "I can't even begin to explain how that happened," she breathes between laughs. "Because I honestly don't remember!" They laugh together only to be interrupted by one of the girls screaming, "Shot o'clock!"

"Gotta catch up, Ev!" Sadie pours her a row of shots. Everyone crowds around chanting, "Shots! Shots! Shots!"

"This probably isn't a good idea guys," she objects. But the cheers ring louder, the music blasts harder, and finally she rolls her eyes and reaches for the glass. She raises hers above her head. "When in Nashville," she hollers, downing the first one.

One shot… two shots… three shots… *oh shit.*

❊

Everyone piles into the cab to head downtown. The car pulls up to let the girls out, each of them a vision in cowboy boots, daisy dukes, and perfected makeup. The moment their summer-tanned legs reach the pavement, they hear the hoots and hollers of men on the street. Sadie leads the pack towards the bar, spinning to give onlookers a better view of her curvaceous body.

Everly wanders anxiously at the back of their group, worrying at the edges of her fake ID until two of the girls turn and link arms with her. They pull her into the excitement and right past the doorman, who's too hopelessly distracted by their seductive eyes and long legs to consider carding them.

"I love this song!" Sadie screeches over the beginning chords. "Let's go!" The music flows over the crowd in rhythmic waves of southern twang. Beers are raised, feet are stomping, and the mob of listeners sings off-key. "Keep going," one of the girls grunts as she pushes into the back of another girl. Everly follows them, helplessly pressing against sweaty bodies of men and women alike. But the comradery of country music makes every stranger a friendly face as they sing along with each other.

Sadie manages to get them all against the stage, close enough to see the red dust on the singer's boots. The speakers project music so powerfully it plays in your bones and reverberates in your heart. Everly allows the music to take over as she lets down her hair and stomps her boots to the beat.

The summer heat and sweaty bodies are nothing compared to the red hot rage building inside Everly's chest as an unwelcome hand ventures up her body.

Turning on her boot heels she finds the culprit intermixed with strangers behind her. From her vantage point, she has to lift her chin to look almost a foot above her at the looming figure. His mouth quirks in a sly, dominant smirk.

Everly softens her expression slightly, an offer to come closer. He moves easily through the bodies between them until he's right in front of her. She smiles sweetly, craning her neck to look him in the eyes. He leans to whisper in her ear, but she's quick to thrust her knee up between his legs. His words cut off in a whimpering gasp. The veins in his neck bulge as his legs buckle, sending him to his knees.

Everly looks down on him, a dominant smirk on her face now. She leans down to whisper in his ear, "I bet your mama would be disappointed in you. Keep your hands to yourself, sweetie."

She turns back around, Sadie cheering for her or the music, she can't tell. "I'm going to grab a drink," she yells to her oblivious group who's focused on the longhaired cowboy singing to them, close enough to touch. She watches as the girls reach for him, his hand moving to hold each of theirs for a moment. They squeal and blush like little kids. But Everly turns, pushing her way through the crowd to the bar for a stiff drink to replace the pain and rage lingering in her chest.

Settling onto the cracked leather barstool, she's scanning her options behind the bar when the bartender extends a fruity cocktail to her. "I didn't order this," she projects over the deafening music. He just gestures down the bar to a guy trying too hard to look nonchalant. She can feel his overconfidence, desperation, and small dick energy wafting over to her.

The way he winks at her before sliding off his barstool unsettles her stomach. A few drinks in and his confidence has reached otherworldly highs as he makes his way towards her, while not so subtly bumping into every female on the way.

Oh, we have another one. Dark eyes watch from the second-floor balcony as a guy moves from his barstool to attempt to woo someone utterly out of his league.

"Howdy." He tips his hat to Everly as he settles into the seat beside her. *So original,* she thinks to herself. "You look lonely, thought I could keep you company." She has to stifle a laugh at his attempt at a southern accent.

No way, she continues to watch from above. *There's no way she's laughing at his pickup line. Girl, look at the new boots, the fake buckle, his hat still has a discount sticker on it.*

Everly relaxes back in her seat, sipping her free drink from the chivalrous poser. "How kind, but I'm not feeling lonely at all actually," she says without paying him any mind.

He attempts to scoot the chair closer to hers. It's painfully awkward when he realizes they are bolted to the floorboards. Everly has to look away to contain her laughter and unease. He clears his throat, sitting back in his stationary spot. "So, uh, where are you from, gorgeous?"

Taking another sip she looks out into the crowd, avoiding his prying eyes. "The Northeast."

"Gotta narrow it down, sweetheart. I gotta know where to visit you." His hand touches her fingers settled on the bar.

God, this is painful to watch. I love it.

Everly pulls away and rolls her eyes, hoping he'll get the hint, but apparently alcohol and an ego bigger than his manhood blocks any sort of rejection signs from processing in his pea brain.

"Bumblefuck, PA." Her smile quirks up at her own answer, knowing it's not what he wanted to hear.

"Funny girl, I see. I like funny girls." He leans in close enough that she can smell the putrid amount of body spray he's probably used since middle school.

Give it a break, dude. Her eyes study the guy as he leans in towards the poor girl who's blatantly uninterested. The girl looks past him towards the crowd of people, probably for her friends. He's talking in her ear. *I bet he smells horrendous,* she giggles to herself. His hand moves to touch hers. No, her drink. The powder dissolves so quickly she could hardly tell. *Oh shit!*

Scrambling from the balcony, she strides through the crowd, down the stairs, taking them two at a time, and shoves her way towards the bar.

Everly sits back in her seat, picking up her drink. "Why don't we get out of here, gorgeous?" Her eyes widen at the absurd suggestion, and her lips bypass the straw for a long swig.

"Oh my god, there you are!" An unfamiliar female voice calls from behind her. Everly turns to meet the deep brown eyes that quickly signal, *Go along with it.*

Everly doesn't miss a beat. "I've been waiting for you!"

The girl leans in to embrace her, whispering something in her ear before pulling away. "The guys are outside waiting for us. Come on." She takes her hand, leading her towards the exit without giving the guy a chance to say a single word.

The cool evening air fills her lungs as her mind starts to fog. "Hey, my name's Jocelyn." Everly's barely aware of the long fingers gripping her shoulders. "That guy put something in your drink. I don't think it was a lot, but you're probably going to feel groggy soon. Do you know where your friends are?" Everly looks down the street, the neon signs shifting in unfocused waves. Everly squints, trying to clear the haziness. "Hey!" Jocelyn shakes her lightly. "What's your name?"

"Ev!" Jocelyn turns to see Sadie and the girls bolting through the bar doors towards them as Everly collapses into Jocelyn's arms.

Chapter 12

The toes of her new boots scrape along the pavement as they drag her into the nearest store. Jocelyn looks up at the tattoo artists who are completely unfazed by the barely conscious girl in her arms, and collectively point to the bathroom past their stations. The girls rush past, breaking off into teams like they've trained for this. One to get her water, another to guard the door, and a third to hold her hair back while Sadie reaches down her throat prompting her stomach to heave.

Everly's eyes widen as she grips the porcelain and retches. "You're going to be okay, Ev." Sadie rubs a soothing hand along her back. Jocelyn stands behind her, holding her hair back. *Thank you*, Sadie mouths to her. She gives a reassuring nod and smile as Everly retches again.

"Good morning, sunshine," a soft voice whispers next to her. Everly blinks at the painfully bright morning light shining on the bedroom walls. She shifts to her side, the movement urging her to heave into the trash can beside the bed. "Can't believe you have anything left in you," Sadie mocks as she pulls back her hair. "How are you feeling?"

Everly sits up, wiping her mouth. "Like I got hit by a truck." She looks up, catching the unfamiliar gaze of deep brown eyes looking at her. "I'm sorry." She shifts the pillows behind her. "I don't remember your name."

"I figured. We met under some pretty strange circumstances last night." Her pink lips spread in a wide smile. "Hi, I'm Jocelyn."

"So, what the hell happened? How'd we get home last night? Did Jocelyn spend the night? I'm starving," Everly rambles as she rests against Sadie's shoulder beside her.

"Jocelyn and some of the other girls left to grab breakfast for everyone. I saw you absolutely humiliate that guy on the dance floor—nice shot by the way. Then you went to the bar. After a couple songs, you still weren't back so we went to find you. After checking the bathrooms, we asked some people around the bar, and some guy said he saw you go outside with someone, so we ran out to find you. My brain thought maybe you found a cute guy, but when we came out you looked awful."

"Wow, thanks."

"Oh, shut up. You got drugged, of course you looked like shit," she giggles, pushing against her. "So anyway, long story short, Jocelyn basically saved you and stayed with us the whole night. She called an Uber for all of us and even made an anonymous phone call to the cops about the dude. I told her that we could call her in the morning to update her, but she really wanted to make sure you were all right so she slept in the armchair." Sadie gestures towards the cushioned chair by the windows.

"That's crazy." Everly sits up, still looking at the chair. Shaking her wavy hair she gazes out the window at the midmorning sun over the large maple tree growing in the yard. "So, did anything happen to the guy?"

"He was caught in possession of an illegal firearm and date-rape drugs. He's probably getting cozy in his cell right about now." Jocelyn pokes her head into the room and leans against the doorframe, smirking. "That piece of shit deserves worse, but some jail time should do him good."

"I don't know how to thank you," Everly starts.

"Stop. We gotta stick together, us girls. I'm just happy you're okay."

"Thank you, Jocelyn. I really—"

"We brought breakfast!" someone hollers from the kitchen.

Jocelyn smiles over her shoulder, then turns to look at Sadie and Everly again. "We picked up some cinnamon rolls and coffee."

"God bless you," Everly laughs, rolling across the bed and over Sadie's lap to race for the coffee and sweets.

"So, what's your story?" Everly reclines on the couch, basking in the sunlight shining in from the lofted skylights.

"What do you mean?" Jocelyn peeks over her coffee mug, the steam drifting lazily around her halo of dark locks.

"Do you typically go around saving lives and such?" Jocelyn laughs at the blatant question.

Looking over her shoulder she analyzes everyone else's whereabouts before leaning towards Everly and speaking in a low voice. "Yes, actually…"

Everly straightens up, placing her plate on her legs. "Wait," she hesitates. "Really?"

Jocelyn falls back into her chair, "No, dummy," she laughs. Everly relaxes back into the couch, a warm blush highlighting her cheekbones. "I do like the idea of protecting the innocent though. I'm going to school for criminal justice."

"No way, the college Sadie and I are going to has an incredible criminology program."

Everly and Jocelyn continue sipping their sweetened coffees until they both nearly spit the contents of their mugs across the room as they realize they'll be going to the same university in the fall. Their conversation ebbs and flows from future plans to past experiences to their similar taste in music and differing taste in men. As everyone else gets ready to explore the shopping district, Everly and Jocelyn remain happily planted on the couch, their conversation flowing without skipping a beat.

When the girls return, the two of them are sprawled across the living room floor, tears streaming down their cheeks as they cackle and cradle their aching stomachs. It's as though they have known each other all their lives. And by chance or fate their meeting has sparked the beginning of a friendship unparalleled by anything either of them has experienced before.

PART II

Chapter 13

"You're good. You're good. Yo, dude." A strong hand shoots up, barring entry. "Ten bucks."

"What the hell? It was five last weekend."

"Yeah, but we gotta pay for the broken window upstairs now. Cough it up, freshman." He holds out his hand waiting for the two crumpled fives, then moves aside, allowing him in. "Welcome, ladies." His eyes rove over the group of girls in their crop tops and tight jeans as they saunter past.

"I need a stiff drink." Sadie wraps her hand around Everly's, and Everly's other hand reaches out for Jocelyn's as they're both half-dragged through the crowded, neon-lit room to the frat's backyard.

"Tough week?" Jocelyn asks over the blaring music.

"You have no idea."

"Want to talk about it?" Everly offers.

"Nope," Sadie coughs out as she downs a shot with no chaser. "Just let loose with me. Please," she begs.

Looking at each other, they contemplate silently, then roll their eyes back to Sadie's pathetic pout. It works every time. "All right, fine!" Jocelyn exclaims. "Pour me one."

"Make that two." Everly drapes her arms over their shoulders, smiling.

"We got next!" Everly projects over the crowd around the beer pong table. "Where'd Sadie go?" She leans against an aged oak tree beside Jocelyn.

"She's over there talking to that girl. You know her?"

Squinting to see clearer, she focuses on the girl's long legs and deep mocha skin, trying to place her. "Oh, yeah. She's in my biology class. I think her name's Raven."

"Damn it!" someone screams from the other end of the table.

"Drink up, losers." Cole and Travis bask in their victory as their opponents chug their final cup and strip down to their boxers. Everyone pulls out their phones to record their naked lap through the streets.

Jocelyn looks at Everly. "We're playing lower stakes, right?"

Everly raises her eyebrows, a mischievous grin on her face. "Depends," she teases. "How confident are you in your ability?" Jocelyn stares at her, wide-eyed. "I'm kidding," she teases. "Sadie, we're up!"

"Guys, this is Raven." Sadie pulls her by the forearm to meet them, her eyes encouraging her to introduce herself.

"Hey—"

"We have a couple classes together," Sadie stammers. "Anyway, we're partners. For the game," she clarifies. "You two are going down!" Her fingers wrap around Raven's arm again, dragging her back to their designated side of the table.

Jocelyn and Everly smile as they too retreat to their side. "Shall we play dare pong?"

"Pass!" Everly blurts out, punching her playfully. Across the table, Sadie sways on her feet, and Raven steadies her with a guiding hand on her hip. "Bring it on!"

The crowd has thinned so the girls can walk into the house without pushing their way past bodies. "We'll get you next time," Sadie slurs, plopping down into the sunken cushions of the sofa beside Raven. She sinks so deep that her legs lift off the ground.

Everly makes eye contact with Raven—they acknowledge that she will be responsible for taking care of Sadie tonight. Jocelyn lies back, her long legs stretching across Everly's lap. "Did you see those guys who played before us?" She glances around in case they're close by.

"You mean Cole and Travis?" She chuckles.

"I think so." She twirls a lock of her dark hair. "He was really cute," Jocelyn giggles. Rarely does she indulge in this much alcohol, let alone allow herself to discuss boys.

"Which one?" Everly asks, poking her ribs.

Jocelyn jumps and slaps her hand away, smiling. "Travis, of course!"

"Did someone say my name?" Jocelyn freezes and Everly's smile expands as she sees Travis stand just behind Jocelyn.

"She did!" Sadie blurts out pointing at Jocelyn. Raven quickly reins her in with a hand over her mouth.

Travis walks around the sofa until he stands a few inches from her, but Jocelyn remains frozen, her legs still sprawled across Everly's lap. "Hi." He reaches out to take her hand in his. "I'm Travis." His lips press against her knuckles, his eyes admiring the deep brown of hers the whole while.

"Say something!" Sadie shouts, and Raven grapples with her, wrestling to cover her mouth again.

Everly gives a gentle nudge to Jocelyn's legs, urging her to sit up. She complies, tucking a loose strand of hair behind her ear. Travis grins as she locks eyes with him. "Hi," he says again.

"Hi," she chokes out, her throat suddenly deathly dry.

"What's your name?" He kneels down until they're eye level. She's silent as she tries to think over the pounding in her brain and the anxiety in her chest.

"Her name's Jocelyn!" Sadie calls out.

"All right, that's it!" Raven swears, then without missing a beat, lifts Sadie's curvaceous body over her shoulder effortlessly. "It was nice meeting you." She looks back at Everly to wave. Sadie giggles uncontrollably until Raven sets her down not too far away, their hands intertwining effortlessly as they make for the exit.

"Jocelyn." It rolls off his tongue. "That's a beautiful name." She smiles up at him, her demeanor more flirtatious now. "And yours?" He looks at Everly.

"Oh. I'm Everly," she reaches out, shaking his hand formally.

"There you are!" A voice closes in from across the room. "Where the hell have you been, dude?"

Travis stands up, throwing an arm around his friend's shoulder. "Cole, this is Jocelyn and Everly." They wave innocently at him.

"Hey." He nods his head at them. "Oh wait, you two played right after us on the pong table, right?"

"Yeah." Jocelyn simply nods.

"We should play," he suggests. "You seemed pretty good."

"I don't know," Everly starts. "I feel like it'd be unfair."

"Why's that?"

"You guys barely won your game." She shrugs, smirking. "And we won by a landslide."

The boys gawk at her, smiling at the challenge. "Fine," Travis counters. "Then it's me and Jocelyn versus you and Cole. Gives us a fighting chance."

Everly stands, pulling Jocelyn to her unsteady feet. "Let's do it. Naked lap for the losers?" Everly calls.

"Hell, no!" Jocelyn squeals.

"Oh, come on, Joce. Everyone's gone."

"Not a chance in hell, Ev. You'd never do it either."

"I totally would, but I never lose." She sticks her tongue out.

Cole leans against the table's edge looking at Everly. "What are the odds?"

She furrows her brow at him. "What do you mean?"

"Pick any number between one and one hundred, and if we yell out the same number, you have to do a naked lap. Deal?"

"Whoa, whoa, whoa. I'm not the loser here," she protests.

"You scared?" he prods. Travis and Jocelyn walk off to sit in the lawn chairs, talking and watching planes fly overhead.

"Fine!" she concedes. "On the count of three."

Together they count, "One…two… three…forty-seven!"

Everly's mouth gapes open, and the color drains from her face. "No way," she protests frantically.

"Let's see it, Everly," Cole cheers. "You said it yourself, 'Everyone's gone' and it's already dark." He licks his pointer finger and holds it up in the air. "Hmm, perfect conditions for a naked lap."

"You can't be serious," she laughs.

"How about just strip down t0 the panties?"

"You'd like that wouldn't you?" she mocks.

"Oh, absolutely I would." He smiles.

"I'll only do it if you do it too," she counters.

He's silent for a moment, thinking. "Yeah, all right."

"Wait." She stares. "What?"

"I said all right. Let's do it." He smiles as he pulls his sweatshirt over his head and throws it on the lawn chair beside Travis. "Chop, chop."

Everly's body boils with dread and adrenaline as she fiddles with the hem of her shirt before pulling it up and over her blonde waves. The cold air kisses her skin as she lowers her jeans inch by inch.

"It's so cold," she blurts out. Jocelyn and Travis have vacated the yard and moved inside to get warm.

"Then let's go," Cole says, jogging in circles around her in his briefs. She shivers when her bare toes touch the brick walkway. Cole reaches out to her, his hands rubbing her shoulders. "It's not that cold, you baby."

Everly looks over her shoulder at him. "Catch me if you can, loser." She takes off down the street.

Chapter 14

The musty smell of aged books lingers about the mahogany shelves as sunbeams highlight the dust drifting on the stale air of their beloved bookstore. Rooms of books stacked in corners from the dingy floorboards to the water-stained ceiling feel like home to them, a safe place to escape the real world. Jocelyn browses the mystery aisle for a plot she's yet to solve, while Everly gets lost in worlds of warlocks and wizards. The rolling ladder screeches with each push towards one particularly intriguing book accentuated by the rainbowed light from the stained glass window. Everly climbs the ladder to retrieve the dust-clad book, but as her fingers slide along the textured cover, an aged rung splinters, sending her crashing to the ground.

The thud shakes the floorboards, sending various piles of books tumbling. She groans, trying to catch her breath, but coughs viciously as her lungs fill with the puffs of dust around her. Resting her head against the stacks and finally catching her breath, she watches as the rainbow light paints the space above her, and a loose page flutters lazily to the floor.

"Are you okay?" Jocelyn calls from behind the stacks.

Jocelyn finds Everly flat on her back surrounded by books bursting with magic, muggles, and demons. She stands there laughing before extending a helping hand. Everly scoffs at her, then accepts it reluctantly. "Thanks."

"What's that?" Jocelyn gestures to the paper in her hand.

Everly raises it to the sunlight and reads aloud:

HELP WANTED

Work Abroad — Earn College Credits

Location: *Mundo de Maravillas* bookshop, Seville, Spain

Employer: Lucía Morales

Job description: Two students will be responsible for ensuring the bookshop is clean, presentable, well stocked, and inviting, as well as assisting Ms. Morales with her daily tasks, which may include, but are not limited to:

- Grocery shopping
- Cleaning/organizing
- Learning English
- Traveling into town, etc.

Compensation: College credits will be awarded to each student upon successful completion of a six-month-long work exchange. Students also receive compensatory housing and food in exchange for their work services.

"No way that's real," Jocelyn exclaims. "Right?"

Everly turns the paper over in her hands. "It looks real," she beams. "And it's for next semester."

Jocelyn snatches it from her fingers, looking for herself. "We *have* to apply, Ev." Everly scrunches her nose. "Can you imagine the two of us living in Spain, working in a bookshop, and just living our best lives?"

Everly paints the image in her mind, the warm sun on her skin, the smell of fresh pastries, and her best friend beside her. Everly meets Jocelyn's hopeful brown eyes. "Let's go to Spain!"

"Yes!" Jocelyn throws her arms around Everly, pulling her into a tight hug that is equally reciprocated and suffocating.

"And so, the adventure begins."

Chapter 15

The latch clicks as she gently pulls the door shut behind her, stepping quietly into the main room. She rubs at her eyes, urging them to adapt to the pitch black as she guides herself along a wall. "Cole," she whispers, hoping it's loud enough for him to hear but quiet enough not to wake anyone else.

Floorboards creak overhead, and she shuffles past the long dining table where she can barely make out the remnants of their most recent party. A loud crunch breaks the silence as she crushes a Solo cup beneath her sneaker. Cursing under her breath, she scurries towards the stairs when she hears another set of feet on the floorboards at the far side of the house.

A light switches on upstairs, illuminating the hallway and casting shadows of the railing spindles along the wall, stopping just before her face. Her breath catches as a shadowy figure emerges at the top of the steps. The figure pauses for a moment before rushing down, two steps at a time. Everly holds her breath, utterly still.

Stopping just a few steps from the bottom, the figure searches the darkness of the room, their eyes likely adjusting to the darkness as hers had. There's a whisper from the stairs.

"Ev?" Everly takes one step forward as she recognizes the voice and lunges as Jocelyn shrieks and falls down the stairs. Everly clasps her hand over Jocelyn's mouth, laughing silently as she settles beside her friend on the floor. Jocelyn bats the hand away. "Jesus, Ev!" Everly holds a finger to her own lips, shushing her. "What the hell are you doing?"

Everly shakes her head, thankful the darkness is hiding her burning cheeks and embarrassed smile. "I…" She pauses, looking up at her friend's dark eyes. "I came to see Cole."

"No, duh, dipshit," Jocelyn snorts quietly. "Why are you lurking around in the dark, is really what I meant." Everly shoulders her.

"I couldn't see anything," she starts.

"We do live in a time of light switches, you know." She teases, poking Everly in the ribs.

"And I just figured he'd come down to meet me," she finishes.

Even in the dark Everly can tell Jocelyn is rolling her eyes. "Well, you're not with him for his well-endowed chivalry." She shrugs.

"Yeah…" she admits. "Wait, how'd you even know I was here?"

"Oh, I chipped you while you were sleeping once," Jocelyn says matter-of-factly. Everly stares at her, almost convinced for a moment she could be telling the truth, until she giggles. "Just kidding. Travis got up to use the bathroom and saw Cole. He told him you were almost here. I figured I'd be your welcoming committee." She throws her arm over Everly's shoulder, head resting gently against hers. "I guess I can be your booty call escort, too. Right this way, milady." Jocelyn offers her arm, and Everly takes it, but only after jabbing her in the ribs.

Without knocking, Jocelyn bumps open the door at the end of the hall. Blue light from the TV casts a glow across the posters of half-naked women hanging on the walls. Cole inclines his head just enough to see the two standing arm in arm with giddy smiles in his doorway. Shifting under his covers, he says, "Took you long enough."

"I could have—"

"She could have gotten up here sooner for her booty call if the booty caller made it easier." Jocelyn clears her throat dramatically. "I had to help her navigate this shithole."

Cole chuckles, accepting the insult. "I'll be sure to clear a path next time."

"Good. Now." Jocelyn wraps Everly in a hug. "I'm going to bed with my *boyfriend*." Everly whirls, squeezing Jocelyn's hand at the news. "Who, might I add, changed the sheets, lit candles, AND made me dinner." She gives Everly a quick hug and wink before flipping her chocolate locks and sauntering down the hallway to Travis' room.

Everly ditches her shoes and flops onto the covers beside Cole. "Boyfriend, huh?"

He looks into her eyes, a smirk painted across his face. "Don't expect that kind of treatment from me," he starts.

She pulls him against her, and the heat burning in her cheeks crawls down to her chest, her stomach, between her legs. "That's not why I'm here," she smiles against his lips. His hands follow the heat along her body, and her breath catches when he pauses on her thigh.

A devilish smile works across her lips as her tongue glides along his neck, and she breathes lightly in his ear. She can feel his body stiffen at the sensation. Her teeth nibble gently on his ear before she whispers ever so quietly, "Do that thing with your tongue—"

His hands grip her neck and waist, flipping her onto her back in one smooth movement. Fighting against the various fabrics restricting his access, his fingers still manage to trace along all the right places. Her hands tangle in the sheets, and goosebumps speckle her skin.

His smile beams as he launches her clothes across the room and pulls her to the edge of the bed. Within minutes her flustered mind is filled with clouds of chaos and euphoric waves that ebb and flow from head to toe.

"Goddamn," he breathes out in rushed huffs. Everly simply nods her agreement. *Buzz… Buzz… Buzz….* Everly takes a deep breath before reaching for her phone, which somehow ended up under the covers at the foot of the bed. "Is it Jocelyn telling us to keep it down?" he smirks. Everly stiffens and sits up against the wall. "Who is it?"

"It's Thomas," she answers, confused.

"Who's he?"

"Um," she starts. "He's, uh, he's my ex." Cole's face shifts for a split second, an emotion she can't place. "He's an asshole, don't worry. I should've deleted his number a long time ago." Cole simply nods.

“Well, anyway, this was fun.” His tone feels like a slap in the face and an invitation to get the hell out. Everly collects her things, getting dressed as she goes, and sneaks out before the rest of the house wakes up. The knot in her stomach tightens as she descends the stairs looking at her phone and those four words.

Four torturous words.

I still love you.

Chapter 16

I still love you.

Thomas, stop.

Ev, please just let me explain.

There's nothing to explain. Delete my number.

Just give me one chance to talk to you in person.

Why should I? Why after all this time do you even wanna meet?

Because you deserve an explanation and an apology for how I treated you.

It's too late for that.

I know. But you deserve to hear it anyway.

"And you're not even a little curious about what he has to say?" Jocelyn leans over the desk staring at her wide-eyed.

"Of course I am. But how could he tell me he still loves me after the way we left things?

"It's been a couple years now, maybe he's finally realized that he lost the most incredible person he'd ever find."

Everly rests back in her chair. "I don't know what to do. Sadie thinks it's a bad idea, but she's always hated him." Gazing up expectantly at her friend, she asks, "What do you think, Joce?"

"Honestly?" Everly nods. "Follow your heart, Ev. If you think things could be different or even if you just want that apology, then there's no harm in seeing him. Nothing has to come of it if you don't want it to."

"You're right," she nods to herself. "You're right."

"Lying, cheating bastard! I'm going to kill him!" Everly races down the sidewalk trying to keep pace. "He really thought I wouldn't find out. What an idiot!"

"Joce, wait up," Everly calls out, jogging to catch up to her. "I want to kill him just as much as you do, but what are we *really* doing?" Jocelyn stops and turns on her heel to smile nefariously at her friend.

"We're going to hit him where it hurts and destroy that pretty little car of his." Jocelyn turns back down the street, but Everly catches her wrist before she can speed away again.

"Joce," she searches in those dark eyes. "Breathe, Joce. Take a deep breath, and think about this for a minute." Shaking her head angrily, her eyes look past Everly as they brim with tears. "Can we try something right now? So we don't end up in jail?" Jocelyn's eyes finally settle on her friend's as she nods. "Okay. Five minutes. You get five minutes to scream, cry, break something, whatever you need to do to get this anger out. But right after that, we're going to take your mind off of it. We'll do something fun or goofy, whatever you want. Okay?"

A nod of agreement.

"Okay. Five minutes starts…now."

December 24th

I know my answer

Answer to what?

You ask why I really wanted to meet and after some thought I know my real answer. If you wanna know

Thomas, I don't care anymore

Please, Ev. Just let me say this

Fine.

Even when we broke up, even with the pain and anger I felt, there wasn't a day that went

by that I didn't wish I had you back.
I'll always love you, Ev.

Why didn't you ever reach out? Why now?

Because I knew you were right. I was awful
to you when we dated. I wanted the chance
to change for you. I wanted to grow into someone
who really deserved you.

I don't think people ever really change.

Well, I have. I was single for almost two years
and it changed me a lot mentally and emotionally.
It's been me focusing on me and because of that
I know that when the time is right, things will
fall into place with us. You've always been the one,
Ev.

Cheaters always cheat.

I was young and dumb. I regret all of that so
much. You have no idea how sorry I am.

I don't know how I could trust you again.

We've both grown and gone through a lot these
past years. I just know that if you give me the
chance I'll do anything to be with you. I want
the ups and downs. Every hardship. I know it
comes with growth and change, and I've done that.
For you.

I don't know what to say.

Then don't say anything. Just meet me a week
from today, New Year's Eve.

I have plans, Thomas. You can't expect
me to upend my life for you.

I'll be there. I'll come to you. Just tell me where.

Chapter 17

The room is clouded with smoke, sweaty bodies and the overwhelming reek of alcohol. "Ten…nine…eight…"

Panicky palpitations surge through Everly's body as she looks to Jocelyn. Her eyes speak for her: *What do I do?* Jocelyn shrugs helplessly at her friend as the crowd screams around them. "Seven…six…five…"

Her fingers ache in clenched fists at her side, palms sweating. "Four… three…" Strong arms find her hips as she moves through the crowd. "Two…one… Happy New Year!"

The room erupts in gleeful squeals followed by the unmistakable silence of passionate kissing. Everly's pulled in by Cole, their lips locking in perfect symmetry. A drunken bliss washes over her, urging her to lean into his embrace until her subconscious and buzzing phone bring her back to reality.

Everly pulls away, her eyes wide with urgency. "I'm sorry," she blurts out as she turns away, shoving her way through the mass of heavy, drunken bodies. Finally, she pushes open the basement door, a chilling gust of new January air stinging her skin. She turns back to see Cole looking after her and sprints out into the night.

Where is he?

The wind nips at her exposed skin, her freckled nose already turning pink. *He said he would be here.*

And he is.

Her racing heart stops right then. He stares into her soul, and the chill of the night melts away immediately.

He came.

Without a second thought, she runs to him. He takes long strides towards her, his arms outstretched, ready to embrace her. They crash into each other, burning against the night. Her body fits against his like a perfect puzzle piece.

Looking into her eyes for the first time in years, he allows himself to smile, taking a long moment to study her face, seeing the ways she's changed. Her rosy cheeks smile at him as he tilts her jaw up and presses a feverishly awaited kiss to her lips.

"Let's get out of here," he says against her smile. His cold hands graze her skin as he lowers her to the ground. She looks up to him, his features illuminated by the midnight moon. His fingers suddenly tense around her waist as he looks past her.

The basement doors stand ajar as some drunken teenagers stumble giddily into the yard, Cole among them. Everly looks over her shoulder to see him moving towards them. "Come on," she says, pulling Thomas towards the car. "Let's just go."

Cole struts across the grass calling out to her. "Oh, I see," he smirks. "Couldn't handle the real thing, so you had to go back to this idiot?"

A group of girls snicker to each other in a huddled circle by the fire. Thomas tenses at his words. "Don't," Everly pleads.

Cole saunters closer to them, his speech slightly slurring. "You know, this is for the best." He pauses, throwing his arm around an unassuming girl. "I wouldn't want *his* seconds anyway."

At that, Thomas rushes at him in furious strides. Everly's feet drag across the wet grass as she pulls helplessly at his wrist. Hands grab onto her from behind, pulling her away from him.

Cole grunts as he throws a hard right hook that Thomas dodges easily and counters with a violent jab straight to the nose. The crack of bone and cartilage is audible even over the yelling and cheering building around them.

More people filter out into the cold night at the commotion, creating a ring around them. Jocelyn moves through the crowd in search of Everly.

Cheers ring out when Cole steadies himself, blood running down his face, coating his teeth. He looks up at Thomas smiling, inviting the challenge. Thomas steps left and swings right, but Cole brings his fist straight up, striking his jawbone. He stumbles backwards, and Cole sprints full force at his opponent, his shoulder crashing into his ribs, grinding him into the ground. An uproar of cheers rings out. The air leaves Thomas' body in a visible whoosh.

Jocelyn pushes past the bordering crowd to see Everly being restrained by Travis and his friend. She writhes in their unyielding grip, her lungs burning with rage and freezing air. When Thomas hits the ground, Everly twists in their grasp, elbowing with all her might at the guy's stomach just as Jocelyn kicks the legs out from underneath Travis and lands a rattling right hook to his cheekbone. She lingers over him a second longer so he can see the triumphant smirk on her lips.

Cole lands a solid punch across Thomas' temple. His ears ring, and the world around him slows. The crowd's roar fades to a gentle hum, and he watches as another set of knuckles comes down towards him. Everly's shriek cuts through the dull humming. Like a lightswitch flicking on, he snaps out of the haze. His mental fog clears immediately, and he uses Cole's momentum to throw him off balance, flinging him savagely to the ground. He rolls quickly, gaining the upper hand as his fists start raining thunderous blows, over and over and over.

"Stop!" Everly shrieks. Thomas continues. Again and again. Everly pleads, pulling on the torn fabric of his flannel.

Cole lays in the frosted grass, his hands trying desperately to protect his face. The crowd quiets slightly as the fight comes to an obvious end. "Please…" Everly begs.

Thomas looks down at Cole's beaten and bloodied face. Their eyes connect for a second. A hush falls over the crowd as Thomas finally stands.

He looms over Cole then looks at the stunned faces around him. He spits the blood from his mouth, intertwines his already bruising fingers with Everly's, and walks her towards his car, leaving an awestruck crowd and defeated opponent behind them.

Chapter 18

The quiet back roads contour the hill on the way up to their spot. The rumbling of dirt and the pop of gravel under the tires means they're close.

"I love you," Thomas says, reaching over to hold Everly's hand. His swollen eyes veer from the road to see her golden hair swirl around in the wintry wind. She's just finished another drink, throwing the bottle out the open window, when she looks back at him.

"What?" she calls over the sound of the rushing air and blaring music.

"I said I love you, Everly!" He smiles at her, the cut on his lip opening again. "Forever and always."

"I heard you." She squeezes his hand. "I just wanted to hear you say it again." She giggles, throwing her head back, breathing in the cool night air.

The car comes to a stop at the edge of the lookout. Moonlight reflects in silver waves across the lake below. Stars twinkle like fireflies behind the wisps of clouds. The earth is silent up here. The noise of the world comes to a halt, and worries melt away with each breath of pine-scented air. This is a place made for special moments: first dates, summer kisses, and maybe even the rekindling of young love.

Everly stares across the lake, wondering how an earth this peaceful can breed such frantic people.

Thomas lowers the music as he looks over at her. "What's going on in your beautiful head?"

She giggles. "Just thinking."

He urges her to continue. "About…?"

She looks up at him, his deep honey eyes analyzing every piece of her that's changed. She studies him too. Studies that angular face that she's looked at, felt, admired, and loved all through high school.

Nothing has changed.

Nothing has changed.

She cracks open another drink, taking a long swig before looking at him. Placing her drink down, she leans towards him over the console. "You really want to know what I was thinking about?" she asks, her voice slow and deep. He nods, a smile creeping across his face in anticipation. She leans in a little closer, whispering quietly into his ear.

That does it. He pulls her into him, and they collide like they always have, feverishly yearning for the other's touch.

Chaptcr 19

Everly paces the tile floor of her small Seville apartment. Jocelyn looks in every now and then to make sure she isn't wearing out the floor. They need to get their deposit back.

She peeks her head around the corner of the kitchen as Everly screams into her phone, "I can't believe I fell for your bullshit again." Her voice strains against the tears she won't let fall. There's a long silence before the rage in her voice scares Jocelyn back into the kitchen. "Don't call me again!" Everly's phone launches across the room toward the couch. *Forever and always* wasn't as lasting as Thomas had promised.

Cautiously, Jocelyn steps into the living room to console her friend. It's less of a living room and more of a shoebox with a small loveseat, laundry lines, a window, and an old TV that has two stations and no volume control. She retrieves the phone from the couch and places it out of harm's way. "Do you want me to listen or do you want me to help?"

Being the closest friend either of them has ever known, they've learned that sometimes you just need to rant and other times you want advice. This question, simple as it may be, has saved their friendship on multiple occasions.

"Am I an idiot for thinking he changed?" Everly asks as she slumps down the fading wallpaper and onto the floor.

"Yes," Jocelyn says pointedly.

They look at each other in silence, then burst into laughter. Jocelyn always knows how to make her smile, even on her hardest days. Their friendship has been pushed to the brink, yet they know that no matter what life throws at them, they are better at handling it when they're together.

Everly is the sun, and Jocelyn is the moon. Opposites that create harmony in a world of chaos.

"Buenos días, chicas," Señora Morales calls up the steep staircase, her sweet voice cracking.

"Buenos días! We'll be right down," Jocelyn replies. It's been three weeks since they packed up and moved across the ocean to live with Señora Morales in Spain.

Jocelyn scurries to Everly's side where she sits against the wall, knees to her chest, head in her hands, reluctant tears streaming down her freckled cheeks. Everly inhales raggedly to say, "Boys are stupid," and exhales sobs of laughter.

"Don't move, I'll be right back." Jocelyn slides across the floor in her socks and returns a few minutes later with her arms full.

"Okay!" she blurts out excitedly. "We're going to get all dressed up and cute, then we're going to go help Señora Morales, and then we're going to go for a walk because it's a beautiful day and the world deserves to see you smile." Everly looks up at her through tears, but Jocelyn knows those are tears of love and admiration. Each tear, a silent *thank you. Thank you for knowing me better than I know myself.*

"Buenos días, Señora Morales. ¿Cómo estás?" Everly asks as she descends the final steps into the bookshop.

"Muy bien, ¿Y tú?"

"Better now. How can we help this morning?"

Lucía looks around her bookshop. It's beautifully quaint but desperately needs some love and attention. The sign above her door once shone with metallic gold outlining bold black letters that read *Mundo de Maravillas,* World of Wonders. Now the gold has lost its luster, and each letter has cracked as worn leather cushions do. The lush ivy and wisteria that once draped elegantly along the outer walls have withered away.

There are charms on the door that chime upon entry, a sweet sound like music flowing over a path of fallen leaves. The heavy wooden door seals the sweet smell of aged flowers and herbs inside. Valencia red roses cinched with thyme grace on the tables. Dried bundles decorate the ceiling, illuminated by streaks of sunlight.

The space feels cozy, and the ambient lighting and well-loved chairs invite guests to explore without haste. Time seems to slow as you walk the narrow aisles, and every now and then an anonymous breeze will flutter the pages of your book, leading you toward a new adventure.

Señora Morales settles her gaze on an overwhelmingly skewed stack of books on her favorite blush-pink armchair. "We start there, to find homes for this books," she announces in her best English, smiling at Everly.

Jocelyn joins her in organizing the array of books. She turns it into a game, creating plotlines for each book based on the title and stringing them together for an outrageously haphazard storyline.

✻

The clouds drift by basking in gold and pink against the blue sky. Everly and Jocelyn, draped in flowery dresses and dingy white sneakers, ramble along the slow-flowing water of the Guadalquivir River. The heavenly sound of a violin drifts on the air as the two of them stare longingly towards the setting sun. Jocelyn skips ahead, spinning joyfully as she goes.

"I found the perfect spot!" she squeals, pointing towards a ledge tucked below the bridge's base but above the meandering water.

They hop down and see it leads to a wider area beneath the bridge. A perfect oasis for them to relax and unwind. They sit on the cool stone ledge watching the sun sparkle across the slight wake of the water.

Everly reaches into her bag, pulling out a bottle of white wine, a fresh baguette, handfuls of strawberries, grapes, and dark chocolate, and the most decadent cheese, recommended by Lucía. Jocelyn scans the scene, from the sunset, the food, the music, to her best friend sitting beside her.

Everly looks at her knowingly. "Don't say anything sappy, just take a swig," she laughs as she shoves the bottle of Albariño at her. Jocelyn lifts the bottle to her lips but does a spit take as Everly screams.

"What! What is it?" Jocelyn exclaims.

There's a man standing over them, hidden by the shadow of the bridge. He's brandishing a weapon over his head. Then he takes a cautious step forward into the sunlight, and Everly sees a bow and violin held up in front of him in the universal sign for *I mean no harm.*

"¡Lo siento, lo siento!" His voice cracks with equal amounts of surprise. "No sabía qué había nadie más aquí."

"You scared the shit out of us," Jocelyn exhales when she realizes there's no real threat.

"Oh, American," he says, caught off guard. "I'm so sorry, I didn't think anyone would be down here. I usually come here after practicing to watch the sunset over the water."

They look him up and down. He's really quite striking. The shadows of the bridge create an intense contrast of sharp lines and angelic softness in his face. Windblown curls frame green eyes and accentuate his sculpted cheekbones. His full lips quirk upward to one side, creating a perfect dimple. In the waning light, he looks like a fallen angel. Hidden in shadows but meant to shine.

Jocelyn finally breaks the silence. "No worries. Would you like to join us?" Everly gives her a look. *What are you doing? We don't know him.* Jocelyn looks back. *Just trust me, it'll be fine.*

"Are you sure that's all right?" he asks politely.

"Absolutely," Jocelyn encourages, patting the stones between them invitingly. "Come sit."

"Was that you playing up on the bridge before? It was beautiful." Everly smiles as he takes his seat beside her, placing his violin next to the wine.

"Yes, I play here most days. I grew up listening to my mother play."

"That's cool," Jocelyn says. "Do you ever play together?"

He hesitates before saying, "She died a few years ago. This bridge was her favorite spot in the city, so I come here to play for her."

There is silence.

"I'm sure she loves it," Everly offers with a comforting smile. He smiles in response, appreciating the kind optimism that his mother can still hear him play.

After nearly an hour of flowing conversation, Jocelyn interjects, "Wait, we still don't know your name!" Everyone laughs at the ridiculous truth.

He flashes a genuine smile that makes his eyes crinkle. "Right," he chuckles, "Hi, I'm Axel."

Chapter 20

March 4th

It's been nearly six weeks since we met Axel. After that first night, we've come to watch the sunset and listen to him play almost every night. He introduced us to his friends who've made us feel like family.

On our days off, we all meet up to hang out. They take us to the best local bars on Fridays and show us the night life of the city. On the weekends, we've started playing pickup fútbol games. I think we're even going to organize a tournament because so many people want to join us.

It's just so lively here. The music, the people, the culture. I love it. And Axel has been amazing. He's really made us feel welcome here. His birthday is next week, so Joce and I are trying to plan a surprise party for him. Lucía says she has something in mind for us. I'm excited to know what it is. Lots of planning to do, fingers crossed it goes well!

⁂

"¿Qué está pasando?" Axel questions as he hesitantly shuffles along behind Everly, trying to adjust his blindfold while holding onto her shoulder.

"No peeking! Just trust me, okay," Everly laughs. He looks like a baby animal just learning to walk, each step uncertain as they make their way down the cobblestone street. Arriving at Lucía's bookshop, Jocelyn opens the door, holding the charms so they don't make noise.

"Do you trust me?" Everly asks, looking up at him. The curls of his hair hang loosely across his blindfold. His dimple appears at the question.

"Of course," he says without hesitation. Everly's heart flutters at his certainty.

"Okay. You can take your blindfold off on three. One…two…two and a half…two and three quarters…"

"Ev!" he exclaims impatiently.

"Three!" His hands bring the blindfold down over his face, and his eyes widen as he takes in the scene.

"¡SORPRESA! SURPRISE!" The room erupts as people jump into view from behind bookshelves and furniture. The first people Axel sees when he opens his eyes are his family. All of them. His dad, two uncles, three aunts, and five cousins who live all across Spain, along with his friends.

"How…" he exhales in a smile. "How did you manage this?" He turns on his heels to face Everly and Jocelyn.

"Hey, don't look at me. I just helped with the decorations." Jocelyn gestures towards the array of balloons, streamers, and lights.

Axel turns his focus to Everly, who blushes slightly at his gaze. "You mentioned your padre likes that cheese we get from the market, so I stopped by one day, and we got to talking," she chuckles as if that answered his question.

"Feliz cumpleaños, mi hijo. Te amo." His father embraces him in a strong hug before kissing both his cheeks.

The bookshop's atmosphere has shifted from quiet little getaway to raging nightclub that happens to have books. Jocelyn's playlist thrums through the store, each beat reverberating through their chests. Axel raises his voice, thanking each person individually for coming. From speaking with his father, Everly knows that Axel has always been an incredibly caring and humble soul. His entire life he has supported others while enduring his own hardships. This is his chance to be appreciated, celebrated, and loved.

The music quiets as Jocelyn and Lucía proceed from the back of the shop, arms full of wrapped books. Everyone watches as Lucía delicately arranges them across the coffee table. Each book is meticulously wrapped in brown paper, tied with twine, and adorned with a single red rose.

Her English has progressed exceptionally over the past month, but she takes a moment to translate her thoughts before speaking. "Happy Birthday, my dear Axel.

Before you are special books, each with distinctly different stories. It has been a tradition in my family for generations to pick at random and receive a glimpse into what your future holds. We have called it *elección de destino*, choice of destiny."

Everyone gathers around, silently deciding which book they'll choose. "Axel, you may choose first," Lucía says.

He contemplates each book, weighing them in his hands, determining if the size of the book might indicate a specific genre. Finally, he settles upon a small, thick package with a large rose, perfectly in bloom.

Carefully, he unties the twine, removing the rose, and allows the paper to fall away revealing his choice. *La Canción de Amor,* The Song of Love. Axel's brow furrows as he reads the title aloud.

His eyes find his father's, and they smile gently at one another. Everyone else lunges at the table to take their pick. Sounds of crumpling paper and laughter fill the bookshop as each person tears open their book with childlike eagerness. Axel drifts through the background of excited chaos to arrive beside Everly.

His closeness sends chills down her spine, and her cheeks flush with the sudden urge to touch him, to feel his skin.

As the room explodes into chatter of book titles and storylines, Axel and Everly hold their breath as his fingers brush against hers. A simple touch that breathes life into their bodies. Everly hides her smile, looking down at her worn sneakers. She chances a glance up, strands of her hair caught in her lashes. The party lights highlight and contour the dimensions of his features. His eyes, typically sage green, look deeper, like a forest of pines on a fall morning. Captivating.

"Everly, open yours," Jocelyn exclaims. Ripping away her attention and her fingers from Axel, Everly comes back to reality. Jocelyn bounces eagerly, reading about the strong-willed characters awaiting her in the pages of her book.

Everyone buzzes about their books and how thrilling it is to see what the future holds for them. Some are more skeptical than others, but everyone seems to enjoy the idea of knowing a little more about life ahead.

Everly reaches for the last remaining book, untying the twine and allowing the brown paper to fall to the floor. The blood-red rose drops delicately to the ground, landing between her dingy white sneakers onto Lucía's favorite Persian rug.

"Well..." Jocelyn urges, "What is it!"

Her fingers trace the etched letters of the leather cover. Everly clears her throat then reads, "The Potential of Heartbreak."

The room stills for a few uncomfortable moments before Axel interjects saying, "Thank you, Lucía, this is wonderful, and I heard someone brought homemade churros…" His smile grows, and everyone perks up, eager to taste the sweet treat.

Everly breathes a sigh of relief as the focus shifts away from her and the strange book.

"¡Gracias a todos! Fue un cumpleaños maravilloso," Axel yells out the door as the guests collectively head back to their homes. "Thanks, guys, that really meant a lot to me," he says, turning to acknowledge Jocelyn and Everly.

"It's the least we could do—you've made us feel like we belong here," Jocelyn replies with a smile. "Well, I'm exhausted. I'm going to bed." She turns to make her way up the stairs but catches Everly's eyes for a split second to wink. "Have fun, you two," she sings as she rounds the top of the stairs.

If it wasn't blatantly obvious with that comment, it's also common knowledge that Jocelyn rarely goes to bed before the early hours of the morning.

The music has been replaced with the low humming of the single-bulb lamp that casts a soft glow across Axel and Everly as they stand beside each other, close enough to touch. An itching warmth agonizes her fingers at her side, urging her to graze his fingers again, but she remains still.

Her eyes look as blue as the depths of the ocean as she lifts her gaze to his. Her heart beats ferociously as their eyes connect, and she can't help but think he might hear it. "Do you want to go for a walk?" he asks, drowning out the noise before he can identify it. Everly nods, and they walk out, the charms on the door serenading them as they go.

The streets are quiet, only the wind whispers and the streetlights hum. Everly cuts the silence, her voice reverberating in the narrow alley. "So, what do you think about your book?" She hesitates. "I mean, do you believe in Lucía's tradition that it could actually predict your future?"

Axel takes a moment to consider this and smiles as he contemplates his response. "Lucía is remarkable, and I have heard many stories of *elección de destino* coming true." He pauses, thinking back to Everly's choice. "But each book can be interpreted differently. If you choose to connect with your book, then it will make sense to you. If not, then it can be just a fun game." His fingers graze the soft skin of her forearm, lighting up her nerves, before settling into her small hand. "You don't have anything to worry about. Your book doesn't have to predict your life if you don't want it to."

She nods, her words stuck in an anxious knot in her throat as her fingers adjust around his. Trying to conceal the blush in her cheeks, she chances a look at him. "Maybe your book was right, though."

"How so?"

"The day we first met, Jocelyn and I heard you playing violin on the bridge before you jumped down and scared the shit out of us," she laughs, remembering the moment.

"Oh, yeah." He bumps her shoulder playfully. "Is that when you fell in love with me?" he mocks.

Everly stiffens at his words, laughing to hide her discomfort. Axel looks down the street at a group of meandering strangers then grabs Everly by the arm, pulling her away from the glow of the streetlights. Her back presses against the cold stone wall of the alley. Axel looks deep into her eyes, his hand coming up to caress her face. "Because that's when I fell in love with you."

Everly's breath escapes her body as their lips press together. Without a moment's hesitation, her hands clasp around his neck pulling him closer, deeper. The chill of the night dissipates with the heat of each kiss. His hand feverishly wanders from her neck, her jaw, into her hair. The other follows the curve of her body to rest on her lower back, pulling her into him.

The group of strangers wanders past, whistling and hollering playfully. Axel pulls back to look at them and snickers at their expressions. His forehead comes to rest on hers, their chests synchronize as they rise and fall breathlessly. His hands rest against the rough stone wall behind her. She can feel the heat emanating from his body. He smells of soap and cloves and comfort.

Axel's hand descends from the wall to brush the hair from her face and tuck it gently behind her ear. His thumb grazes the freckled skin of her cheeks, and his palm rests along her jaw. Everly's eyes study him. The way his body leans over her in a dominant arch. The way his shirt rides up ever so slightly to reveal the smooth golden skin of his muscular torso. The way the veins along his forearms and biceps pulse with the beat of his heart. She revels in the way his simple gaze feels like the press of warm lips against her skin, a tenderness that only new love evokes in fragile souls.

Carefully turning the knob, Everly opens the heavy wooden door to the bookshop as quietly as she can, but the charms make it nearly impossible. Axel grabs her hand before she can walk inside, and she spins into his arms, his lips meeting hers before she can close her eyes. He kisses against her smile, then sets her steadily on her feet again before lifting her hand to his mouth. His eyes never leave hers as his lips touch the smooth skin of her knuckles. Everly's heart flutters at the chivalrous act. He must have noticed because his dimple appears as he releases her hand.

"Buenas noches," he whispers as he turns to walk away.

"Goodnight," she breathes into the chilling night air.

Everly's body is not her own. It maneuvers through the bookshop, avoiding tossed shoes by the door, sidestepping piles of brown wrapping paper, and carrying her up the stairs effortlessly without distracting her from replaying tonight's events in her mind.

Her eyes see nothing but the shadows of his face, the moisture on his lips, the golden skin of his biceps, and the dark ruffled curls of his hair highlighted by the moon's glow.

Trying not to wake Jocelyn, she opens the door of their shared room as gently as possible. Once there is space for her to fit, she slides her body into the room and softly clicks the door closed. Tiptoeing towards her bed, only a few feet from Jocelyn's, she sits on the squeaky narrow mattress.

The light snaps on.

Jocelyn is sitting up, fully awake but obviously ready for bed with her hair twisted around towels and a facemask coating her skin.

“Tell. Me. Everything.” She scrambles to resituate herself on her bed, crossing her legs and resting her elbows on her knees with her chin in her hands attentively.

The girls spend the rest of their night squealing quietly, trying not to burst with excitement or wake up Señora Morales in the process.

Chapter 21

His hands trace her jaw as he gazes into her clear eyes with admiration. Her lips hover so close to his he can almost taste their sweetness. His eagerness gets the best of him as his hands brush through her hair and push her against the smooth marble wall of the corridor. Their lips collide in passionate heat and intensity. Everly giggles at his overflowing desire, but he presses his nimble finger gently to her lips.

"Shhh," he leans in close, his breath tickling her neck, "you'll get us caught." His lips brush seductively along her ear. Each kiss as light as butterflies wings. A small gasp escapes her throat when his hand runs down her arm and around her waist agonizingly slowly.

"Oye," a security guard barks. "Oye, ¡no puedes estar aquí!"

Axel laces Everly's fingers into his as they flee across the museum corridor weaving between statues and *cerrado* signs. They are a beautiful mess of youthful love, laughing as they sprint through exhibits until finally blending into the sea of people.

⁂

Golden sunlight illuminates their faces. Everly quickens her steps to accommodate Axel's long strides. Her arms wrap around his bicep, pulling him close to her, settling her head against his shoulder. As they cross the bridge where they first met, she pulls him to its edge. The sun sets over the rippling water each night, but each sunset is like none before it. They are intricate masterpieces, each one a perfectly crafted closing scene. Tonight the sun burns golden with deep hues of orange and pink above the horizon.

Her skin tingles where his eyes linger. The beautiful intensity of his gaze makes her want to melt into him like the sun on the horizon. She guides him with her hands until his back is pressed against the guard rail. Sunlight casts light shadows of his long lashes across his cheeks.

"I love you," she whispers as she stretches on her tiptoes to press her lips to his. His hands come to rest on either side of her face as he looks deeply into her eyes. The sun has darkened the freckles on her nose.

He smiles at her intently before kissing her forehead. She leans into it, reveling in his touch. "I want to show you something," he says, leading her across the bridge towards home.

⁕

Everly knows Axel's father enjoys painting but never imagined he'd have a studio in their home where he creates such exceptional art. The room is perfectly square with an exquisitely large window that lets the sunlight pour in from the horizon. She drifts towards the window, feeling called to bathe in the wash of light. Axel opens the bay window, sitting on its ledge, where Everly comes to join him.

"My father paints the sunsets from here. He says my mother put them all to shame with her beauty." He bows his head, worrying at his palms.

Everly reaches over to steady his hands. "I'm sure these sunsets are nothing compared to her."

Axel looks back towards the setting sun and the drifting water of the river. "You know they met on that bridge." He pauses. "He always said I would meet my soulmate on that bridge, too."

Everly's heart burns hotter than the sunlight melting across the skyline. *Soulmate.* Her hand tightens around his at the thought, and he squeezes hers in response. "I'll be right back," he says as he sneaks a kiss on her cheek, hopping off the ledge and bouncing out of the room.

Everly slides off the windowsill, ambling about the studio. Her fingers trace the textured lips of stacked canvases. Her smile brightens when she discovers a record player beneath stacks of unfinished canvases. The crackle of the vinyl interrupts the silence of the impending night as she adjusts the arm and drops the needle on the record.

The rich notes of a violin drift into the empty spaces, filling the room with a sense of comfort and familiarity. Everly moves her hips to the smooth rhythm, allowing her arms to sway freely above her head. The door swings open, and Axel stands motionless with a bottle of wine and a baguette in his hands. He's never looked at her like this before. A look of utter disbelief.

"What?" Everly urges, moving to turn off the music. "I'm sorry," she says. "I shouldn't have touched anything."

He lingers in the doorway a moment longer before clearing his throat and setting down the items in his hands. "Nothing." He pauses. "It's okay. That's just…a song my mother wrote." His voice finds its composure. "I just haven't heard that in a long time. She wrote it for my dad."

Their silhouettes dance across the wall of golden sunlight as they embrace. They laugh over the music and stumble in blissful chaos as Axel attempts to teach Everly how to dance. Her hair cascades over her shoulders and falls wildly around her face. Standing on her tiptoes, she loses her balance with each sway. Axel tries to guide her steps, but she's never been one to relinquish control.

"Just follow my lead," he laughs as she steps on his toes.

"Then lead better," she teases.

His arm tightens around her waist, and he pulls her body close against his, so she relaxes and finally lets go. The music flows in beautiful rhythms—it sounds like meeting old friends after years apart.

Everly's head rests perfectly against his shoulder as they move about the room. The sun's intense rays momentarily blind Axel, and he missteps, catching his foot on the table leg and sending them tumbling to the ground. Axel's back thuds against the aged wood floor, and his breath leaves him. Everly's body collapses helplessly atop him. Unfinished watercolors and sheet music flutter to the floor around them, and paint splatters across their clothes.

"Ev, I'm so sorry, your dress," he apologizes, looking at the new array of colors on the fabric. She looks down at her dress, then back at him. Her eyes are unreadable for a moment as she dips her fingers into the blue paint puddle beside him, and then she smiles, smearing it across his cheek. His mouth falls open in surprise, his dimple creasing the wet paint.

Orange paint drips steadily from the table top. In a swift motion he leverages himself, flipping Everly on her back, his legs straddling her hips. Her breath catches. Axel has her arms pinned above her head on the floor. His face is serious, intense. The world stands still as she looks at him, even the dripping paint seems to slow. He leans in closer, one hand holding her arms still and the other bracing his weight. Her lips ache with anticipation as he lingers a breath above her.

His freshly painted dimple reappears as he smears orange paint across her neck and chest. She bursts out in a fit of laughter and resistance, trying to get the upper hand.

He catches her escaped hand before it can spread the new-found yellow paint across his chin, but it splatters him anyway. His arms wrap around her waist, and he rolls with her, purple splotches covering him as he lies back on the floor, Everly atop him again.

Axel's orange handprints linger on her skin. His hand rises to touch her neck, gently tracing her collarbone. The tips of his fingers find the textured cotton strap of her dress, slowly guiding it down her arm.

Her breath catches, her skin burns with each touch. He's found the second strap. His eyes hold her gaze as he slides it off her shoulder. Her eyes invite him to look. She can feel him holding his breath as his eyes trace her body, the gentle slope of her neck, the freckled skin of her shoulders, the smooth lines of her torso, and the luminous curves of her breasts.

The sun's gentle glow lingers on the horizon until the moon offers to take its place. He sits up slowly, adjusting her legs around his waist, until they are face to face. The chill of impending twilight dances along her bare skin. His tongue and lips gently press to her throat. Each kiss sparks warmth in her as his mouth wanders purposefully along her jaw. Her legs shift around him as she tilts her head back allowing a soft moan to escape. She can feel him smile against her skin at the sound.

His teeth nibble gently at her ear, and he exhales deeply, sending shivers down her spine, awakening her body. Her hands entangle his hair between her fingers, gripping it tighter as his lips travel lower. Drowning in anticipation, she lowers her hands, tracing the contracting muscles of his back, reaching for the hem of his shirt. Her hands travel along the smooth canvas of his skin as her nails drag knowingly down his back. His lips press deeper into her in response.

They are creating a language of their own design, each movement a poet's phrase.

Her hips press into his, and a moan catches in his throat before he allows it to escape. In one swift motion, his hand cups the back of her neck, the other wraps around her waist, and she's suddenly on her back again.

The dark curls of his hair drape along his brow, but the fire in his eyes shines through the shadows. A breeze drifts through the open window, but the chill of night cannot overpower the intensifying heat between them.

All at once they collide, and the room's set ablaze. Everly's hands rip his shirt over taut muscles, and he straightens up to pull it over his head, tossing it aside. His lips crash into hers with fierce yearning. Her hands pull him closer, grabbing his hair and digging her nails into his back. He releases a deep moan as her nails leave marks on his skin.

His lips and tongue travel down her collarbone to her chest, and she shudders at the sensation. While his tongue traces her body, his hands move to pull her dress past her hips.

Her eyes close, heightening her senses. The way he kisses her stomach is maddening, leading with his tongue followed by the gentle press of his lips. He moves lower, and lower still. His hands cradle her hips as his lips dance across them tortuously. Her back arches against the wooden floor, begging.

The darkening sky welcomes each star into the quiet night until Everly's breathless moans disrupt the tranquility.

Chapter 22

April 28th

Ours is the perfect kind of love story. The one you see in movies. The love poets write about. A love that people pray for.

True love.

May 5th

My parents called me today. They don't know about Axel yet. I feel guilty hiding such a major part of my life from them, but I want this chapter of my life to be easy. No expectations, no explanations to anyone else. Just me and him in our own world. Together.

May 12th

Axel and I have been spending time in the park having picnics and reading his book as often as we can. He rests against our favorite tree, and I lay my head in his lap, watching the sun shine through the dense leaves and listening to the sweet words roll off his tongue.

La Canción de Amor, *The Song of Love. It's the book he chose on his birthday. The story follows two young souls who reconnect after years apart. At first I thought about Thomas, but as he's kept reading I see that it's actually like us. Young lovers, separated in the prime of their story only to fall deeper in love later on.*

I leave in just over a month, but I know we will make this work because ours is the type of love you fight for.

May 16th

I love watching Axel's green eyes trace along the words of his book, the way his dimple appears when he reads certain words, and the way he pauses sometimes to translate in his head. He's read it nearly every day since he started it.

I wish I could say the same, but my book sits on the nightstand of my room collecting dust. What would make someone want to read a book titled The Potential of Heartbreak *anyway? I may end up leaving it for the next person to find or sneaking it back into the stacks when Lucía isn't looking.*

June 1st

Two weeks. I only have two more weeks with my friends, Lucía, and the love of my life. They say that love comes when you least expect it, and I believe that to be fully accurate. We met when I was brokenhearted over someone who didn't deserve a second chance, when I was mad at the world and stuck feeling sorry for myself. He changed my life. He taught me a new language, how to dance, how to slow down and appreciate the little things.

I love my life here. I love my life with him. But Joce and I leave in two weeks.

I'm just not ready to go. I'm not ready to go without him.

June 7th

I have this horrible feeling in the pit of my stomach that's growing bigger each day now. My impending departure hangs over my head like a stormcloud, but I can also feel a discomfort and distancing coming from Axel.

Maybe he thinks it'll make for an easier goodbye if he pulls away, but I won't let that happen. This is going to be a hard change for us both, but I'm confident that we can make it work.

I've been rehearsing what I want to say to him all morning, but we're meeting up with everyone for brunch, so we'll talk about it later today.

Chapter 23

"Don't walk away from me," Axel's voice reverberates through the stone stairwell.

"You're not even listening to me anyway!" Everly snaps back at him, continuing down the steps.

"Why did you hide this from me?"

"What are you talking about?" She stops in her tracks to glare at him. "We're all friends. He's *your* friend."

"Then why didn't you tell me you went out with him?" A dark flame ignites the forest in his eyes.

"All of us went out *except* you. I don't understand why you're so upset," she says, her voice softening.

"Because you shouldn't have gone out without me."

"Are you kidding?" Everly scoffs. "I love you, but that does *not* mean you can control what I can or cannot do."

"So that gives you the right to go out and *fuck* whoever you want then?" Everly misses a step as she walks, physically stunned by his words.

"Axel, I would never do that," her voice strains. "You know me."

Leaning into the railing, he exhales deeply. "Maybe I *don't* know you." The words fall like anvils through the floor, shaking her to the core.

"What do you mean?" Her voice wavers against an onslaught of emotions. "Is this because I'm leaving?" She pauses. "I know it'll be hard, especially because of classes and the time difference, but this is worth saving. Right?" There's a long silence. "I love you." She silently begs for a response.

"What are we doing, Ev?" The anger in his voice dissipates as his true frustration comes to light.

"What do you mean?"

"You leave in a week." He throws up his hands. Everly stands silently, waiting for him to say what he really thinks. He moves impatiently, wanting her to respond.

She doesn't.

Everly's pulse quickens, waiting for him to explain himself.

"I met someone," Axel blurts out.

Everly's breath catches in her lungs. Like a flame under a glass, her heart fights to remain lit, but his words suffocate her and extinguish her flame.

"I finished my book," he nearly whispers.

Everly's eyes shine with unshed tears and confusion. "What?"

"I finished my book," he repeats. "*La Canción de Amor.*" He looks at her as if his response explains everything. "I don't know how to explain it."

"Try," she demands.

"*La Canción de Amor,*" he starts. "It's the same title as the song my mom wrote for my dad." Everly looks up at him, utterly confused, as he paces along the stairs. "I can't explain it, but the moment I picked up that book, even from the first sentence, I knew it was about her."

"Who is she?" Her voice is barely audible over the deep, painful thudding in her chest.

"I'm so sorry, Ev."

"Who is she?" she demands again.

"My first love." The words cleave her chest, rip the air from her lungs. "She moved away when we were young, and we lost touch, but once I started to read that book…" He pauses. "...every word was for her."

Her eyes, restless like stormy seas, look out the stairwell window onto the street below. "You read those pages to me," she says, her voice a painful whisper.

He stops pacing.

"What's her name…"

If love ever had a name, it was hers. "Alicia," he breathes. "Her name is Alicia."

Everly sinks to the floor in the stairwell as Axel recounts the past two weeks.

"The night all of you went out, I felt an urge to stay home. To go practice, actually. When I took my violin to the bridge, I heard the familiar deep tones of my mother's song being played. I've never heard anyone else play it before, so I followed the sound." He pauses. "She had her back to me, but as I ran over I knew without a doubt it was her." He fails at hiding his smile.

"I couldn't believe it was actually her." The memory of her makes him blush slightly, his dimple creasing. "I can't explain it, but once I saw her again it all made sense. I felt like my mom called me to that bridge to see her again. When she turned around it was like no time had passed at all, like she was the same girl I'd loved my whole young life standing right in front of me." He hesitates, seeing Everly wipe the tears from her chin. "I love you, Ev. This was real. I never want you to doubt that." His voice strains. "But it was never going to end well."

Gathering herself from the floor, she stands up, wipes the tears from her cheeks, and looks him in the eyes as steadily as she can. Her mind whirls in endless spirals of misery.

Axel now sits on the narrow lip of the windowsill between two apartment doors. His gaze, once warm and comforting, is now unfamiliar and distant.

Everly stands strong, a powerful statue of resilience and composure. Her voice is flat and unwavering as she looks into his eyes. "How foolish of me to give my heart to a stranger, and how cruel of you to have let me." She passes him without a second glance and descends the marble stairs, holding her breath until she hits the cobblestone street.

Those green eyes poisoned my soul with hope and flooded my veins with fictitious love.

Chapter 24

The afternoon sun shines through the windows of the bookshop, illuminating the floating particles Lucía calls fairy dust. A warm glow engulfs the shop like a comforting hug, inviting passersby to come in.

Jocelyn spends her morning sleeping in but manages to get up in time for brunch with their friends. Everly and Axel are supposed to meet them at the cafe, but they haven't appeared.

"I'm sure they're busy." She winks at everyone around the table, and they giggle in understanding.

Jocelyn waves goodbye to her friends as they pass the bookshop on their walk into town. There are few things in the world that Jocelyn loves more than a good nap, especially after a good brunch, and that's exactly what she's planning to do.

The sound of the charms against the bookshop door makes her smile every time they welcome her in. The front bifolding windows are open, allowing the warm summer breeze to breathe life back into the tired books.

"Buenas tardes, Lucía. I brought you some fresh orange juice from the market," she calls out. The shop is unusually quiet. She listens intently for movement upstairs. Nothing. Then a ragged inhalation comes from the hidden romance section of the shop.

As she goes down the few steps into the beautifully intimate room lined from floor to ceiling with love stories, she sees Everly curled up in the corner with her hair curtaining her face. "Oh, love, what happened?" Jocelyn goes to her, falling to her knees and embracing her friend without hesitation.

They sit like this for a while until Everly composes herself enough to speak. "He's in love with someone else." Her breath catches on the words.

"I'm so sorry, Ev." She pauses. Her hand moves to Everly's chin, tilting it up so they can look into each other's eyes. Jocelyn smiles empathetically at her, wiping the tears from her cheeks and brushing strands of hair behind her ears.

"He's an idiot to let you go—everyone knows you're as good as it gets. I mean, come on," she exclaims. "Look at the rack on you!"

Everly's tears escape her eyes as she bursts out laughing. Jocelyn always knows just what to say to make her smile. Even when it feels like the world is collapsing around her, Jocelyn is always there to brace her.

"Buenas tardes, chicas," Lucía calls, the front door latching behind her. "I brought you jugo de naranja del mercado."

"Great minds think alike, I guess," Jocelyn chuckles to Everly, looking at the orange juice beside them. "Hola, Lucía," she calls out. "Un momento!" Jocelyn springs up, holding her hands out to Everly. "All right, lovebug, here's what's going to happen. First, we're going to get up and drink some orange juice, because it's actually really good, and I want you to try it." Everly smiles at her ridiculousness. "Second, we're going to do our five-to-one routine. And then…" she exaggerates the words, "we are going out to a nice dinner, getting all fancy, ordering some wine, and enjoying the time we have left in this beautiful city." Her hands open and close, urging Everly to grab them. "What do you say?"

Everly looks up at her best friend. "Déjà vu."

"I know, right? Stop letting boys stomp on your heart, doofus." She sticks out her tongue.

"I'm a hopeless romantic, what can I say?" Everly shrugs, tucking her hair behind her ears.

"Wrong. You're a *hopeful* romantic, because one day all this heartache and bullshit will be worth it. There is hope for you, Ev. I know it." Holding out her hands, she looks down at Everly, inviting her again to take them. "Now, get off your butt!"

Taking her hands, Jocelyn leads her out into the bookshop where Señora Morales is basking in the sunlight as she thumbs through a book in her favorite pink armchair.

She looks up as they approach, noticing Everly's swollen eyes. "Oh, bella, ¿qué pasó?" Her arms open wide, offering an embrace. Over the past six months, they've grown exceptionally close, Lucía like an honorary grandmother to the girls and they, her granddaughters.

Everly accepts the hug without hesitation, falling into her lovingly. Jocelyn takes a seat across from them on the soft cushions of a vintage green couch they found a few months earlier.

"What happened, mi amor?" Lucía asks.

Everly pulls away from the hug, throwing her arms up exaggeratedly. "The usual," she jokes. "Just boys playing with my heart again." She laughs coldly.

Lucía processes this for a few long moments before speaking. "My darling girl, may I offer some advice?" Everly nods as Lucía silently composes and translates her thoughts.

"To live merely as one pleases is no life of value, for there is always potential in the hardest of times." Her tanned skin creases as she smiles at Everly. "My dear, there is always potential in heartbreak."

Everly blows out a deep breath and falls onto the green couch and into Jocelyn's lap. "I know…" she whines. "And you just want me to read that stupid book."

Lucía's eyes squint with her wide smile and silent laugh. "Do you know what I do when I am going through a hard time?" she offers. Everly looks at her, her head still in Jocelyn's lap. She shakes her head, awaiting the answer.

"I read."

"Of course you do," Everly laughs as she throws up her arms, stretching across the couch. Jocelyn and Everly smile at each other.

It is peacefully quiet. Jocelyn rests her head back on the couch, basking in the afternoon sunlight and playing with Everly's hair as she stares up at the ceiling. The old wooden beams match the bookshelves, and the dried roses and thyme shift in the subtle breeze drifting in. Lucía sips happily on her orange juice, looking lost in thought.

"How'd you know?" Everly questioned Lucía.

Her lips shift as she smiles knowingly. "¿Qué?"

"The books. How'd you know which ones people would choose?"

"I don't. The books know which of you needs them." Everly and Jocelyn glance at each other then look back to her.

"I joke," she smirks. "Although I selected each of those with hopes you'd all choose the right one."

Everly sits up. "Was mine the one you wanted me to pick, then?"

"Well, if you would read it," Lucía says, narrowing her eyes playfully, "maybe you'd realize it is the one *you* wanted to pick."

Everly sits forward on the couch to finish her orange juice while Jocelyn explains their five-to-one routine to Lucía and how it prevented her from setting her cheating boyfriend's car on fire in a fit of rage.

"When something happens to either of us, we do this to get through it. It's five minutes of screaming, crying, throwing things, or whatever else you need to do to get those feelings out. Then it's one hour of doing something that will bring you joy and help you to move on from those hurt feelings."

"That is a wonderful idea, chicas. Maybe do it away from the shop then," she teases.

"Oh, but I was really hoping to demolish the romance section and burn some classics," Everly teases back.

⁂

A few blocks from the bookshop is a long alleyway where the two of them sneak off to smoke during breaks, a bad habit they've picked up over the past few months. The afternoon light doesn't touch the cold stones of the alley but highlights each end like golden doorways.

Jocelyn looks at Everly. "What do you need?"

"A cigarette and space." Jocelyn extends a cigarette to her. Everly's lips tense around it as she lights it up and inhales deeply.

"Your time starts… now." Jocelyn presses *start* on her phone and backs away slowly.

Everly exhales the smoke like a dragon craving destruction.

"All this time I've been thinking this was it. That this was some sort of true love bullshit. But two weeks? Two fucking weeks of him fawning over someone else only to pick a fight with me because he didn't have the guts to tell me. What a coward!" She paces past Jocelyn waving her hands in frustration. "I shouldn't be surprised though, it's not like I have a good track record with guys. But why does this keep happening?" Her hand rakes through her hair as she takes another drag of smoke that silences her for a moment.

Breathing out a cloud, she quiets. "Am I not worth it? Am I ever going to be good enough to be someone's first choice?" Everly's eyes glisten as she looks at Jocelyn. Once again, Everly sinks to the ground sobbing helplessly. She draws a shuddering breath. "I just want to be someone's first choice."

"Time," Jocelyn says quietly. She looks Everly in the eyes. "Ev, you deserve the kind of love that will fight to keep you. The kind of love that can't imagine life without you. A love that breathes life into your soul." She pauses to make sure it's resonating, then continues.

"I have never met anyone else in my life who is more deserving of true happiness than you, Ev. I've also never met a man who comes close to what you deserve. And so, yeah, you'll have to fall in love with assholes, be broken-hearted, and then put yourself back together. But each wrong guy, each two-timing loser, is a step closer to finding someone who truly deserves you.

"Like Lucía said earlier, 'There is so much potential in heartbreak,' and I think she's right. Ev, you deserve the moon, and Axel can't give it to you. But someday, someone will come into your life and do anything they can to give you everything you deserve."

Chapter 25

"Jocelyn, come back!" Everly yells, her breath billowing in chilled puffs of night air. She pauses to collect her thoughts and forcibly sober her brain. Wrangling Jocelyn on a night out has proven to be even harder since the summer.

"Cam!" Jocelyn squeals excitedly into her phone. Her long legs carry her in uncoordinated strides along the sidewalk, and her speech slurs. "Wait…what's your address again?" She pauses to look up at the house numbers around her. "Forty-two, right?"

Everly catches up to her breathlessly. "Joce, stop running away—" She's interrupted by Jocelyn's hand covering her mouth.

"Shit," Jocelyn exhales in a breathy laugh. "Okay, we'll be there in five." She shoves her phone into her bag, grabs Everly's hand, and drags her down the street as she nurses her flask. "It's twenty-four, not forty-two," she laughs.

"Oh shit." Jocelyn smiles as they approach the scene. The house is overflowing with partygoers in the front lawn cheering for those playing beer die and on the rooftop pouring drinks on unaware people below. The flashing lights illuminate the doorway and windows where hordes of people are dancing to the heavy beat.

Everly's lips quirk into a mischievous smile. "This is going to be fun." She takes a swig from her flask before linking arms with Jocelyn and skipping towards the mayhem.

"Cam!" Jocelyn pushes past the mass of sweaty bodies to collide with her boyfriend. They were meant to be a summer fling, but Jocelyn has always been more girlfriend material than a casual hookup.

He lifts her up, her legs entangling around him, and their lips smash against each other in unapologetic desire as people shuffle past.

I need a drink, Everly thinks to herself. Her heart hasn't fully recovered from her tragic love affair with Axel. The music thrums through the crowd, shaking the walls as everyone screams the words out of tune. Bottles of vodka are passed around, and Everly clasps one in her palms and takes a significant swig before passing it along.

"Ev!" She turns to see who's calling to her. She can't identify the voice in the densely packed room where her eye level is at most peoples' chest level. "Everly!" Climbing a few steps, she scans the room from a higher vantage point and finally lands on a familiar face by the pong table.

"Oh my god, Sadie!" Everly races down the stairs, shoving her way through the crowd until they crash into each other with flailing limbs and drunken giggles. They haven't seen each other since her return to the States.

"Be my partner, pretty please?" Her hazel eyes glisten and her lips pout, hoping to elicit a *yes*.

Everly picks up the ball, looks at Sadie, and without breaking eye contact arcs it across the table into a red Solo cup. The onlookers cheer rabidly. Sadie's eyes open wide as she looks back and forth from the cup to Everly.

"Let's play."

⁕

"Undefeated, bitches!" The crowd cheers as Everly and Sadie dance across the table top, basking in their victory. "Joce, come dance with us!"

The mob of college students has somehow doubled during the time they played; now there's hardly enough space to breathe. Cameron clears a path for Jocelyn to get through, making sure no one touches her. He grabs her hips, spinning her around for a kiss before lifting her onto the table next to Everly.

A new song blares through the speakers, igniting commotion in the crowd as people jump, dance, and sing. The lights strobe across everyone in blinding flashes, the sea of people seeming to move in slow motion. Everly pulls Jocelyn in beside her when someone spills a drink on Sadie's shoes, and she jerks back, knocking Everly off the tabletop. The strobe lights make her feel like she's falling in slow motion, or maybe it's the alcohol. The bass pulses deeper and slower through her body as she squeezes her eyes closed, preparing for the hard impact. The collision is softer than she'd expected, more comforting.

Her eyes are still squinted shut when she recognizes the feeling of a large arm cradling her back, long fingers wrapped around her leg, a sturdy chest pressed to her side. Before she can open her eyes, she's placed gently onto the tabletop beside her friends. Only a moment later, the crowd and pulsating lights have already swallowed the identity of her savior.

"Ev, I'm so sorry!" Sadie wraps her in a tight hug, "Are you okay?"

"Yeah, I'm fine. Did you see who that was?" Sadie shakes her head, Jocelyn too. Shaking it off, they pull her safely between them as they lead her dancing and singing in a wild haze of youthful chaos.

⁂

Stumbling up the staircase, Everly walks down the hallway to Cam's room, avoiding the couples making out in dark corners. "Joce," she calls, knocking on the door twice before opening it. "Oh god." She covers her eyes with her hand. "Don't mind me. Just getting my jacket."

"Ev!" Jocelyn sits up, unabashedly naked. "Text me when you get home." She smiles. "Want a hug before you leave?" She lunges out of bed, and Everly laughs, racing out the door. "Love you!" Jocelyn calls from behind the door.

"Love you too!"

⁂

Walking back to their apartment, Everly stares down the street, trying to remember which way they came. *Walk down to the street lights, then a left for three blocks, then right for two more. Or was it another left? Fuck.*

A group of girls, comparably drunk, brave the uneven sidewalk across the street in their heeled shoes. Having enough common sense to look each way before crossing the street, she calls out to them, "Hey." They look at her with blurry judgment. "Do any of you know how to…" *Oh fuck.* Everly races to the nearest alleyway and retches into the darkness, her hair falling around her face. Moments later, one of the girls is holding it back for her and rubbing her soothingly as her stomach lurches again, rejecting her earlier decisions.

Bracing herself against the cold brick, she wipes her mouth and stands up straight. "I'm so sorry…" she starts, turning around only to see the shadowy figure of a broad-shouldered man before her.

She trips over herself as she steps away, and his arm moves fast to catch her before she can stumble into the wall. The smooth tone of his voice shocks her system, igniting her nerves and making her more aware of the cold night air. "Are you okay? I didn't mean to startle you." He steadies her before taking two steps back. He's intimidatingly large compared to her slight frame, but her nerves calm as he respects her space.

Everly takes a deep breath, trying to settle her mind and stomach. "I'm fine." She looks down the street. No one else in sight.

"Did you just come from Cam's house?"

She narrows her eyes at him. "Yeah…why?"

"I was there too. Saw you wreck everyone in pong." He smiles, his face too shadowed for her to see. "You need help? Looked like you were lost."

"So you were stalking me," she accuses, half-joking.

"Oh, absolutely. Can't let a girl like you slip away." He leans back on the streetlamp behind him, finally illuminating his face. Everly's stomach flutters again, this time pleasurably as she notes the high cheekbones and straight lines of the stranger's jaw. "So, do you need help?"

"Nope." She shakes her head. A mistake. She braces both hands against the wall as she heaves. His large hand collects her hair and rubs her back again.

"Let it out," he says as she gasps. She spits onto the brick and leans against the rough wall, catching her breath and wiping the sweat from her brow. "Okay, either let me walk you home or sleep on my couch. I live a block down the street."

"No way." Her head lolls back as she looks up at his towering figure. "I just need to call her." Her words stumble over her tongue. Rummaging through her pockets, she groans frantically. "Where?" She turns to check the ground around her. "Where is it?"

"Where's what?"

"My phone." She looks at her pockets. Jocelyn's pockets. Jocelyn's jacket. "Fuck!" she blurts out.

"Do you know her number? I could call her for you."

"My key, too."

"Everly, right? It's late and cold, so come crash on my couch. You can figure things out in the morning, yeah?"

"Think you're clever? I know how this story ends, dude. I'm not going to be the idiot who lets some college dirtbag pretending to be a nice guy take me home, especially in this sta—" Her knees buckle and hit the ground hard. "This state," she finishes.

"Well, I'll have you know, I really *am* a nice guy, and as far as I can see, I'm the only one willing to help you." He holds his hands out to her, the lamp light shining on his dirty blonde hair. The sleeves of his flannel are rolled up to his elbows, revealing tight muscles under smooth skin littered with scars. Each one a perfect circle of healed skin. His broad shoulders balance his sturdy figure and height.

But his eyes. *Wow,* Everly thinks to herself.

As her eyes reflect the ocean's vast horizons, his mirror the depths of glaciers. Piercing, beautiful, and undeniably mesmerizing.

He holds out his hands, urging her to take them. "I'll be a perfect gentleman for you. I swear it." She glares at him. "I just can't stand the thought of you out here in the cold all night." She reaches out her hands apprehensively. "I'm just trying to help," he reassures as he lifts her to her feet.

"Fine." She turns on her heel, releasing his hands. "Let's go."

He clears his throat, and she turns to see him pointing in the opposite direction and trying to hide his amusement.

Chapter 26

Everly stretches her stiff muscles, the soft, cotton sheets entangling her legs. *Oh god.* Her eyes protest against the sunlight streaming through the window, and her brain slams against the walls of her skull. She forces her reluctant body to sit up. Rubbing her eyes, which still have makeup on them, she looks around the room.

Shit.

She rips herself out of the comfortable bed, her body feeling like a bag of wet cement, to stumble into the bathroom. She splashes her face with cold water, removing the smeared makeup and forcing her senses to wake up.

The mirror reflects her disheveled hair and lack of clothing. Only a large white t-shirt hangs from her body, making her feel exposed. Grabbing the nearest article of clothing to drape over herself, she charges into the unfamiliar living room.

"'*I'll be a perfect gentleman*,' my ass!" Her outburst causes his spatula to fling a steaming pancake across the room to land inches from her feet.

Turning to face her, he smirks at the way his bathrobe hangs around her, swallowing her small figure. "Good morning to you too," he chuckles.

"Don't be smug. Where the hell are my clothes?" He motions to the couch where her shoes, pants, top, panties, and bra lay in a neat folded stack. "What the hell is this?" She looks at him, disgusted.

The smirk still lingers on his face as he combs his fingers through his hair. "So, what exactly do you remember from last night?"

"Is this a fucking game to you?" She looks at him, dumbfounded. He waits for her to answer the question. "I remember walking over here like an absolute *idiot* and passing out on the couch. So, tell me. How. The. Hell. Did I wake up in your bed, naked, in what I can only assume is your bigass shirt?"

He chuckles to himself but quickly stops when her eyes shoot daggers at him. "I'm sorry, I'm sorry," he clears the laughter from his throat. "You're right. We came in, and you immediately passed out on the couch. I grabbed you a blanket and left you alone, I swear it."

"That doesn't explain this," she gestures to her body underneath the gigantic robe.

"I'm getting there," he insists with a grin. "So, you passed out on the couch, and I went to sleep in my bed, but in the middle of the night you barged in there looking for the bathroom. Scared the shit out of me by the way," he smiles. "I thought you were going to be sick again, so I went in after you."

"And then?" Everly demands.

"Well, you really wanted to shower." He tries to suppress a smile as he watches the horror on her face. "I'd like to note that, firstly, you left the door wide open, and secondly, I didn't want to be responsible for you drowning or getting a concussion in my shower." Everly stares at him, utterly still. "I sat outside the door until you were done and gave you one of my shirts to change into, then you just climbed straight into my bed." Her eyes turn wild. "Don't worry. I took the couch. You snore anyway."

"I do not!" she blurts out.

"Do too," he laughs, turning back to tend to the pancakes. "And now my pancakes are burning." The smell wafts over, and her stomach growls, begging for them.

"God, I'm such an idiot," she says to herself, but he responds.

"Hey, it could've been worse." He shuffles the pancakes onto a plate beside the stove.

"How could this have been any worse?"

"You could've slept on the street, been picked up by some weirdo—"

"Not yet convinced that isn't the case," she whispers. "I've done some stupid shit in my life, but this is probably in the top three." Her hands rake down her face. "Wait," she blurts out. "I don't even know your name." That aggravating grin is back as he places two plates stacked with pancakes on the countertop between them, the burnt ones closest to her. "So," she insists. "You got a name, bigfoot?" He fakes an exaggerated look of hurt before smiling.

"I'm Liam," he says in a voice more charming than before. "And you get the burnt ones." He slides the plate in front of her and settles himself against the counter's edge with that stupid smirk as he digs into his perfectly fluffy pancakes.

Chapter 27

Before piling into the car, Sadie and Everly shove their suitcases in the trunk. "How was your last final?" Sadie asks.

Everly slumps down in the passenger seat, "Rough. How was yours?"

A shy smile appears on her face. "It actually went really well. Did a lot of studying with Raven." Everly leans on the center console to raise an eyebrow. "Oh, shut up. We *actually* studied." Glancing quickly at Everly she turns back to watch the road. "Mostly," she confesses.

They laugh together, squealing. "I think Joce is calling, one sec." Everly rummages through her bag, pulling out her phone. "Hello?"

"Hi…" Her heart stops dead. That voice. That rough, familiar voice. "Can we talk?"

She hangs up, chucking her phone in the back seat. "Whoa," Sadie looks at her surprised. "Who was it?" Everly stares ahead, wringing her fingers. She takes a deep breath before speaking.

"Jax."

⁂

Plush pillows and downy blankets comfort her as she rests against the windowsill in her childhood bedroom, staring out at the worn shingles where they used to lie together. *Why now?*

Picking up her phone she scrolls to the Js. She leans her head back against the wall, closing her eyes. *Ring… Ring… Ring…* "Hello?"

"Hey, can we talk?"

"Of course, Ev. What's going on?" Jocelyn replies.

For nearly two hours Everly talks about him. How they grew up together, their friendship, their first kiss, the heartache and abandonment she felt when he left, and now this. "What do you think he wants now?" Jocelyn asks.

"I have no idea."

"Are you going to call him back?"

"I don't know," she pauses. "What if it's the same situation as Thomas? I can't deal with something like that again."

"I know. Just take some time and really think about it. I don't want to see you heartbroken again, especially over someone who's been radio silent for nearly six years."

"I don't even know what I'd say to him."

"You don't have to say anything, Ev. Just remember that you deserve someone who would do anything for you. You are the prize."

"Thanks, Joce. I needed to hear that."

❊

The sweet smell of cinnamon rolls baking and fresh coffee brewing still isn't enough to wake them from their restful sleep. Three light knocks on the door. "Good morning." The bed groans as he sits on its edge. "Merry Christmas, my girl."

Everly extends her limbs, stretching like a starfish. "Merry Christmas, Dad," she says, squinting her eyes.

"Come enjoy some breakfast before we go to church." Everly turns over, groaning into her pillow. "Please, Ev. It's Christmas," he begs.

"Okay."

"Great, I'll wake your brother and poke the mama bear."

"Good luck."

❊

It's always the same. *Wow, you've grown! What are you up to now? How's school going?* Smiling and nodding, avoiding deep topics, and shuffling farther from the older crowd waiting to plant too-wet kisses on her cheeks.

Midmorning sun shines through the stained glass windows, projecting rainbows onto the parishioners. Babies babble and kids color as the priest walks down the aisle, acknowledging his people in silent prayer. Everly looks up to find him standing beside her. Reaching out, he takes her hand in his and whispers lightly, "May God soothe your soul, my dear." Mystified, she stares at him as a single tear rolls down her cheek and into her lap.

Breathing steadily with his palms up, he walks purposefully back to the altar to deliver his sermon. "Today is a reminder of new possibilities, unconditional love, and defying the odds set against us, for Jesus has been born this day."

Prayer, Everly thinks. *A useless means of complaining to a mythical being about your problems. Well, I've got a couple problems I'd love some answers to, so here goes nothing.*

Um... Hi, God. I don't know what I'm doing. I haven't prayed since I was a kid, and I haven't known what I'm doing in life since I got here, she chuckles silently. *But really, I need to know why I'm never anyone's first choice. And don't give me any of that, 'you have to wait for the right one' bullshit. I get that. I've done that. But they always pick someone else. There are so many ways to get your heart broken, but mine has shattered multiple times because I've never been good enough. Why?*

Silence.

I knew this was a stupid idea. What good is a God who doesn't help his people?

More silence.

Chapter 28

"Everly," her mother calls up the stairs. "Come say goodbye before you head out, okay?"

"Okay!" Her suitcase thuds down each step until it rolls across the dark wood of the foyer.

"You out of here, kiddo?" Her dad looks up from his book.

"Yeah. Sadie's going to drop me off at the apartment, and then Joce is getting back this weekend."

"That'll be nice. Tell them Happy New Year from us."

"I will. Love you."

"Love you more." Her parents squeeze her tightly between them until she pushes away for air. "Text us when you get back." They stand on the front porch waving as she hops into Sadie's passenger seat. They don't stop waving until the car turns down the street, out of sight.

❊

"Are you and Raven coming to the New Year's party this weekend?" she asks as they turn the corner onto her street.

"I think we're going to stay in and do our own thing."

"That'll be nice. I'm going to head to the store in a bit, do you need anything? Condoms maybe?" Laughter fills the car.

"Yeah," Sadie cackles. "Magnum, please. She's packing!"

Everly wheezes. When she's finally calm enough to speak, she asks again, "Do you actually need anything, though?"

"Maybe some chocolate dip and strawberries. That's her favorite." She smiles.

"I love how your face lights up when you talk about her." Grabbing her keys, she turns back to Sadie for a moment. "Wish I could find someone as thoughtful as you."

"You will, Ev. But you're not my type, sorry." Everly closes the car door behind her, smiling as she drags her bags inside and watches Sadie drive off.

⁕

"Hello?" The phone call plays loudly in the car speakers.

"Ev, it's Mom. Do you have time to talk?"

"Hey, Mama. Yeah, what's up?"

"It's about Jackson."

Silence.

"His mom is sick. She's been going through chemo recently, but the doctors say the cancer's spread." She pauses. "There's nothing more they can do."

Silence.

"You should reach out and check on him. I know it's been a while, but I think he could use a friend right now."

"Oh… Okay."

"I love you, sweetpea. Drive safe."

"Yeah… I love you too, Mom." A horn blares behind her, and she looks up to see the light is green. The words process slowly in her mind, each one twisting the rusted blade of grief through flesh and bone.

She's sick. The cancer's spread. Nothing more they can do. He could use a friend.

Before she can pull off the road, tears stream fiercely down her face and sobs steal the air from her lungs.

Make it stop, she begs silently. *She doesn't deserve this.* Thoughts whirl through her mind in anxious spirals. Ignoring Jackson's call, how Miss Amy was like her second mother, how evil God must be to allow someone so pure to endure such pain. "Save her, you bastard!" The plea comes out in a hopeless howl of desperation. "Please," she whimpers.

⁕

"You've reached Jackson, leave a message, and I'll get back to you… *Beep.*"

"Hey…it's me again. Give me a call back when you get this."

Sadie and Raven walk through the door as she sets her phone on the coffee table. "Still no answer?"

"Nope." She pulls a pillow into her lap, resting her chin on its soft edge. "I'm starting to get worried."

"He'll call back when he's ready, Ev."

"Yeah…" she breathes out.

⁕

"¡Buenos días, chicas!" Jocelyn screams up the stairs as she drags her humongous bag up the front steps.

"Chica," Everly corrects her as she comes down to help. "Just me. Sadie and Raven are staying in tonight."

"Guess we'll have to drink enough for two, then." Those dark eyes land on Everly, looking excited and mischievous until they analyze her expression. "What's wrong with you, Mr. Grumpypants?"

She grabs hold of the bag's handles, helping her bring it up the staircase. "Jax."

"Did you call him? I thought you decided against it?"

Dropping the bag on the landing, Everly turns to face her. "His mom is dying." There's silence until Jocelyn lunges for her friend, embracing her in a tight hug and allowing all her emotions to escape.

"Oh, Ev. I can't imagine how hard this is. I know how close you were with Miss Amy growing up." Her long fingers brush away the hair sticking to her damp cheeks.

"He hasn't answered any of my calls," she stammers.

"I'm sure he's just trying to process this, just like you are." Rubbing her back lightly, she rests her head against Everly's. "Give him time. When he needs you, he'll reach out again." Pulling away to look in her friend's eyes she asks, "Okay?"

Everly's lip quivers as she nods. "Okay."

⁂

I started writing a letter to Jax since he won't answer any of my calls. Thinking about his mom and her losing battle broke my heart, but once I wrote that first letter I started writing a second.

One about how angry I am at him for leaving. For only coming back to tell me his mom is dying, a woman we both love endlessly. I'm so angry at him, it makes me sick.

I don't know how I'd be able to talk to him again without losing it. I desperately want to slap the shit out of him and cry in his arms at the same time.

Who knows. Maybe I wouldn't even recognize him now. Or maybe it'd feel like no time has passed at all.

Chapter 29

Jocelyn tears through the crowd as she sees Cameron's bright hair across the room. Liam walks alongside him, a couple inches taller.

Everly follows hesitantly. She's staring at her feet when she meets his large white sneakers toe-to-toe. *Shit.* Her gaze pans upward over form-fitting jeans to the layering of a t-shirt, flannel, and hoodie along the smooth skin of his neck, finally landing on those icy spheres that pierce through her.

His lips thin into a smirk as he looks at her. The pulse at the base of her throat thrums visibly.

"Hey, Bigfoot," she sneers. "Long time, no see."

"Hey, Pancake, how you been?"

"Pancake, really?" she mocks.

"You know, it was the first thing that came to mind," he offers defensively.

"Well, I'm glad that's the first thing you thought of…"

"I mean, technically, that wasn't really the *first* thing. But, you know. It was the first appropriate thing." Liam can't help but chuckle.

Everly turns the same shade of red he's seen before. "I need a drink." Striding across the room she finds Cameron and Jocelyn sitting in a circle of people. She scooches between Jocelyn and another girl and without a word grabs Jocelyn's drink, taking swift gulps.

"God, Joce, what is this? Sugar water?" Jocelyn giggles at her, she's blissfully buzzed already. "I need something stronger." Everly moves towards the kitchen.

"But not too strong!" Jocelyn yells across the room, turning heads. "Remember what happened last time!" Everly rolls her eyes. She can hear her and Cameron snickering to themselves.

"Ev, come play!" Jocelyn searches for her in the crowd, finding her on the couch staring incredulously at her phone. The words twisting around in her mind.

I need to see you.

Who is this? She replies.

"Ev, come play!" She grabs at Everly's wrist, dragging her towards the pong table.

"I'm not in the mood, Joce." She pulls her wrist back. "Plus, I don't have a partner," she says as an excuse.

"I'll be your partner." Her stomach drops as she feels his presence behind her. She can tell he's smiling without even turning around to see. She senses someone else's presence too. She sits up, looking around. The blur of someone she thought she knew hurries past and out of sight.

Liam clears his throat. "If I'm remembering correctly, you're pretty damn good at this."

"Not better than me!" Jocelyn interrupts from the other end of the table, drawing Everly's attention back. Jocelyn faces her with a deviant grin. Neither of them can turn down a challenge. "Now, come on, lovebirds, let's play!" Everly checks her phone again for any new messages. Nothing.

"Ladies first," Liam says, extending the ball to her. She reaches for it, but he closes it in his fist until she uses both hands to pry it out. She rolls her eyes, and he smiles down at her as she prepares to start the game.

"Wait, wait, wait." Jocelyn interjects before Everly can shoot. "This isn't like normal pong."

Her brows furrow, and she can feel the heat emanating from Liam, who's moved closer to her now. "What do you mean?"

"Welcome to Dare Pong, ladies and gentlemen. Under each cup is a dare. When the ball lands in your cup, you can either do the dare or skip it and take a drink. But to make things more interesting, both teams only have two skips."

"What, why?" Everly protests.

"Because I know you'd drink every single drink here before doing one of those dares. Or are you a quitter, Ev?"

Everly's chest starts to burn, with competitiveness, alcohol, and the feeling that someone is watching her. Someone in the crowd she can't find.

Liam leans over, nudging her lightly and bringing her mind back to the game. "We got this."

"All right, fine. Let's just start." She shakes the feeling off.

"Oh, but I haven't told you the best part." Jocelyn rubs her hands together like she's scheming a wicked plan. "We get to write the dares for the opposing team."

I can't catch a goddamn break.

"Let's start off with a shot, then. Yeah?" Everly downs her glass before anyone else can even respond, then drinks Liam's too. "Let's go."

Plunk. Jocelyn picks up the cup Everly's ball lands in and reads the dare aloud, "Switch clothes." She cups her hands around her mouth and whispers loudly, "Parentheses, everything!" Without hesitation she leads Cameron to the bathroom. A minute later Jocelyn comes strutting out of the door with jeans pooling around her ankles, a belt cinching her waist, an oversized burgundy t-shirt, and backwards baseball cap.

Everyone applauds as she dances around, embracing her new look. All eyes turn to the bathroom door waiting for Cameron to emerge. He sticks his head out only enough to see the crowd watching him, then retreats back into the room.

"Come on, Cam!" Everly cheers, her face burning from the shot she's just downed. "Show us what you got!"

Suddenly, the door flies open, and Cameron comes bursting out, strutting to the music and making his way through the crowd that's parted for him. The guttural laughter drowns out the music as he sashays across the room. Jocelyn's slinky black dress clings to every muscle, and appendage, on Cameron's body. The crowd roars with ecstatic cheers, pushing the players to continue the game.

Cameron & Jocelyn:

~~Swap clothes (everything!)~~

~~Give the other team a lap dance~~

The crowd hollers as Cameron immediately grabs a chair, pulling it to the opposing side of the table, and pushes Liam into it. He lifts his leg up, straddling his friend as the spectators erupt. "Dude!" Liam protests. "We never said you couldn't change back into your own clothes. For the love of God put some pants on!" Everly collapses with laughter as she watches Cameron turn, flip his imaginary locks, and drop it low so his rear is right in Liam's face. Liam leans back, trying to distance himself from Cameron's ass, but his chair flips backwards, and his feet catch Cameron's groin. Both guys lie on the floor groaning as the room explodes with laughter and cheers.

Naked lap:

"Nope, never going to happen, Ev!" Jocelyn protests as Everly cackles at her from across the table.

~~Read the last sext conversation you had~~

"Oh, this is a good one," Jocelyn announces. "I want you to put your—"

"No!" Everly interjects. "Stop, I regret writing this one."

Jocelyn narrows her eyes at her friend, that deviant smirk appearing again as she continues to read and Everly fake gags.

Everly & Liam:

T~~ake an article of clothing off each other with only your teeth~~

Everly turns to him, a warning on her face. "You can take off my sock."

"Ev, that doesn't count!" Jocelyn argues.

"You weren't specific. It counts." Liam lowers himself to his knees, locking eyes with her as he removes her heeled boot. He holds her foot up, his finger lightly stroking her ankle. Leaning forward, he presses his lips to her smooth skin before baring his teeth to grab the sock and pull it over her toes.

"Lame!" Jocelyn exclaims, her smile beaming.

Body shots

"Don't you even think about it." Everly simply holds out the cup, waiting for Liam to drink.

~~Tell everyone how you lost your virginity~~

"It was like a fairytale," Liam starts, dramatically looking off into the distance. "It lasted about thirty seconds, and she was definitely unsatisfied." Everyone bursts out cackling.

"Too true," Cameron exclaims.

"How about you, Ev? Don't think I've heard this story yet." Jocelyn leans forward on the table waiting.

"One sec!" She skips into the next room, coming back with a bottle of tequila. "All right," she takes a swig. "He was an asshole I'd been dating for a while. His parents went away. I snuck out to go see him, and it really hurt." She leans against the wall beside the table, taking another long swig as people stare. "Anyway," she waves her hand. "Give me that." She takes the ball and shoots it perfectly into an opposing cup.

~~Get handcuffed together for the rest of the game~~

"Would you move over!"

"We're handcuffed, genius. How do you expect me to move?"

"You have to throw with me."

"I'm trying! You just have terrible aim anyway."

Give your partner a hickey

"Pass!" Everly protests as soon as Liam reads it aloud. "We'll take our chances with whatever's left."

One cup left for each team. It's down to the wire. Jocelyn lines up her shot. "There's no way you're doing this dare," she laughs. The ball flies through the air, rotating, and hits the lip of the cup. Everly and Liam high five each other, excited by the prospect of winning. But it's Cameron's turn. He steps up to take his shot. Everly and Liam jump around, waving their arms frantically, trying to distract him.

It's no use. The ball splashes perfectly into the final cup.

"Wait, we can still have redemption if we do the dare!" Everly yells at no one in particular, her words slurring slightly.

Liam picks up the paper to read out loud. His facial expression says it all. They're going to lose.

"What is it?" Everly snatches the paper from him.

He exhales with a reluctant smile. "Seven minutes in heaven."

Everly whirls around to look at Jocelyn. "What is this, middle school or something?"

Jocelyn just laughs, then says, "Feel free to pass. I'll gladly take the win." She sticks out her tongue, taunting her friend.

"Oh, hell no. Let's go." Everly stomps off towards the closest room. Liam follows close behind, their hands still cuffed together. The door slams shut. "Start the timer!" Everly yells.

"You know it's almost midnight, right?" Liam grins at her as she kneels, trying to detach the handcuffs.

She looks up at him. "Don't get any ideas, Bigfoot."

"Just a thought." His hands raise defensively just as Everly's hand slips free from her cuff.

"We just have to stay in here for the seven minutes, and then we'll use our redemption shot to put this game into overtime." She moves about the room looking for something to occupy herself. "If Joce wins, I'll never hear the end of it. She's usually my partner, but not since she and Cameron started dating."

Liam sits at the foot of the bed in what seems to be a guest room. Everly wanders aimlessly about, trying to create distance between the two of them.

It's a simple room. One abstract art piece hangs above the queen-size bed, a small closet to the left, long dresser and floor-length mirror opposite the bed, and a connecting bathroom to the right.

Everly whirls at a knock on the door, but Liam reaches out, grabbing her wrist before she can open it.

"Has it been seven minutes yet?" Everly shouts over the music and chaos of the party outside.

No answer.

Liam stands up from the bed, and Everly moves back warily as he passes her and heads into the bathroom.

Who knocked? The cheers outside the door drown out her thoughts as everyone chants, counting down to midnight. "Ten…nine…eight…"

"You know," Liam projects from behind the bathroom door, "I feel like there's been a lot of tension between us since we first met."

Everly blushes. "You think so?" she says, her question dripping with sarcasm.

"Seven…six…five…"

"Yeah, and I'm pretty sure I know how to solve our problem." His voice is barely audible over the crowd.

"Oh, yeah, how's that?" Everly responds.

"Four…three…"

"We need to level the playing field." The door cracks open. Everly is still occupying herself with the room's decor.

"Two…one…"

She turns to the open bathroom door, and her mouth gapes open in utter shock.

"HAPPY NEW YEAR!" The house shakes with thunderous cheers as Liam stands in the doorway completely naked, his arms braced against the top of the doorframe.

Chapter 30

Buzz... Buzz... Buzz.... Her hand fumbles across the nightstand in search of her phone. Pulling it to her ear she lets out a pained, "Hello?"

"Everly? Everly!" someone shouts into the receiver.

She winces at the noise. "What?" she demands, pressing the phone back to her ear.

"Ev, it's Mom. I'm so glad you're okay. You didn't answer any of my texts," she stammers.

"Mom, I'm fine. What's wrong?" Her eyes remain shut, and she turns away from the sunlight beaming in through the window. Her stomach churns, and it feels like any sudden movement might push her over the edge.

"Oh, Ev. There was a horrible accident last night right by you. Two severely injured and one dead." Her mom chokes on the words. "I just…" she mumbles. "I just needed to know you were okay."

"I'm okay, Mom." She waits until the sniffles subside. "Mom," she says, her heart suddenly sinking to her stomach, "I need to call Sadie and Joce. I'll talk to you later." She hangs up the phone immediately.

Ring... Ring... Ring... Ring... Ring... "Hello?"

"Goddamn it, Joce! I thought you were dead for a second!"

"Jeez, quit screaming, Ev. I'm not dead, all right? What's going on?"

"My mom said there was a fatal accident in town last night. I have to call Sadie." She hangs up.

Ring... Ring... Ring... "Hello?" A throaty female voice answers the phone, and Everly's heart collapses into her guts. "Hello?" the voice says again.

"Where's Sadie?" Everly demands.

"She's sleeping. Is everything all right, Everly?" Raven asks.

"Thank God." She exhales a sob. "I uh… I just…" she starts. "Yeah. Everything's fine." She clears her throat. "How was your New Year's Eve?"

She can sense Raven's smile through the phone. "It was really nice. We stayed up watching our favorite movie, made some brownies, and watched the ball drop. How was yours?"

"It was…" She contemplates for a moment. "It was pretty interesting," she giggles. "Definitely a memorable night."

"I'm glad," Raven replies. "Are you and Jocelyn free to come over for dinner tonight?"

"We'd love to," she smiles.

"We'll see you two tonight then."

"Sounds good. Bye, Raven."

"Bye, Everly."

Chapter 31

Everly takes a seat amid the endless rows in the lecture hall. She chooses one a few rows from the front but left of center so she's not in the professor's direct view. The room slowly fills with the lazy shuffle of college students back from winter break. Everly prepares herself, riffling through her bag for a pencil and notebook when someone taps her on the shoulder. She looks over to see ice blue eyes that immediately send shivers down her spine.

"Hey, Shortstack." Liam smiles at her surprise and the redness that creeps up her throat and settles in her cheeks.

Everly blinks and sits up, composing herself before responding. "Shortstack, really?"

"Oh, come on, it's clever, and you know it." His nose scrunches with a sweet smile she almost finds attractive.

"Welcome to Microeconomics." The room quiets down. Facing the large wall of whiteboards, the professor scribbles his name, saying it as slowly as he writes. "My name is Professor Rob-in-son."

"You know, he kind of looks like a naked mole rat," Liam whispers in Everly's ear, his breath warm against her neck. She can't help but let out a giggle, noting the bald head and squinting eyes. Professor Robinson glares in their direction, then turns to start his lecture.

"Class dismissed," he announces to the lecture hall of half-sleeping students. "Don't forget to get your textbook and read chapters one through five for next class," he projects over the stampede of kids exiting the room.

"Damn, that's a lot of reading," Liam complains, collecting his bookbag. He looks at Everly for a response. She doesn't give him one. "You know, we could split it up and work together," he proposes.

"Hmm, and why would I trust the guy who barely passed his first year of college to actually be helpful?" Everly questions.

"Because I'm a changed man," he smirks, straightening his back to tower over her confidently. He steps over the row of seats to sit beside her as she collects her things. "I really do want to do well this semester, though. You're the motivation I need. If I know that you're relying on me then I will never miss an assignment or reading again." It's a genuine answer, which catches Everly off guard.

She looks over at him, contemplating. She steps past his long legs, turning to walk up the awkwardly spaced steps out of the lecture hall, then looks back, inviting him to join her. He takes the stairs two at a time, catching up in seconds. She pauses a few steps up, making her almost his height. "Okay," she starts. "We can split the work, but the second you start slacking you're on your own. Got it?"

"Yes, ma'am." She can't tell because he starts walking ahead, but she thinks his cheeks are rosier than usual.

⁂

"What are five ways microeconomics is important in business decision making?"

"Oh god." Liam lies back on his bed.

"You know this," she encourages.

"It helps business managers learn about how to sell stuff."

"Well, duh." She waits for him to try again but answers for him when he remains silent. "It guides business managers in optimal resource utilization, demand analysis, cost analysis, optimal production decision, and pricing policy."

"Isn't that what I said?" He rolls over to stare at Everly sprawled out on his bedroom floor.

"Not quite," she jokes.

"You know, you can come up here. It's comfier than the floor."

"I'll take my chances."

"You know you're safe with me, right?"

She sits up to glare at him. "Why would you say that?"

"Because I can sense it. You don't trust me." He sits up on the bed.

Her eyes try to decipher his expression. "I don't trust a lot of people." She pauses, staring at him harder. "I don't know what kind of game you're playing, but I'm not falling for it, okay?" Shuffling her papers into her backpack, she moves for the door.

He shifts toward her, his arm reaching out to brace himself against the wall in front of her. She recoils from him, and he steps back. "What happened that makes you not trust anyone?"

She stares, bewildered at his audacious question. "None of your business. Now get out of my way." She shoves him aside, slamming the door in his face as she storms off.

Wow, good one, Liam, he thinks, falling back onto the bed.

⁂

The silence unsettles her as she looks back over each page, making sure she's answered everything to the best of her ability. Exhaling her anxious thoughts, she gathers her bag, hands Professor Robinson her exam, and moves to exit the lecture hall when Liam appears between her and the doorway. They stare at each other for a moment before she shoves past him.

A light dusting of snow covers the pavement outside of the business building as her footprints clear the path for others. She can hear the door fling open and the pounding of footsteps coming nearer. Even when he's beside her, she walks at a steady pace, ignoring him fully.

"Everly," he starts, "I'm sorry. For whatever I did that made you not want to talk to me anymore."

She continues her quick pace.

"Please," he begs. "I just want to know what happened. The least you could do is tell me what I did wrong."

Everly stops dead in her tracks and faces him. Her demeanor somehow makes her seem taller than him. "Because I can't do it again," she nearly screams.

Liam stands in front of her, bewildered. "Do *what* again?"

"This!" She gestures between them. "I'm done letting guys take advantage of me just to turn around and find someone better."

"Everly…"

"Don't." She turns to walk away, but Liam lightly catches her wrist, pulling gently until she faces him again.

"Everly, I'm sorry. For overstepping and making you uncomfortable but especially on behalf of the idiots who have mistreated you before. You deserve so much better." Her throat aches as a rush of emotion bombards her. "You deserve to be someone's first choice."

Chapter 32

February 12th

Liam came over the other night. We started studying, then gave up to watch a movie. I don't know when it happened, but at some point I rested my head on his shoulder. I could feel his heart beating out of his chest, which made me smile.

He made me watch a scary movie so when something jumped out, I flung the popcorn all over him. It was hilarious. He even snorted!

He called that a "study date," but I told him I'm not ready to date anyone, and he's understanding about that.

February 18th

I haven't seen Joce in a while. She's basically lived at Cameron's since getting back from break. She said they're training for some fitness thing together, and sleeping there makes it easier to stay consistent. But we have plans this weekend, so it'll be nice to catch up.

Haven't seen Sadie much either. Raven had a really hard roommate situation, so she moved in with Sadie. They seem really happy together, but that all happened so fast.

Then there's me. It's nice having the apartment to myself, but it gets lonely so Liam comes over sometimes. I was making dinner for myself last night but used the recipe I use for me and Joce, so I had a lot more than I could eat. I don't know why, but I called Liam and told him to come over for dinner and a movie.

I made sure he knew it still wasn't a date. I was just bored and had more food than I could eat...

February 22th

Liam's been walking with me to class recently. He lives closer to campus than I do but still walks nearly a mile to my place so we can walk together to class.

He's also doing really well in microeconomics, which I'm actually impressed with. We sit next to each other every class and split up note taking, even though his handwriting is horrendous.

February 24th

He tried to kiss me.

We were studying while lying on my bed. I leaned over to correct one of his answers, and when I turned to look at him he was already staring at me. He moved in, but I pulled away.

He immediately apologized, but so did I. I was so embarrassed, but he told me not to be. He was really understanding and didn't make me feel bad about it. It's so different than when I was with Thomas.

I feel safe with him.

February 28th

I kissed him.

It was amazing.

My stomach is still trying to calm the frantic butterflies.

This is what happened...

Knock... knock... knock... Everly skips down the staircase, swinging the door open to see Jocelyn standing before her. "Ahhh," they squeal, embracing each other tightly. Everly's arms wrap further around Jocelyn than they ever have before. "Wow, you look amazing, Joce." Everly stands back, taking in her friend's slim figure.

"Thanks, Ev. We've been training like crazy for the competition this summer."

"Yeah, if she keeps this up, she has a chance at winning for sure." Cameron walks up the pathway behind her.

"Well, you know I'll be there with signs and sparklers and cookies." Everly winks.

"Oh, what I wouldn't do for a cookie right now." Jocelyn looks like her mouth might actually start watering.

"Come in!" Everly opens the door wider. "You're acting like you don't live here anymore."

"I feel like I don't. We've just been really busy with school and then training. But I miss you, Ev. I'm glad we're doing this."

"Me too." They hug from the side, resting their heads together. "I think Liam might come by too." Jocelyn raises an eyebrow. "Oh, shut up," she scoffs. "We've just become really good friends."

"Who have seen each other naked," Cameron says under his breath.

Everly whips around to look at Jocelyn. "You told him!"

She covers her laughing grin. "How could I not," she defends. "You can't tell me that's not the funniest story you've ever heard." Everly concedes, putting a hand to her face and laughing along with them.

"So, what do you two want on your pizzas? I have pepperoni, olives, chick —"

"Actually, we brought our own food," Cameron cuts in.

"You brought your own food to pizza night?" Everly leans against the counter staring at Jocelyn. "Doesn't that defeat the purpose?" she giggles. Jocelyn just shrugs. "Okay then, more for me."

Knock... Knock... Knock... "I got it!" Jocelyn races to the door, swinging it open. Liam steps back at the sudden movement.

"Hey, Joce." He smiles.

"Hey, Liam. We're just about to make pizzas." She opens the door wider so he can pass through. Cameron and Liam converse for a moment before he makes his way to the kitchen to see Everly, her hair tied up in a beautiful mess, dancing around the kitchen with pizza sauce on her cheek. Jocelyn and Cameron settle into the plush couch cushions and set up their game on the coffee table. Music wafts through the air, mingling with the savory smells coming from the oven.

"Hey," Everly says without turning around. "What do you want on your pizza?" Liam leans forward on the counter top, looking over her small frame to see his options. Once he's made up his mind, Everly expertly organizes the ingredients on his personal pizza, designing a giant foot outline. She turns to mock him, and he squeezes her side playfully, sending her into a fit of squeals. "What! You don't like it, Bigfoot?"

"We're going to start without you," Jocelyn calls from the living room. Everly looks up into Liam's piercing blue eyes, his smile crinkling them at the sides. She puts his pizza in the oven beside hers and grabs his hand lightly, guiding him to the couch.

"Wow, that smells amazing." Jocelyn collides into Everly, sniffing her plate.

"Joce, just have a slice. It won't kill you," she chuckles.

"No, but Cam might." She flops back on the cushions.

"I won't tell, if you don't." She looks slyly at Jocelyn before turning a wicked glance at Liam. He throws his hands up defensively and nods his head in agreement.

"Okay," she blurts out. "One bite before he comes back." She picks up the slice, and her eyes fix on it like it's the most beautiful thing she's seen in her lifetime. Her lips part as she takes a bite, the cheese stretching between her and the slice as she moves to put it back on the plate. Everly laughs when the cheese string is nearly two feet long before it breaks and falls into her lap.

Cameron fidgets with the finicky lock before his footsteps beat along the hallway and into the living room. Jocelyn swallows the bite in a hardy gulp, turning quickly to the game.

"Ready to go, Joce?"

She takes a big swig of water before answering, making sure to wash away all evidence. "Yeah, I'm ready." Collecting her bag, now filled with extra clothing and toiletries to bring to Cameron's house, she hugs Everly tightly before heading out. "Love you, Ev."

"Love you too, Joce."

The door closes heavily behind them. Only the quiet music and ticking of the wall clock fill the room as Everly and Liam sit across from each other. Liam stands, and Everly's heartbeat jumps nervously. He collects their plates and glasses, taking them to the kitchen. "Oh, you don't have to do that." She follows him.

"I know," he continues.

"Why?"

He turns to face her, his brows furrowed in confusion. "Why what?"

She shakes her head, the smile on her lips growing wider. "Why are you so kind to me?" They stare at each other for a moment until she continues. "I definitely haven't earned it," she laughs. "All I do is make fun of you, or argue with you, or yell when you beat me in games or spoil movies."

His eyes, that chilling blue, burrow into her soul and send shivers through her entire being. Somehow the chills turn to fire in her veins when he finally speaks. "You don't have to *earn* kindness, Ev. You just deserve it."

Grabbing his collar, she pulls him into her, and their lips collide in helpless yearning. He effortlessly lifts her onto the countertop, her legs straddling his waist, pulling him closer. Kissing purposefully along her jaw and moving back to her lips, his smile grows and hers widens to match.

"What?" she asks. Their lips linger a breath's distance apart, her eyes dancing back and forth between his, trying to see which is her favorite.

"You are so beautiful, Everly." Her lungs empty as she looks at his face, fully and undeniably truthful. Her chest swells with happiness, and a deep urge to laugh and cry at once chokes her throat, but she silences it by pulling his mouth to hers once more.

The rhythmic pressure of their lips releases a feeling of freedom she's refused to allow herself since putting up strongholds around her heart.

His lips liberate her and fan the fire she thought had been snuffed out.

Chapter 33

His tongue traces light circles along the base of her throat, his lips parting into a smile as he feels the moans reverberate under his touch. Orange sunlight beams through the blinds, highlighting the curves of her body as she moves against the sheets. Long fingers trace down her jaw to her collarbone and move agonizingly slowly over the supple mounds of her breasts. Her breath catches as he guides the loose strap over her sunkissed shoulder. Sunlight, wet paint, and music flood her memory only to be blotted out with anger, tears, and pain. Her body shudders against the feelings.

Liam sits up immediately. "Ev, are you okay? I'm sorry. We don't have to."

"No, I just…" She rests back on her elbows, replaying the pictures in her head. "I'm sorry."

"Don't be sorry, Ev. We don't have to rush anything." She nods, looking out of the second story window to see the sun nuzzle against the horizon, preparing to rest for the night. Leaning over the bedside, she grapples for the covers, dragging them over her exposed skin. "Do you want to talk about it?" Liam asks, trying to read the look on her face.

Settling back into her pillows, she looks up at him. Those icy eyes stare at her, chilling her soul as she talks. "It's just…" she starts. "Have you ever been in love?" His eyes widen, not expecting the question. "Or thought you'd been in love," she corrects. His features harden as he thinks back. She can tell this may be a sore subject for him as he cracks his knuckles and fiddles with his fingers, deep in thought. "I'm sorry. You don't have to answer that."

"No, no. It's okay." He clears his throat. "I guess I thought I was in love once."

"What happened?"

He looks down at her, his face unreadable. "It just wasn't meant to be. Long story short, everything seemed fine until one day she ambushed me with her friends and broke it off."

"Liam, I'm so sorry. That's horrible." Her hand reaches out to hold his. He smiles looking down at her hand dwarfed against his.

"It's all right. It led me to where I am now." His lips press against her forehead, and she leans into the warmth of it. "What about you? Have you ever been in love?"

"I thought I was. A few times, actually." She pulls her hand away, fidgeting with the sheet. "I was never good enough for them, though."

Liam shifts forward and turns to face her, his hand comforting on her knee. "You are and always have been enough, Ev. You just never had someone who appreciated you the way you deserve. Until now." His thumb and forefinger lift her chin so he can press a soft kiss on her freckled nose. Her smile creases her eyes, and she allows them to close, melting into the security of his arms as he pulls her in to lie back on the cool sheets. She nestles against his steady heartbeat, her one leg draping over his torso. Her hand traces along his neck and outlines the shape of his pectoral muscles. His heart beats against her ear as she drags her fingers lightly down his abdomen in slow circles. Shifting herself against him and lowering her leg, she sneaks her fingers under the hem of his shirt to feel the soft skin covering taut muscles. The breath catches in his throat as she lazily follows his waistband, her fingers dipping lower. She smiles, feeling his muscles contract against her touch.

He turns to her, lifting her chin for another kiss, but she presses him back into the bed, a devilish grin on her face. Again, her touch teases along his waistline, torturously slow, then lightly traces the skin between his torso and thigh. His body jumps and writhes at the sensation. Bracing herself on her elbow, she watches his face as she palms him.

He barks a curse.

She laughs quietly, moves to kiss his neck, and fully grasps him in her hand, the moan in his throat vibrating against her lips. In an instant she's on her back. Her mouth goes dry at the sight of him.

Liam is built to play football with his wide body and thick muscled limbs, yet he hovers over Everly's slight body so gently. Everly looks up into those ravenously piercing eyes, her mouth parting to loose a breath. "Are you okay?" he asks, his voice hoarse. Staring steadily into those blue eyes, she nods and guides the straps off her shoulders. She watches as his eyes wander over her shoulders, her throat, then down over her newly exposed skin. Leaning forward he kisses her lips. Slow. Soft. A hand slides along the smooth skin of her torso while he lowers himself over her, his hips nestling into hers. Her breath catches at the touch, and she exhales shakily as his hand floats along her ribs and over her breasts.

Arching her back, she presses into his palm and their lips connect in fiery passion. Her hands search for the hem of his shirt, pulling it over his head as he scrambles to throw his pants to the side, taking his undershorts with them. Pulling her to the edge of the bed, he kisses her as his long arms remove her shorts and toss them against the door.

Liam falls to his knees, his arms hooked around her thighs as he admires her. Their eyes connect, and they each huff a laugh. Everly drags her fingers through his short hair until he lowers himself out of reach, and her body arches and writhes against his warm tongue, whimpering happily as her mind fogs.

⁕

Exhaling elated exhaustion, they lay sprawled on the sheets, the fan chilling their sweat and casting goosebumps across their skin.

"Wow," Liam huffs. Everly turns toward him, her hair spilling over the pillow in golden waves. Her smile radiates as she looks at his expression of utter contentment. She searches for the comforter with her hand, but it's been flung in a pile on the floor. Settling for the thin sheet, she yanks it over her and spreads it across Liam's lengthy body. Reaching for her small figure, he pulls her into him, gifting some of his warmth.

"This is crazy," she giggles lightly.

"What is?"

"Us."

"How so?"

"Because the first time we met I was blackout drunk, throwing up in an alley, and stealing your bed from you after walking around naked wanting to shower." Her hands fly to her face, covering her embarrassment and muffling her laughs.

"That wasn't actually the first time we met." Everly bolts upright.

"What?"

"Yeah, we *technically* met earlier that night." He smirks, watching her face crinkle as she racks her brain. "You nearly broke your ass when Sadie pushed you off the tabletop." Liam watches her face as she pieces together the events. "Luckily, I have good reflexes."

"That was you?" She cranes her head forward. He nods, half smiling. "Wow. I always wondered."

"I told you I'm a good guy." They both grimace, remembering their first verbal interaction. "I'll always protect you, Ev. No matter what." Settling back into his arms, she allows her brain to replay the murky memories of that night.

"When did you and Cam first meet? At college or before then?

He shakes his head. "No, we grew up in the same town, so we've known each other since we were kids, actually. But we weren't really friends until we both started playing football in high school." Nodding at his response, she waits for him to continue. "He was actually a jerk growing up. Always the alpha male type."

"That makes sense. Seems like he's more muscle than brains sometimes," she teases. "But he really cares about Joce, so that's all I care about."

"Sometimes those muscles get the best of him."

"What do you mean?"

"Nothing, really. Just when we were growing up, he hit his growth spurt before everyone else and made sure people knew it." Everly shuffles her pillows behind her to sit up. Liam does the same, sitting up next to her.

"So, he was a bully?"

"Oh yeah," Liam chuckles. "He was always getting in trouble for fighting when we were younger. Especially when we got to high school."

"What happened in high school?"

"I just remember this one time specifically, we had an away game. A guy from the other team ran it back for a touchdown, and Cameron was pissed. I knew something was going to go down when I saw the look in his eyes right before the snap. Anyway, he absolutely wrecked their quarterback, broke his arm I think." Everly gapes at him, recognizing the event. "The play stopped and people took a knee. Everyone except Cam, who walked over and spit on the kid. All hell broke loose after that."

"That was him?" she whispers under her breath.

"I remember trying to pull Cam away, and then the arrogant prick who just ran it back for a touchdown came out of nowhere and tackled me. Everything went to hell after that."

The memory of a moshpit of fists, shouts, and toxic aggression floods her mind. "I was at that game." She looks up to see Liam's dumbfounded expression. "That was my high school. My ex—" she pauses. "Never mind."

"You were there? I can't believe we were in the same place at the same time. I guess our paths were meant to cross." His lips press against her forehead as he pulls her into his arms again.

"Has Cam always been like that?"

"What do you mean?"

"Has he always been an aggressive asshole?"

"I wouldn't say he's an asshole. All the time," he clarifies. "Although, his exes in high school would probably say otherwise."

"Why?"

"He just had a reputation in high school. We don't have to talk about it."

Everly pulls back from him, searching his face. "No, I want to know. What kind of reputation?"

"I don't want to talk bad about the dude. We've become good friends."

"I don't care—he's dating my *best friend.* What kind of reputation did he have?" she insists.

"Okay." He reaches over to hold her hand. "I only really know about the one girl, Casey." She nods, urging him to continue. "We were actually friends before Cam and I started hanging out." The room settles into the quiet of night, the only sound a soft wind blowing against the screened windows. "Long story short, I'd heard he was controlling with his girlfriends, but hearing what Casey had to say was kind of wild. She was so infatuated with him at the beginning, too. It's that damn charisma, I guess. One day, she just stopped showing up to school. I never found out why."

Everly leans forward. "Well, what do people think happened?"

"Rumors spread that she dropped out because Cam leaked photos of her, other people said Cam broke up with her so she stopped eating and ended up in the hospital, and I heard other people say she snapped and got put in a psych ward."

"What did you do?"

"What do you mean?"

"Did you shut down the rumors? You two were friends right?"

"Yeah, we were, but I didn't know what happened."

"You didn't even defend her?" she snaps. "Why didn't you tell me this sooner?"

"I'm sorry, Ev." Liam sits up in the bed, reaching for her hand as she gets up. "Where are you going?"

"To get Joce."

"Right now? Ev, they were just here, and she seemed fine."

"Did she? She looked skeletal, Liam."

"Aren't they training for a competition though?"

"She literally had to hide the fact that she took one bite of pizza from Cam. I should've noticed earlier."

"Noticed what?"

"She needs me. I have to go." Everly pulls on a jacket and shuffles through a pile on the floor for her sneakers.

"Right now? Do you want me to come with you?"

"No!" The shout rings in his ears. "No, I'm sorry. I just need to talk to her alone."

❊

"Joce!" Everly calls out as she rhythmically bangs on the front door of Cameron's frat house. "Joce, I need to talk to you!"

The door flies open as one of Cameron's shirtless frat brothers starts to yell, "What the fu—" but Everly shoves right past him, heading up the stairs.

Cameron's broad body blocks the path to his room. "What do you want, Ev?" Cameron asks dismissively.

"I need to talk to Joce." She moves to get past him. He blocks her way with his arm. She looks up at him determinedly. "Move, Cam."

"She doesn't want to see you."

"Then let her tell me that." Everly shoves him, but his heavy muscled body doesn't budge. His hands are quick to grab her wrists, painfully tight. Her eyes widen at the aggression. "Joce!" she yells down the hall.

The door to his room opens a crack. Cameron looks back, his expression unreadable from Everly's angle.

"Go home, Ev." Jocelyn's voice nearly whispers.

Everly tries to move against the tight grip of Cameron's hands, trying to see Jocelyn in the doorway. "Joce, come home with me," she begs.

Her voice rises slightly, "I said go home, Ev." The door clicks shut.

"Told you," Cameron mocks, releasing her wrists and pushing her back.

"Oh, fuck off, Cam." Everly projects her voice past him. "Ask him about Casey!" His face contorts at the name, and she smirks, knowing she's struck a nerve.

Everly marches down the hallway towards the stairs. Every door is open with dumbfounded guys gaping at her. "You enjoy the show?" she shouts at no one in particular.

She slams the door shut behind her, holding herself together until she's swallowed by darkness, away from probing eyes. Finally, she crumples onto the pavement, sobbing helplessly on the curb.

⁕

Everly nuzzles her head against the plush cushions of the couch, Liam caressing her legs on his lap while they watch a movie. Her mind wanders from the movie's plot to assignments that are due to the incident with Jocelyn and Cameron nearly two weeks ago now. She hasn't heard from her since.

Liam catches her dazed expression and touches her face. "You did everything you could." She nods, thinking back on it and willing herself not to cry.

As the credits roll up the screen, Everly has finally escaped the gloom of her mind. She stands to head to the bathroom, but Liam leans forward, catching her fingers and spinning her around to face his smile. “Ev,” he starts.

She smiles, curious as to what’s so important it can’t wait until she relieves her bladder. She looks at him expectantly. He shifts to the edge of the couch, a soft smile across his face. “Can you hug me,” he asks purely.

“Can I pee first?” she chuckles. He releases her hand, laughing as she skips to the bathroom.

She emerges from the shadowed nook, sliding across the floor in her mismatched socks. The circular shag rug beneath the coffee table stops her just short, and she stumbles into his arms. Their laughter mingles as their lips collide happily.

Her arms wrap around his neck, her head resting on the slope of his neck and shoulder. Liam smells of fresh cedarwood and warm comfort. His long arms envelop her, each circling around her body to rest on the other.

“Hey, Ev?” His deep voice reverberates.

“Hey, Bigfoot,” she speaks into his neck.

His voice is caught in his throat; she can feel his need to say something, but he remains silent. His grip around her tightens slightly, as if urging his own words to escape.

“I love you.”

The apartment door swings open. Jocelyn stands in the doorway, tears streaming down her bloodied and bruising face.

“Oh my god, Joce!” Everly tears herself away from Liam, sprinting with open arms to catch Jocelyn as her knees buckle. They collide, and Everly slides against the door, holding Jocelyn’s weight in her arms, until they reach the floor. Cradling her head in her lap, Everly soothes her shaking body, stroking her hair rhythmically. The evening breeze rushes through the open door to help dry her tears.

“Breathe with me, Joce. Just like this.” She takes deep, steadying breaths. Jocelyn fights against the hard, jagged inhales spasming in her chest.

“Ev…” Liam approaches them cautiously. Everly motions out the door with her head, quickly turning her attention back to Jocelyn.

Liam walks out the door, looking back at the silhouette of the two perfect friends, in a world where only they exist together.

Chapter 34

Last night Joce and I didn't even talk. We didn't need to. She just cried herself to sleep as I held her.

I'm so mad at myself for not noticing it sooner. She's mentioned struggling with an eating disorder in high school, but I just thought this was different. Looking at her now I can see the patterns, but the physical effects were hard to discern while she's been training.

I can see it on her face, though. The purple under her eyes and how they've started to sink in, the way her collarbones are more pronounced than before.

I should've been there to help her.

She's still upstairs sleeping. I barely slept trying to think of different ways to kill Cameron. I am livid thinking about how this motherfu—

"Good morning," Jocelyn says, rounding the bottom of the steps. Everly closes her journal immediately, startled by her presence.

"Hey, girly, how you feeling?" Everly pats the couch cushion beside her, inviting her to sit.

"I'm good. Just embarrassed," Jocelyn looks down at the floor before flopping onto the couch. "I owe you an explanation."

"Joce. You don't owe me anything. I'm here to listen whenever you're ready to talk." Everly puts an arm around her, and she leans into it, resting her head on Everly's shoulder.

"I love you," Jocelyn whispers through her tight throat.

"I love you back." Everly squeezes her in response.

⁂

Liam picks up his phone to dial Everly's number again. It rings a few times before being declined and sent to voicemail for the third time.

"Hey, you've reached Ev. Leave a message, and I'll call you back when I get a chance." *Beep.*

"Hey, Ev, I know you're helping Joce with everything, but I really need to talk to you." He pauses. "Just give me a call when you get this." He hangs up, throwing his phone against the couch.

⁂

The sun seeps through the blinds of their cozy apartment, warming their skin. Everly rests her head atop Jocelyn's. "What do you want for breakfast?" Jocelyn shrugs passively.

"I can make something, we can go out, I can pick something up. Whatever you want."

"I'm not hungry," is all Jocelyn offers in response.

"You sure? I know how much you love breakfast. What if I make some pancakes and coffee?"

"I said *no*."

Everly straightens up at her curt response. "Okay, sorry," she says, standing up to go make her own coffee. Jocelyn can sense her unease. There's silence as Everly finds her favorite mug, avoiding eye contact.

"Ev, I'm sorry." Jocelyn stands, moving towards the kitchen.

"It's okay, Joce."

"It's not. You're just trying to help." Jocelyn sits at the countertop, watching Everly prepare her coffee. There is a long silence before Jocelyn looks up, tears in her eyes. "I think I need help…"

⁂

Jocelyn races for the door, slamming it in Cameron's face and locking it before collapsing onto the bathroom floor.

"Open the goddamn door, Joce!" Cameron's fists thrash against the door. "Open the fucking door!"

Jocelyn cowers helplessly in the farthest corner of the shower. The beating stops, and she can hear Cameron's breath steadying. "Joce," he calls calmly. "Please come out. Let's just talk about this."

Jocelyn wipes her cheeks and clears her throat before speaking the words that have tortured her for weeks. "Who's Casey?"

"Come out here, and I'll tell you," he counters.

Jocelyn holds her ground, keeping silent. She can hear him pacing outside the door, his tension and frustration building.

"Okay, fine," he shouts. "You want to know about Casey?" His pace quickens with agitation. "She was some bitch that I fucked with in high school. End of story."

"What happened to her?"

Cameron laughs manically, running his fingers through his hair. "She went fucking crazy is what happened. I don't know what you want me to tell you, Joce."

"Is that what you'll say about me?" she asks almost to herself.

"Don't say that. I need you, Joce."

"You don't." She pauses, trying to compose herself. "You've changed me... I don't even recognize myself anymore." She stands in front of the bathroom mirror watching her bony fingers touch her sunken cheeks.

"What the fuck are you talking about? I'm trying to help you, to make you better. If that makes me a bad person then so be it, but don't you come crying to me when you realize you're nothing more than the person I've built."

Silence.

He exhales exaggeratedly. "Joce, I didn't mean that. Please come out, and let's talk about this, okay?"

Jocelyn yanks the door open, anger boiling over. "You beg me to stay, promise you'll change. Every fucking week you say you'll change, but you never will! You're just going to be an angry, manipulative narcissist who makes people think they'd be lost without you. Well, guess what, I'm good enough without you. I always have been, and I always will be. So fuck you, Cam!" She tears through the room towards the door.

Cameron shadows her movements, his rage building with each of her words. Jocelyn opens the door only inches before Cameron's hand slams it shut. His arms barricade her on either side. His words come slowly, each one pushing him closer to the edge. "Is that what you think?" He pauses, smiling as she tries to squirm away from him. "I've done nothing but love you, Joce. Think about how I've always helped you."

Jocelyn pushes against his chest. "You mean the ways you've controlled me? What I eat. Who I see. What about when you deleted messages from Everly on my phone to make me think she didn't care?" Her dark eyes glow with rage as she looks up at his shadowed face. "If you don't let me out of this room in two seconds, I'm going to scream."

Cameron's smile twists unnaturally as he scans Jocelyn up and down. He shifts his weight back slightly only to thrust his palm powerfully against her throat, slamming her brutally into the wall.

⁕

There's a knock on the apartment door, tearing Everly away from Jocelyn's story.

Jocelyn flinches at the sudden noise. Everly rubs her arm reassuringly. "I'll see who it is." She stands, walking towards the anonymous knocker. Pressing to her tippy toes, she peers through the peephole. The fish-eye lens shows Liam pacing back and forth on the front steps.

Are you kidding me? Everly exhales, swinging the door open. Liam turns, smiling broadly when he sees her. "Hi."

"What do you need?" she asks pointedly.

His smile dissipates and brows furrow, confused by her terse response. He clears his throat. "I just wanted to talk." His voice trails off. "We never got to finish our conversation, and you haven't been returning my calls or texts."

Everly turns to look at Jocelyn. "I'll be right back," she smiles, shutting the door gently and stepping out into the brisk morning air. Once the door is closed, she whirls to look at Liam. They stand almost eye to eye because of the steps. "What is your problem?!"

Although the door is now shut, Jocelyn can clearly hear the shouts. “You know that I need to be with Joce right now.” Her hands wave, projecting her frustration.

Liam looks less confident than when he first knocked. “I know, I’m sorry, but we were having a really important conversation, and we never got to finish it.”

Everly’s eyes could burn holes in him if he’d stay in one spot. She takes a deep breath, trying to compose herself before the urge to scream overwhelms her. “Okay.” Her eyes close, steadying her thoughts. “Yes, I know we were having a serious talk, and it got interrupted, but you have to understand that this is a more immediate issue than that.” She pauses, opening her eyes to look at him. “Right?” Her impatience burns in her chest as she waits for a response, the way a mother waits for a toddler.

“Yeah.” He nods reluctantly. “Yeah, I get that, but I feel like the least you could’ve done was call me back.”

Everly’s hands rake through her knotted hair, her fists clenching in frustration. “The least *you* could’ve done was give me a fucking *day* to help my friend!” Liam’s eyes widen in shock at her sudden intensity. “I’m sorry that I didn’t get the chance to say ‘I love you too’ because my friend walked through the goddamn door battered and bruised!”

Liam smiles immediately at her words. “So, you love me too?”

Exasperation thrums through Everly’s body like an electric charge. She composes herself with another deep breath, forces a smile, and nods stiffly. “Now, can we please talk about this another time? I have to be with Joce.”

Liam takes a step up and wraps his long arms around her. She reciprocates the action reluctantly, irritation still gnawing at her. “I’m going to be helping Joce work through a few things the next couple days, okay? I might not be able to text or talk much because she deserves my attention right now.” A moment passes without acknowledgement. “Okay?” she urges.

Liam nods in agreement. “Okay, I’ll be waiting for you whenever you’re free.”

Everly rests her hand on his cheek, wrestling internally with whether to caress it adoringly or slap the stupid out of him. “Thank you,” is all she says.

The door clicks shut behind her as she turns to face Jocelyn who is smirking mischievously.

Everly's brows crinkle. "What?"

Jocelyn's eyes narrow. "That boy's been a sucker for you from the moment you met."

Everly rolls her eyes and plops down, sighing exaggeratedly, onto the couch beside Jocelyn. "Shut up," she snickers.

"It's cute, Ev. And you deserve that kind of love and attention. It's a little quick though." She lets out a genuine laugh. Everly marvels at the sound, thinking back to the first time they'd talked and laughed together. The day they became friends.

"You think?" Everly teases, poking her in her bony rib cage. Jocelyn squirms at the ticklish touch but pulls a pillow into her stomach, clutching at it with her bruised hands. Everly clears her throat. "Tell me what you need."

Her brown eyes brim with hot tears before she can speak. "I need you to know everything that happened."

Everly nods. "Okay. I'm listening."

⁂

Cameron's grip tightens around her throat, crushing the screams that could save her. "You know," Cameron says passively, "you've always been too emotional, and now I'm realizing that no matter how much I try to help you, you're always going to be the pathetic little bitch everyone thinks you are." He snickers to himself, loosening his grip slightly. "You're lying to yourself if you think I'm the manipulator in this relationship, Joce. I've only tried to help you, to make you better. I'm the only reason people know who the fuck you are."

The purpling of her face is hidden in the shadows of the room but his eyes monitor her. He releases his hand from her throat. She gasps for air, her lungs burning.

"Fuck you, Cam," she spits, her voice hoarse and painful.

"Fuck me? Oh yeah, you wanna fuck me, Joce?" He moves closer, pressing her breathless body against the wall. Cameron's hand tightens on her lean face, his other hand grappling to hold her arms over her head.

She lets out a gasp as his grip crushes her wrists. "Cam, stop." Jocelyn tries pushing against the weight of his body.

"What's wrong, Joce? You don't love me anymore?" he whispers in her ear. "You've had no problem being a whorish little slut for me since we met." His lips trace down her neck, and she shrinks from his touch.

"Cam, please," she begs.

"Oh," he pauses, pressing his lips to her collarbone. "You don't have to beg, baby." He looks her in the eyes as his hand glides against the smooth skin of her thigh.

"Hel—" Jocelyn yells just before Cameron clasps his hand over her mouth. Panicked breaths escape through her nose, and her eyes search the room frantically. Her muffled cries are silenced by his heavy hand.

Cameron's body crushes her against the wall as his free hand lifts the hem of her skirt. His hungry eyes drop down just in time to see Jocelyn's knee move forcefully towards him.

His breath leaves him as he collapses to the floor. Jocelyn dives for the door screaming, "HELP!" Cameron's long arms grapple at her ankles, forcing her down. "HELP ME!" she shrieks. The door flies open, the edge striking Jocelyn's face. She yelps in pain as people flood into the room.

Two guys carry her from the room out of harm's way. She fights her way out of their arms, unable to look anyone in the eye. When her bare feet finally hit the cold pavement outside, she doesn't stop running until she's staring helplessly into the only eyes she trusts.

Chapter 35

"I feel like I haven't seen you in forever," Liam says, enveloping Everly in his signature bear hug.

She hugs him back, her ear resting over his steady heart. "Okay, okay," Everly breathes as she starts to feel claustrophobic.

"Sorry, I just missed you," he smiles down at her.

"I missed you too, Bigfoot," she teases back. "How about we go away this weekend? Joce is home with her family getting some help, and I could definitely use a break from all the chaos that's been going on."

His eyes crinkle at the corners as his face widens with his beautifully white smile. "That sounds perfect, my love."

⁂

The sound of gravel under the tires reminds her of when she was little. Her stuffed animal cushioning her head against the car door during the long drive. How her young eyelashes flutter with blissful dreams only to awaken to this same sound of gravel. Like a bird's instinct to fly south, her heart knows her destination is close.

Liam drives the entire way. He doesn't like compromise when it comes to being a *gentleman*. Their fingers rest loosely intertwined on her lap as the car jounces along the rough path. Everly leans forward looking up at the towering pine trees on either side of the road. "It's up here on the right." She squeezes his hand.

Kicking up dust, they pull into the unpaved driveway and stop in front of Everly's family lake house. The wooden exterior still glows with the vibrancy of her memories even after years exposed to the elements. Her grandfather built every inch of this house. His favorite part was the custom front door he built to welcome the people he loved into his space. Each carved detail perfectly placed with hard work, intention, and love.

Liam admires the architecture before pushing the solid door open. A gust of stale air eagerly escapes into the pines. "Wow," he says, looking at the high ceilings and vast windows that invite the warm afternoon light to stream through.

"My grandpa built this whole thing." She pauses in her nostalgia. "Check this out." She walks to the wall of glass windows facing the west. The lake shimmers in the afternoon light amid the blooming trees.

"Let's go," Liam says, dropping their bags to the floor and pulling the sleeve of her sweater.

She giggles, pulling back lightly. "Go where?"

"In!" Before she can react, he sweeps her off her feet and over his shoulder.

She squeals like a child being tickled. "No way! The water's freezing!"

"Guess we'll have to keep each other warm then," Liam says, sliding open the glass door and descending the back stairs toward the lapping shore.

"You're crazy!" Everly squirms in his arms. The hem of her sweater slides over her helpless, inverted body. Liam takes this moment to pull it the rest of the way over her head, throwing it to the side as he strides closer to the water.

Everly squeals as the fresh air dances across her nerves. She laughs uncontrollably as her fingers fumble with his belt, her arms trying to wrap around him to find the buckle.

Liam swings her around to cradle her in his strong arms. For a moment her heart skips. It's like she's seeing him in a new light. Her eyes trace his jaw, the smooth skin of his lips, the rigid contours of his nose and cheeks, to those eyes that send shivers down her spine. Her eyelashes flutter until their eyes connect. Deeply, intimately.

Everly's freckled cheekbones shift with her smile. He looks down at her adoringly. "What?" he asks.

"You're beautiful," she breathes out, nearly whispering.

He chuckles slightly at the unusual compliment. He leans forward to kiss her temple. "Takes one to know one."

"I don't think that applies to this," she snickers at him.

He rolls his eyes and sticks his tongue out mockingly. "Whatever, you know what I mean."

He sets her down gently, and she shivers, realizing how exposed she is. His belt buckle is almost undone, but he's perfectly content in his long sleeves and jeans. Her eyes look him up and down. He grins at her curiously. "What?"

"Oh, nothing," she says innocently, "just want to level the playing field." She grabs either side of his jeans, yanking them down to his ankles and baring the wintry pallor of his long legs to the sun.

"Hey!" Liam objects. Everly laughs to the point of tears. "What?" he demands over her cackles.

"You're just so pale," she wheezes, wiping at her eyes.

Within seconds Liam is tugging her pants down by the pockets. Everly's eyes widen as she's jerked forward by his powerful grip. The afternoon sun does little to warm her exposed body. Liam looks her up and down, admiring his work.

"God, it's cold! Let's just go back inside and make a fire," Everly pleads.

Liam looks up at the house on the hill. "Okay, fine," he whines. Everly moves to pull up her pants and search for her sweater when Liam's warm hands wrap around her torso, dragging her after him into the frigid water.

Shrieks of laughter ring out across the lake, and birds scatter from the treetops. Her breath catches as the ice-cold water laps at her waist. Most of Liam's torso still lingers above the water as he releases one arm to pull his sweater over his head, throwing it back to the shore. His icy eyes pierce her heart as he pulls her into him and deeper into the water.

Everly wraps her arms around his neck and her legs around his waist, trapping the little body heat they have left. Her teeth chatter rapidly in the cold. Liam's hands linger at her hips below the surface, his fingers dancing across her nerves. He looks at her adoringly; her sweet freckled skin, her frantic smile, the beautiful curve of her cheeks.

The cold seems to dissipate as he looks at her. His gaze ignites a warm spark within her. "You're beautiful." He tucks a lone strand of hair behind her ear before placing a comforting hand on her cheek.

Shivering uncontrollably, Everly manages to say, "Takes one to know one."

Liam's fingers entangle in her hair, pulling her to him. Their smiles collide against each other, his warm tongue heating her body. Everly's fingers comb through his hair as his lips caress her throat. A growing heat spreads through her body with each kiss. Gentle moans escape her when his hands graze her smooth skin beneath the water's surface.

Her legs loosen around his waist to create space. His lips pull away from her skin, his eyes penetrating her soul. He watches her face, each minute movement, as his fingers trace along her inner thigh. Shivers of cold are replaced with the deep heat of desire within them both.

Pressing herself against him now, she whines frustratedly, waiting for his touch. Liam's lips contort into a sardonic grin, his eyes still pleasantly analyzing her movements. Impatience consumes her as she pulls herself against his taut torso. Her ravenous lips explore his collarbones, throat and neck, while her hand sneaks below the water to venture elsewhere.

Liam's body shivers at the sudden sensation. He takes hold of her hair, tugging her head back. A small gasp escapes her throat, followed by an enticing smile. His body tells her he's ready so Everly clasps her arms around Liam's neck as he raises them from the water, her legs encircling his slippery body. He strides with purpose past their discarded clothes towards the house.

*

Out of breath, their chests rise and fall synchronously. Golden sunlight streaks through the windows, bathing them in its gentle glow. The birds twitter and rustle about as they prepare for the impending twilight. A choir of creatures preparing to rest invites the sun to relax as it highlights the tops of the trees.

Liam supports himself on his elbow, gazing down at Everly's bare skin. His cheeks crease with an adoring smile as his fingers tenderly trace along her figure. "We should get some firewood before it gets too dark."

Everly sits up, pulling the plush blanket up with her. "That's a good idea." She leans forward to kiss him. It's like he's a new person here; no past or future can touch them in this moment. This moment of pure contentment.

One kiss turns into two, two turns into four, then before she can continue, he groans. "Come on, it'll be dark soon."

Everly falls back to the floor, splaying her limbs dramatically. "Fine. But you're making dinner, I'm building the fire."

He chuckles. "No way, I'll make the fire, and you make dinner."

"I'm definitely the better fire builder in this relationship," she insists.

He chuckles because they both know that to be true. "All right, let's go, love. Up and at 'em!" He yanks her to her feet and slaps her backside before making his way to the kitchen.

The aroma of baking bread fills the air along with Liam's enthusiastic, offkey baritone. Everly welcomes the subtle warmth of the house as she brings in armfuls of wood. Maneuvering around the strewn pillows, she sets the logs, kindling, and tinder on the cool stone hearth.

Within minutes the fire gently crackles, its warmth radiating throughout the space as Liam saunters into the living area with plates of seasoned pasta and golden bread. Everly's mouth starts watering before she even sees it. He settles onto the floor beside her.

"Wow, you *are* good at that," Liam admits, gesturing towards the fire.

Everly flips her hair knowingly. "Told you." Her hands extend to accept one of the plates. "This smells amazing!" She nearly sticks her entire nose into the pasta to capture every whiff. "Where did you learn to cook so well?"

"My grandma taught me a little bit before she died." He pauses, looking down at his plate. "She taught me everything I know." Everly looks up from her plate to his lowered eyes. He continues. "Basically, my dad constantly traveled for work, so I rarely saw him growing up. My mom, on the other hand, was always around, just not in a good way." She reaches a comforting hand to rest on his knee. "She's uh… just struggled with some mental health stuff and made it hard for us to be around her." He shrugs passively. "So, yeah. My grandma taught me a lot. But she died when I was twelve." He clears the tension from his throat before speaking again. "Anyway, it's not a big deal. Just made me who I am, I guess."

"Well, I think you turned out pretty damn good." Everly smiles, resting her head on his shoulder.

"How about you, Rosie the Riveter?" Liam's smile glows orange with the hues of the fire's flames. "Are you just a pyromaniac, or did someone teach you how to build fires?"

Everly giggles. "I've always been hardheaded, as you may or may not already know," she smirks.

"Oh, really? Never noticed," he says, his words dripping with sarcasm.

"Oh, hush. Anyway, the summer after high school, I went out on a solo road trip, and along the way I met amazing people. My second night I met a family, and they taught me how to build a fire almost instantly. I remember leaving for that trip and sobbing nearly the whole drive because I didn't know what I was doing, but I met such kind strangers along the way and learned a lot." She leans back, smiling at the memories. "About myself mostly."

Liam places a delicate kiss on her forehead. "Well, I was right."

Everly looks up at him, her mouth now full of pasta. "Right about what?"

He grins down at her. "You're a badass."

Everly leans back on a pile of pillows, arms flopped out to either side. "I'm so full," she groans. "Look at my food baby." She cradles her distended belly.

Liam rests on the ground beside her. His hand comes up to rest at the base of her stomach. "Our babies are going to be so cute," he whispers.

Everly's heart drops. She nods in dazed agreement. He moves to snuggle closer to her, "How many kids should we have?"

Everly stays silent, but he breaks the silence offering his answer. "I've always wanted a big family, so maybe five kids." She remains quiet. "Is that weird? Should I not have brought it up?"

She shakes her head. "No. I just…" she stammers. "It's just that my ex and I had this conversation once. He, uh…he didn't want to talk about our future much."

"Oh." He sits up. "How long ago was that?"

"It was in high school."

"Oh," he exclaims. "That's not a big deal. It's not like young relationships like that last anyway."

She nods. "Yeah, and he was an asshole. Cheated on me more times than I could count, and somehow I ended up apologizing every time."

"Well, you never have to worry about that with me, love. You're my one and only. Always." He kisses her temple as they move closer to the dwindling fire.

"Let's change the subject."

"Okay. So, what made you decide to take that solo trip after high school?"

She contemplates for a long moment before answering. "I think I was looking for a fresh start. A chance to be on my own and reflect for once."

"What did you learn from that?"

"That I never want to have to rely on other people again. That I am more capable than I thought, and I don't need anyone else."

"Ev." She gazes deep into the embers, unfazed. "Ev," he says again. "It's okay to need people."

She shakes her head. "It always hurts in the end."

"I won't hurt you, Ev. I promise I'll keep you safe. Okay?"

She nods. The fire starts to wane as exhaustion washes over them. The gentle pop of sparks and sizzling of coals finally lull them to sleep.

Chapter 36

"Ev, I'm heading to the grocery store. Do we need anything else for pizza night tonight?" Jocelyn yells up the stairs as she grabs her keys.

"Could you grab some more pepperoni and a tin of anchovies," she calls back.

Jocelyn stops dead in her tracks, gagging at the thought. "Absolutely not." Moments later Everly skips down the steps. "Who the hell wants anchovies on their pizza?"

Everly throws her head back, laughing. "No one. I just wanted to gross you out."

"You're the worst!"

"And yet, you love me anyway." Wrapping her arm around Jocelyn's shoulders, she hugs her before they exit the door at the same time. Jocelyn waves from her car as Everly continues walking down the street towards her favorite coffee shop.

The comforting aroma of coffee and freshly baked pastries welcomes Everly as she roams the coffee shop looking for a place to relax. It reminds her of Señora Morales' bookshop with its eclectic collection of sofas and armchairs.

"Vanilla latte for Everly!" The barista scans the room for recognition.

"Over here." Everly leans forward from her armchair, smiling at the beautiful girl holding her coffee. Long black eyelashes cast shadows over her dark, almond-shaped eyes. A thick black braid trails down her back, a few loose strands framing her round face. Her reddish-brown skin glows in the warm rays of sun streaming through the skylight.

She grins in acknowledgement, walking to the back corner where Everly clears space on the small side table for her drink. The girl maneuvers around bulky furniture and inconveniently placed lamps as she makes her way. Everly looks up as she approaches with a wide mug, seeing the impressive foam art she's created.

Everly starts to say 'thank you,' when the girl's foot catches on the rug, sending her hard to the ground, shattering the mug and spilling coffee everywhere. In a single second Everly is on her feet. "Are you okay?" The entire cafe pauses to assess the commotion. Everly waves them off as a deep shade of red creeps across the girl's face.

She pulls herself to her knees. "Oh god, I am so sorry," she starts.

"Don't worry about it at all. Are you okay? Let me help you up." Everly guides her up, holding her forearm.

"I'll clean this up right away." The girl turns to walk away, but Everly catches her arm.

"You're bleeding." The girl looks down to see scarlet streaks covering her palm.

"Let me help you," Everly offers with a warm smile. She leads her to the bathroom and carefully cleans where the shattered coffee mug has cut her hands, wrapping them in simple bandages from the shop's first aid kit.

The girl continues to avoid eye contact, only staring at the tiled floor. "What's your name?" Everly asks.

She looks up at the question. "Grace." Everly works through the urge to snicker at the irony.

"My name's Everly," she smiles. "This should help those cuts for now, but make sure to—"

"Oh my gosh, your clothes," Grace interrupts, seeing the splatters across Everly's jeans and blouse. "I'm so sorry."

"Don't worry about it," she says calmly. "I'm washable." She grins.

The coffee and ceramic shards have been cleaned up by the time they exit the bathroom. Grace rushes towards the counter to make Everly a fresh cup. As she walks over a second time, her steps are calculated and slow, making sure to lift her foot enough so it can't catch the rug's lifted corner.

"Thank you," Everly says, cupping her hands around the steaming mug.

Before she can walk away, Everly reaches out, catching her wrist. "What time do you get off work?"

She looks at the clock behind her. "Ten minutes ago," she grins.

"Would you like to sit with me?" Everly offers kindly.

Grace looks at her apprehensively for a moment, then nods. "I'd love to."

⁂

"Joce is the only person I know who could be late to a party at her own house," Everly jokes. The room erupts with laughter. Antonne picks up the broom and uses it to bang on the ceiling, "Joce! Hurry up, or I'll eat your pizza!" That gets her attention. Everyone can hear her footsteps pound across the hallway upstairs. Finally, she flies down the stairs, skipping two at a time until she's waltzing around the living room hugging each person on her way to the kitchen. Caleb and Raven sit on the couch setting up the games, while everyone else puts the finishing touches on their homemade pizzas.

"Antonne, you're not even helping! Stop eating my toppings," Sadie shoves him away from her pizza. Jocelyn scooches past Liam's broad figure to turn up the music on the speaker and instantly grabs Sadie and Everly by the wrists, pulling them into the living room with her. They all skip over to grab Raven's hands, dragging her into dance with them.

The boys watch in dazed curiosity as they whip their hair around, holding hands and laughing uncontrollably. Jocelyn reaches out to pull Caleb into the chaos, but he sits back heavily into the couch.

When there's a knock on the door, Caleb's the only one close enough to hear it over the thumping music. Stepping around the coffee table and avoiding the flailing limbs, he opens the door.

His eyes widen and the breath leaves his body as he stares into the deepest brown eyes he's ever seen. *Whoa.* He shakes his head, composing himself. "Hi… uh," he stutters.

"Hi," Grace blushes, looking up for only a second before staring back at her feet. A long moment passes silently between them. She looks up again, tucking a loose strand behind her ear.

"Sorry," he blurts out, moving away from the doorway. "Come in."

"Thanks." Looking past him at the chaos, she stumbles suddenly on the threshold. Caleb reaches out, catching her around the waist. He looks into her eyes, searching to see if she's all right. Her rosy cheeks flush an even deeper red as she nods away his worries. His hands tingle against her cool skin, a warm heat creeping up to highlight his cheeks as well.

"Sorry." He shakes away his nerves. "I'm Caleb." He shifts, extending his hand out to her, grinning awkwardly.

Fighting to settle the butterflies in her stomach, she smiles up at him. "Hi, I'm—"

"Grace!" Everly rushes over, cutting through the tension she's utterly oblivious to. "I'm so glad you made it!" She embraces her new friend.

"Joce!" Everly yells over the music. "Turn it down!" Jocelyn dances over to the speaker to do as she's asked. "Guys, this is Grace," Everly announces. The room erupts in warm welcomes and friendly smiles, and for the first time in a long time Grace feels like she's found a safe place to rest her heart.

Everyone takes a seat around the table waiting for the game to start. "Have you played Pictionary before?" asks Sadie, leaning over to Grace. She shakes her head. "You can be on my team," she smiles.

Caleb interjects, "Whoa, whoa, whoa. Everyone knows I'm the Pictionary champion. She should be on my team." Grace's bronze complexion helps hide the subtle burning of her cheeks every time he looks at her.

Sadie holds her hands up, conceding. "She's all yours."

"Ev! Can you bring over my pizza," Jocelyn calls from the couch.

"Can you grab my drink, too," Antonne adds.

"Mine, too," Raven smiles.

"Anything else?" Everly responds. "Anyone need a kidney? My spleen, perhaps?" She can hear them chuckling from the kitchen.

"What a drama queen," Sadie teases, heading over to help, allowing Caleb to steal her seat on the couch next to Grace.

As everyone's requested items are delivered to them, Everly asks Liam to grab a sweatshirt from her room. He takes the stairs three at a time, his long legs too impatient for each step.

Opening the door to her room is like walking into a war zone. Piles of clothes litter the floor, pillows and sheets are strewn across the bed, shoes languish without mates. Everly likes to call herself a "tornado cleaner"—she allows the mess to accumulate until she gets an overwhelming urge to clean everything all at once. This week's storm looks like it's lasted longer than usual.

Liam can't help but organize as he searches for a sweatshirt, clearing discarded clothes off her unmade bed. As he adjusts the skewed comforter and pillows, a book topples onto the floor. *The Potential of Heartbreak. What a weird title,* he thinks to himself. He places the book on her nightstand where her journal sits open to its newest entry. Another guy's name litters the pages, one he's only heard in hushed whispers before.

Looking over his shoulder, he only hears the distant laughter coming from downstairs. His fingers fiddle with the bent corners of the pages as he begins to scan the entry. The veins in his neck bulge as he silently swallows each word. And finds the letter.

He jolts upright when Everly's voice calls out from downstairs, "Liam, hurry up!"

The tension in his fingers peaks as he tears the page from the book, crushing the name in his grasp.

"Fireworks! Dress! Girl! MILF!" Antonne screams at the drawing.

"MILF?" Raven cackles.

"Time," Jocelyn announces. "What was it?"

"Cheerleader, stupid." Raven throws her marker at Antonne.

He flinches, trying to catch it. "I was close," he teases.

"Okay," Jocelyn calls for attention. "Sadie sucks at this game, so we're out," she says, sticking her tongue out at her partner. "Ev and Liam didn't stand a chance this time, and Antonne was too focused on MILFs to actually guess."

"It was a valid answer!" he defends proudly as everyone laughs.

"Looks like Caleb and Grace won this week." Everyone cheers for their victory.

"Told you I was the best," Caleb brags, shouldering his partner. Grace giggles, grabbing onto his arm to steady herself. There's a moment when everyone is aware of them, their closeness. Grace notices their looks and pulls away, but Caleb shifts into her again unfazed by the staring.

Jocelyn leans into Everly. "They're adorable," she whispers.

"I know, it's so cute," she squeals quietly.

"Bye, guys, thanks for coming," Everly calls after hugging each person like it'll be months until they see each other again. Jocelyn skips up the stairs, ready to lie in bed and watch her favorite show as Everly flops down onto the couch beside Liam in the empty living room.

"You okay? You seemed a little off tonight. We usually destroy everyone," she smiles at him.

"I'm fine," he snaps.

She hesitates for a moment, "Okay." Sitting up, she moves to collect dishes from the coffee table. She catches a glimpse as he sinks deeper into the cushions of the couch. "Okay, what's wrong?" She sits in the armchair opposite of him, setting the dishes down.

He breathes out sadly. "You know, Ev. I thought we were fine. I thought after talking things through and learning more about each other that we'd be closer than ever. But then I see this." He holds out the crumbled page.

Everly looks at him. "What is that?"

"I went upstairs to grab your sweatshirt, and your journal was open." He pauses. "I read your journal." Everly gapes at him, horrified. "I'm sorry I did, but I saw his name and then all the things you wrote and…"

"You did what?" she asks slowly.

"Who's Jackson, Ev?"

"He's none of your goddamn business, Liam!" She jumps up from the chair. "He's no one. No one I've known for a *very* long time."

"Okay."

"I can't believe this." She rushes into the kitchen to stress-clean the dishes. Liam gets up to follow her. "Don't!" she warns. "Just… get out."

"Ev," he pleads.

"Get out!"

Chapter 37

"Please come in. Take a seat."

Everly walks guardedly into the room, taking a moment to decide whether to sit on the long couch nearest to the woman or in the single armchair across the room.

The armchair it is. She sits back in the deep seat, arms crossed over her chest, feet dangling slightly above the ground.

"My name is Stella. Jocelyn has told me a lot of great things about you, Everly." Her smile is the only warm thing in this cool-toned room. "She said you'd be apprehensive about this. So, let's start with the basics, shall we?" Everly can feel Stella's eyes lingering on her as her own dart about the room avoiding eye contact desperately. "What brings you in today?"

The words settle onto her chest like an overwhelming weight. Then the walls around her crumble as tears well behind her eyes with searing heat, and her throat burns as she fights to restrain her sobs.

Stella observes the internal battle Everly's waging with herself. "What are you feeling right now? What's going through your head?"

She shakes her head, wiping the tears away in frustration. "Therapy's for weak people," she huffs.

"Would you consider Jocelyn weak for coming to therapy?"

Her eyes snap up. "No," she defends. "She needs therapy. She needs help for all the shit she's been through. She's brave for going back into treatment."

"And what about you, Everly? Don't you deserve help?"

Silence.

"Whether you think you deserve to be helped or not, let's discuss what brings you in today."

More silence.

"Okay, let's start with an easier question then. Do you have a significant other?"

Everly narrows her eyes. Jocelyn must have mentioned Liam to her before. "Yes. I mean, I think so." She scoffs at herself. "It's complicated right now."

"How so?" Stella waits patiently in the long silent moments before Everly speaks.

"He read my journal last weekend, and I've been ignoring him since." The air conditioner powers on, shifting her hair lightly and spreading goosebumps across her exposed skin.

"Are you upset that he read your journal or about *what* he read in your journal?"

Everly looks up at her incredulously. "Both?" she questions herself. "*What* he read, actually. It didn't even mean anything, I was just venting. That's what journals are for. You don't expect anyone to read them so why the fuck—sorry."

"That's all right." Stella smiles. "I curse all the fucking time." She winks.

Everly smiles at her, relaxing deeper into her seat. "You don't expect anyone to read your journal, so you don't have to filter anything. I don't even know why I wrote that stuff about Jackson anyway."

Stella scribbles across her notepad for a few long moments before looking back at Everly. "Who is Jackson?"

Everly shuffles through her bag, pulling out a well-used notebook with two envelopes stuck inside it. Looking up at Stella, she flips towards the beginning of the book and starts to read.

I never want this feeling to end. It feels like my heart is smiling and butterflies are migrating around my body all the time. Jax kissed me today. Time stopped, the way they say it does in books and movies. It felt like we lived in that moment alone together for years and I never wanted to leave but reality pulled us back.

She continues.

Miss Amy let us have a movie night in their basement. Jax and I cuddled on the couch holding hands but every time we heard the door open we'd push apart. We don't want anyone to know yet.

It's our perfect secret.

Another entry.

Everything hurts. My heart is utterly shattered. I don't want to see him. He leaves in the morning and I don't want to see him so I won't have to say goodbye.

I've never felt this kind of pain before. It feels like I'm being crushed under a weight while someone wrings out everything that's ever been in my heart until it's an empty, useless husk.

How do people survive this hurt? The loss of the only person you'll ever love?

And another.

Liam and I went up to grandpa's cabin over the weekend. When we got there I couldn't help but see the memories of our families laughing together. Jax and I used to hide out in the attic for hours or sneak off to the big rock by the water where there used to be a rope swing. That was the first place we held hands.

It felt good to be there, but it felt wrong to be with Liam. I'd look at him and sometimes wish it was Jax.

But Liam is good. He's good for me. And Jax left.

But Miss Amy's sick. Maybe he needs me now.

But he left me when I needed him.

But I can't ignore him when he truly needs me.

But he hasn't returned my calls or reached out.

But I know he needs me. The way I've always needed him.

Everly pulls out the two envelopes tucked into the pages. "I wrote him a letter. Two actually. But I never sent them."

"Why not?"

"I've been meaning to. I just… I guess I'm afraid to get a response. Or not get one."

"And there are two letters?"

"Yes. The first one is an apology. That I wasn't there when he reached out with the news about his mom getting sick."

"And the second?"

A muffled laugh breaks from her lips as she looks up through her tears. "The second one is all the things I never got the chance to scream at him."

Stella makes a note. "Why did you decide not to send them?"

"I meant to. The first one, anyway."

"Why not the second?"

Everly looks up at Stella like she's a kid who thinks it'd be funny to eat a bug. "Because," she explains, "he has enough to deal with. He doesn't deserve to hear about all the issues I've had with him over the past six years."

"And why not?"

"What?" Everly looks at her, dumbfounded.

"Don't you think *you* deserve for him to know how you've felt all these years?"

"I mean…" she contemplates. "No. Not now, at least."

"What about Liam?"

"What about him?"

"Do you think he deserves to know how you've been feeling towards him recently?"

"I—"

"Here's your homework for this week—" Stella tears the page from her notebook, holding it out to Everly. "Sit down with Liam and discuss how you've been feeling. He may not like it. You will likely hate it." She smiles knowingly. "But it is important for you to address issues as they come up, because as long as you hold onto those feelings without telling the other person, it's like drinking poison and expecting the other person to die. Don't drink the poison, Everly."

Everly stares at her in disbelief.

"And send those letters to Jackson. Both of them. I'll see you next week."

Chapter 38

"Liam—"

"Ev, I love you. Please don't do this." She looks up at him confused. "Just tell me what I can do."

"What are you talking about?"

"Wait," he starts. "You're not breaking up with me?"

Everly laughs out loud. "No, you idiot. We just need to talk some things through."

"Oh, thank God." He wraps his long arms around her, pulling her tight against him.

"Okay, okay," she growls, pushing back. "That's one of the things I need to talk to you about." He sits back into the sofa attentively. Everly stays standing, pacing back and forth in the living room of his apartment. "Actually, let's start with the big thing. You read my journal—"

"And I'm so sorry, I never should have done that, and I swear on—"

"Let me finish." She stares daggers at him, his large frame shrinking under her gaze. Clearing her throat, she continues. "You read my journal and although that is a *huge* invasion of privacy, I know that what I wrote probably hurt your feelings. You asked me who Jackson was. We grew up together. Our families were closer than most, but his moved away the summer before high school, and we haven't talked since then. But then he called me a few months ago to tell me his mom is dying." Pacing a furrow in the blue rug, she takes three composing breaths. "She's an amazing woman." She smiles despite her glossy eyes. "I hung up on him before he had a chance to tell me, and now I can't get a hold of him. So, he's been on my mind a lot recently." Liam nods.

"Then the whole Jocelyn thing happened, and that took a lot of my attention. It's still happening. She's working through her recovery at a place near home until the fall, which is the best thing for her right now. She went there in high school too to help her through her eating disorder.

"Anyway, that hasn't left a lot of time for you, and I'm sorry about that. You deserve my attention, too."

"Ev," Liam interrupts before she can continue. "*You* deserve attention, too. From me, from our friends, but especially from yourself. Okay?" Everly nods.

"I just—" Her tears get the best of her, and she chokes on a sob. Liam stands up, collecting her in his arms and settling them both down onto the leather cushions of his couch.

"Everything is going to be okay, Ev. I've got you." She nestles into the smooth skin of his neck and shoulder, releasing the sobs she's fought against for too long. "I love you."

⁜

Dear Jax,

I'm here. I'm here whenever you need me. I can't imagine the pain you must be going through. Please give it to me. I'll take it all if that's what you need.

I love your mom like she's my own.

Words will never be able to express how sorry I am for hanging up that call. I get if you're mad at me or confused, but please just answer my calls. Respond to this letter even. I just need to know you're okay.

Let me be there for you. Please.

Love,

Lele

Dear Jax,

Six years. It's taken six years and a woman we both love to suffer a cruel fate for you to reach out to me.

You're a pathetic lying bastard. I wish I could hate you as much as you deserve to be hated.

I waited. I waited months. Then years. I waited for a hopeless dream that I should've known was nothing more than empty promises and torturous lies.

Thank you, truly. You've made it easier to hate you by coming back only to break my heart all over again.

I just hope you know that the young, naive girl you once knew isn't here anymore. The scars you left on her heart have never faded, and because of you she'll never trust or love as fully as she deserves.

You did this. You broke her.

Everly

Everly looks over the letters once more before sealing the envelope, her tongue dragging across the mint-flavored flap. Turning them over in her hands, double and triple checking the address, she finally pulls open the one-way hopper of the mailbox and drops them in. Her hands shake at her sides as she releases them into the dark, metal container with no way of retrieving them now.

It's done.

⁂

"Come in, take a seat." Everly walks quickly to her spot in the opposing armchair, noting the new pair of thin glasses perched on Stella's nose. "How was your week?" she asks, diving right in.

"It was…" She contemplates for a moment. "Good, actually."

"How did your conversation with Liam go?"

"It went a lot better than I expected. I told him about Jackson, and he seems understanding of the situation."

"I'm happy to hear that, Everly. Did you send *both* letters?"

She nods.

"How did that make you feel?"

Looking around the room, her eyes study the abstract paintings on the wall. The cool blues, grays, and whites intermingle in randomized splatters. "I feel guilty." She catches the movement of Stella's pen out of the corner of her eye.

"Do you often feel guilty?"

"What do you mean?"

"When expressing how you feel or how others have made you feel. Does that make you feel guilty?"

She nods, subconsciously.

"What was life like growing up, Everly?"

She wastes no time answering. "I had an amazing childhood. I have two happy parents who are still madly in love and an older brother I get along with, and I've never had to worry about what I was going to eat or wear."

Stella makes another quick note. "I'm happy to hear you were provided with all the necessary things to survive growing up." Everly cocks her head at the word *survive*. "How was growing up for you emotionally?"

"I don't understand the question."

"Let me rephrase it then. When you accomplished something or were unbelievably happy, how was that emotion met by your parents?"

"They were always happy when I was happy. They've always been my number one fans and encouraged me to try my best."

"How about when you were sad or trying to discuss a difficult topic? How would those emotions be met?"

Thinking back, the fog of memories clouds her head. "With anger or discomfort."

"Why do you think that is?"

"Because they don't know how to help. My mom told me that once." Her gaze wanders across the coffee table that displays a fake plant, a stack of self-help books, and a lit candle that smells of fall. "She gets upset when she doesn't know how to help me, so she gets angry."

"And your father?"

"He ignores the bad feelings all together."

"Can you give an example?"

Everly shares about a time when she'd struggled with a bout of depression that left her in bed, crying, and mentally worn down for weeks, and how her parents' interactions with her did more harm than good. *"Just focus on the good." "Think about all the people who are worse off than you." "Just get up and do something."*

She talks about past relationships, like when she tried to address issues in her relationship with Thomas, and how he'd shut down the conversation or turn it back onto her. *"The only reason you think something is going on with me and that cheerleader is because you're insecure."*

And when Axel tried to accuse her of doing something behind his back because he was too afraid to confess that that's exactly what he had been doing. *"So that gives you the right to go out and fuck whoever you want then?" When what he was really trying to say was, "I met someone else."*

"Everly," Stella interjects before she can continue. "Some people play the victim to crimes they have committed. Don't be burned by fires you didn't start." All at once Everly crumbles, shaking and sobbing as the clock strikes the hour.

Chapter 39

"Joce!" she calls, racing out the door.

"Ev!" she yells, dropping her bags on the walkway and opening her arms wide.

Colliding into each other's arms, they bury themselves in the tangle of gold and dark chocolate hair. Everly's arms wrap around her friend, and she feels the healthy weight Jocelyn was desperately afraid of gaining.

Pulling away from each other, Everly holds onto Jocelyn's thin fingers and smiles, looking in her deep brown eyes. "You look…" She contemplates for a moment. "Healthy."

Jocelyn squeezes Everly's fingers and smiles back at her. "I *feel* healthy. For the first time in a long time, I feel like I have control over my life again."

"That's amazing, Joce. We should—"

"Hey, Joce," someone interrupts. Turning towards the voice, they see Liam taking his long-limbed strides down the sidewalk. Approaching them, he wraps his arms around them both, squishing them between his brawny arms. "Glad you made it out alive," he jokes.

Everly whirls out of his grasp and stares at him incredulously. Jocelyn laughs it off with an award giggle and nods.

"Joce, can you give us a minute?" Everly asks, still staring daggers at Liam's oblivious expression.

"Here, let me help you with those bags first." Liam interjects, grabbing the handles of her two overstuffed duffles and heading for the door.

"I'm sorry," Everly whispers to Jocelyn.

"It's okay, Ev."

"No. It's really not." They follow Liam into the apartment, closing the heavy wooden door behind them.

"So, Joce," Liam calls out as he descends the stairs after putting her bags in her room. "What was the hospital like? Was it like the movies?"

Jocelyn's face pales as Everly's ignites to a deep shade of red. "Liam!" she snaps. "What is wrong with you?"

"What?" he defends, settling into their plush sofa. "I'm just curious."

Shaking her head, feeling as though it might actually explode, she storms over to the door and hauls it open, its hinges squeaking against the movement. "Get out."

"What?" He leans forward slightly.

"Get the fuck out!" Liam's eyes widen as he stares at Everly's burning face, then turns to see Jocelyn leaning against the counter hugging herself, the color drained from her face.

Standing up, he tries to make eye contact with Jocelyn, but her eyes avoid it. "Sorry, Joce." Stepping closer to Everly he catches her eyes and whispers in a hushed tone, "I was just trying to lighten the mood."

"Well, you sure did a shit job of that. Get out." Everly slams the door on him the moment he steps out.

For fuck's sake, she thinks to herself, then open her arms to Jocelyn.

⁂

"Ev, there's a package down here for you," Jocelyn calls up the stairs. Footsteps pad across the upstairs hallway as she makes her way. Taking the last couple steps down, she spots Jocelyn reading the note attached to the square package. "Liam says he's really, really, *really* sorry for being insensitive."

"Did he write that to me or you?"

"You," she replies, handing over the card before tearing open the wrapped box.

"Of course," Everly says, rolling her eyes.

"Oh, I love 'forgive me' chocolates!" Jocelyn rummages through the sweets, landing on the dark chocolate hazelnut.

"You can have them. They should be for you anyway."

⁂

"And then what happened?"

"I told him that he needed to apologize to Joce, not me. So, he sent her the same exact thing. The same note with chocolates."

"How did you feel when he did that?"

"I was pissed. He just needed to actually apologize, not copy and paste whatever bullshit he thought would make us feel better. I'm just so sick of him acting like an idiot and then trying to make up for it. But even more than that, I'm sick of yelling at him like he's a goddamn kid and I'm his mother!"

"What situations have occurred where you have felt like a mother reprimanding her child in your relationship with Liam?"

"Don't even get me started," Everly smirks without humor.

Stella takes notes as Everly relays story after story of Liam's thoughtless actions or comments that she's had to address and how each of those little incidents has started to create microfractures within their otherwise healthy relationship.

⁂

"I don't get what the big deal is," Liam sighs.

"It's not a 'big deal,' it's little issues that have just been adding up."

"Ev, I'm sorry. I promise I'll do better. I won't smother you, or talk about Jocelyn being in the mental ward, or—"

"Right there!" Everly yells. "You can't say shit like that, Liam. She wasn't in a fucking mental hospital for crazy people, she was getting the help she needed for a really difficult situation that she's struggled with her whole life."

Liam nods. "Okay, okay. So I can't say *mental ward*?"

"Oh my god, Liam." She rakes her hands through her hair frustratedly. "Just don't be a dick and then make fake apologies for the shit you say!"

"Okay, I'm sorry, Ev. I promise I'll be better. I'll do anything for us. *Anything*. I swear it."

Everly nods, hoping he's telling the truth.

Chapter 40

"I think we should break up…" It's nearly a whisper. Liam's eyes bulge at the sudden statement.

"What? What are you talking about?" His pain cuts her like a knife, raw emotions drip like poison on the blade. "Ev, I love you." He slides towards her on the dark leather couch. "I can change. Just tell me what to do. Tell me how to fix this," he pleads helplessly.

"I have told you. I've told you over and over again, and you promise to change, but you never do." Her blue eyes glisten as she stands up.

"Ev, please. I swear I'll do whatever it takes. I love you."

Turning away, she speaks over her shoulder. "It's too little, too late, Liam." His hands grasp at hers, their grip tightening like his throat around the suffocating sobs he's fighting against. He pulls her back to face him, but she avoids his glassy stare. "I'm sorry." A single tear connects the constellation of freckles on her cheek until it falls onto their entwined hands.

The world shifts in slow motion when she rises to her feet. Their hands linger in one another's grasp until she moves out of reach. His eyes pierce her soul as she turns the door handle. He begs one more time, "Don't do this." The door clicks shut behind her. "Please," he pleads in the silence.

⁂

It's been months now. Months of insistent texts, of feeling his eyes on me everywhere I go, even avoiding my favorite places because I might see him there.

His hair's grown out and he looks like he hasn't slept in days. I don't know what to do but avoid him at this point. I've tried being nice, even attempting to 'stay friends' but that blew up in my face really quickly.

He says he'll wait for me. No matter how long it takes.

I hate this.

⁂

"Ev," a shaky voice utters over the phone. Before the awful words reach her ears, Everly's legs buckle, and she slides to the ground, her chest constricting. "I'm so sorry, Ev," her mother breathes.

After nearly a year in hospice, Miss Amy took to planning her own funeral, to make it as lively as possible, despite the obvious irony. Stepping out of the car proves to be the most difficult thing Everly has had to do in a very long time. That step, that single movement towards the church, means it's real. It can't be real.

A loving hand eases the door open and guides her feet to the pavement. As she rests against the car door, her mother cups her face in her palms, searching past the blank stare to connect with her daughter. Pressing a kiss to her cheek, she whispers lightly into her ear. "Go find him. He needs you."

Misery turns to anxious waves of nausea. A slow fog fills her brain as she meanders past teary-eyed women in mourning clothes and oblivious children skipping through the halls. Everything slows to an agonizing pace. Her lethargic gaze scans the room, and only after a moment, or maybe it's minutes, she realizes he's likely to be taller now. How else will he have changed? Will he still have a wild mop of tawny hair or has he cut it so that she can't shuffle it back from his eyes anymore? Will his eyes be the same? Or will they be darker from the devastation he's suffered?

Where is he?

A hand gently catches at her wrist. She refuses to turn until her heart starts to beat again. Her eyes flutter, urging back her tears as she turns to face into the broad chest.

Liam?

Retreating, she stumbles away from him. Her eyes rake over him like he's just shot an innocent right in front of her. "What?" The word slips from her lips.

"Ev..." He reaches out for her.

"Don't!" she erupts. People turn and chatter in hushed tones as they observe the two at the center of the room. Tears cling to her cheeks, then are the only indicator she was ever there, a trail of droplets where she stood.

Gasping, clutching at anything along the narrow hallway to keep her upright, her hand latches onto a door handle at the end of the hall. Snot and tears coat her face as she charges into the room, collapsing onto the cool tiles. Inexorable sobs wrack her body. Dragging herself desperately along the floor, her legs useless and numb, she cradles a small trash can in her arms, heaving relentlessly.

She's vaguely aware of the door opening as she retches again. A long-fingered hand pulls back her hair and rubs firm circles against her back. She shakes her head, unable to speak against the acid coating her throat. "Jax?" she manages to cough out.

"They found me unconscious on the floor after the service," Everly says, staring blankly at the flame burning lower in the clay-colored candle. She collapses in on herself in the familiar fit of sobs Stella has become accustomed to waiting out.

Chapter 41

"He did what?" Grace blares over the phone. Everly remains silent on the other end. "Ev, I'm so sorry. What are you going to do?"

Sinking further into her plush cushions and wrapping herself tighter in the fuzzy blankets, she shakes her head, exhaustion warping her face into a hollow shell. "I don't know," she breathes out lightly.

The door swings open on its newly oiled hinges, and Everly shrieks, launching her phone at the person storming in. "Ev!" Grace screams into the phone as it flies through the air.

Jocelyn drops her bag and fumbles with the phone as it bounces between her hands and clatters to the floor. Bending to pick up the phone, Jocelyn holds it to her ear. "I've got her, Grace. We'll talk to you soon." She hangs up. Looking at Everly's shaking body, she pads over to stand before her, arms outstretched. Everly shifts her blankets to the side, welcoming Jocelyn into her cocoon. "Everything is going to be fine, Ev." She rests her temple on her friend's shoulder, her dark locks draping across the white blanket. "I'm here for you."

*

"Has he tried to contact you since then?" She nods.

Clearing her throat she elaborates. "He used someone else's phone. I've blocked his number, all of his accounts, and he's still trying to talk to me."

"He's an obsessive weirdo, Ev. I think you have to get a restraining order."

"Really?"

"Wouldn't it make you feel safer if he couldn't contact you? Or show up at someone's funeral he never knew just to talk to you? This is what I study, Ev. I think it's the best way to keep him away from you for now." She nods again. "We'll go down to the police station this afternoon to fill out some forms and get that going. Okay?"

"Okay."

"So, Joce is going with you to file the restraining order?"

"Yeah. She knows what to do, so it's really nice having her help me through this."

"For sure. I'm so sorry you have to deal with this, Ev. I really thought he was a nice guy for a while. It's amazing how deceptive people can be." Everly gazes out the window, her stare unfocused.

"On a brighter note," Grace beams, captivating Everly's attention.

She sits, smiling broadly until Everly pushes against her shoulder. "What!"

"Caleb and I are official!" she blurts out, the words escaping in one quick breath.

Everly squeals, hugging her friend. People walking past turn at the commotion. "It's about time!"

Grace looks around at the people staring. "Ev," she giggles. "Shut up, you're so loud."

"Oh, oh. Sorry," she whispers. "I'm just excited that my friend has a BOYFRIEND!" Grace hides her face in her hands as more people turn and stare.

"You suck," she giggles.

"You love me," Everly teases, laying her head on her shoulder. "You want to come join me and Joce for this wonderfully uncomfortable visit to fill out countless forms about my stalker?" She laughs without humor.

"Think I'm going to pass on that enticing offer. Caleb and I are starting to study for finals."

Everly narrows her eyes at her. "Mhmm. Have fun 'studying.'" She makes exaggerated air quotes in Grace's face. Grace laughs, slapping them away.

"Oh, hush, we're meeting at the library."

"Sexy," she teases.

"It's a bunch of people from our class," she clarifies.

"Hey, whatever you're into." Grace cackles, shoving her friend.

"You're ridiculous," she says getting up. "Good luck with the Liam thing. Let me know how it goes later."

"Will do," she smiles, watching her friend stroll down the sidewalk.

⁜

A chilling breeze lazily passes, carrying clusters of brown leaves from the once-beautiful fall. The wind whispers that winter is coming, and it nips at her exposed ears. As she walks up the street, her senses heighten as a memory flashes. Blurred vision. Cold brick. Towering figure. Striking eyes. *This is where we met.*

A shiver rushes down her spine just as the vibration of her phone pulls her from the thought.

Ev, I'm running a little late. Wait for me there.

Everly's fingers move effortlessly across the screen; she glances up as the traffic lights turn yellow. Anticipating the light change, she steps out into the street to cross. An engine revs as a car speeds through the red light, and Everly's yanked back off her feet onto the sidewalk, her head smashing hard against the pavement.

Coughing and gasping for air, she claws at the concrete, turning on her side. The edges of her vision darken, and the scene lags in time as she rolls onto a figure beside her.

Her name. The faint calling of her name is barely audible over the pounding in her skull and the shrill ringing in her ears. The sun burns against her sensitive eyes, obscuring the details of the silhouetted figure that hovers over her. Deep shouts pound against her brain like a sledgehammer. A long-fingered hand touches her cheek, and another cradles the back of her head, sending searing waves of agony through her body. Her eyes try to refocus and the world moves in slow ripples as the silhouette blots out the winter sun and the darkness consumes her.

Chapter 42

A wave of nausea washes over her as she shifts upright. Her pulse thuds against her skull, and she fights to open her eyes. Planting her feet on the ground, Everly drags her heavy body upward just as the world shifts again, sending her crumbling to the ground.

"Whoa, whoa, whoa. Take it easy, Ev." Her eyes squint open in search of the voice, when she's lifted into the air and placed back onto the couch. She winces when her head touches the leather. "You're okay, Ev. Don't worry, I'll take care of you."

She pleads for her eyes to open. To make sense of where she is and why her head's pounding in time with her heart like either of them might explode at any time. Her mouth is dry when she tries to speak. "What…what happened?"

"I saved your life, Ev." There's a pause. "I told you I'd always protect you."

Holding on to what's left of her consciousness, she begs, "Joce…help."

Chapter 43

"Hey, Ev, I'm starting to get worried. This is my fourth time calling. I'm outside the station. If you got cold feet that's okay, just call me back, please." Jocelyn sighs as she places her phone beside her.

Tapping her feet anxiously against the metal leg of the bench, she looks at her surroundings. The busy afternoon streets, couples walking hand in hand down the sidewalks giggling, an old woman shuffling beside her patient dog towards her bench, a group of homeless men lingering near an alley.

Flinching at a startling sensation, she turns to find a Yorkshire Terrier licking her ankle, his face peppered with gray. Looking up, she sees the woman, likely in her eighties, staggering nearer pulling at the dog's leash. "Milo, stop that. I'm sorry, love. He's really quite friendly." Jocelyn leans down to caress the dog's soft coat.

"It's no bother at all. He's very sweet. Milo, is it?"

The old woman nods, her white hair falling in puffy curls. "Would you mind if we sit with you, dear?"

"Please," Jocelyn scooches over invitingly, placing her phone on the arm of the bench.

"What a beautiful day it is." The woman gazes up at the sky, its blue reflected in her eyes. Jocelyn nods, following her gaze to the clouds drifting lazily above. "What do you see?" The woman's squinting eyes shift the skin on her face into thoughtful lines. Her smile, outlined in precisely applied pink lipstick, broadens when she catches her stare. "In the clouds, I mean." she clarifies.

Jocelyn cranes her neck to search the cumulus clouds for meaning. "I'm not sure. I just see clouds."

"Look harder." Lifting her thin arm, leaning in closer, and pointing with her arthritic finger, the woman outlines a particular portion of the large cloud. "I see two swans in love." Jocelyn blinks at the sky, finding where two blobs connect around a hollow heart shape.

"Where the heart is?" she asks.

"Exactly." The woman turns to look at her. "Did you know swans are a symbol of everlasting love because once they are bonded, they are bonded for life?"

"I didn't know that," Jocelyn replies, looking back towards the clouds only to see them shifted into new nondescript blobs.

"Do you have a swan?" the woman asks.

Jocelyn turns to her, nodding a greeting at a man walking past when he lunges for her phone and takes off down the street. "Hey!" Jocelyn yells after him, her long legs pumping in pursuit. "Hey!" He turns the street corner, and Jocelyn pushes off her feet, her brown hair flying behind her as she gains speed. Taking the corner, she makes it mere feet before colliding into a uniformed man, tackling him to the ground.

Scrambling to her feet, she sees the culprit beside them on the ground, handcuffed. Gazing around incredulously, she sees her phone in the hand of the man she's just collided with.

"Oh god. I'm so sorry." she starts, holding out her hand to help him up. He takes it, a small smile growing across his lips.

"Nice tackle. I'm assuming this is yours." He holds out the phone to her.

"I am so sorry, officer…" She glances at his name badge. "Jeong."

"You can call me David." Jocelyn can feel a prickling heat crawl along her collarbones and up her neck when she sees the bright smile on his face. "I was just on my way into work. Would you like to accompany me and our friend here to give a report?" Jocelyn turns to the man in cuffs beside them and nods. "Great."

As they turn the corner to walk towards the police station, the old woman watches. Before they pass, she reaches out to catch Jocelyn's wrist. "Is this your swan?"

David stops beside her, pausing his reading of the Miranda Rights for a moment. "No." Jocelyn shakes her head. That prickly heat shifts to her cheeks now.

"Look harder." The woman smiles up at her, releasing her hand to pet Milo.

"All right, that's everything I need from you."

"Great." She pauses. "Actually, I came here today to help my friend with a restraining order."

"No problem." He shuffles through some paperwork, pulling out a clipboard and a thick manila folder. "We just need her to be here to start the process."

"She was supposed to meet me here an hour ago."

"Well, it is common for victims to get cold feet before coming in. It can be a challenging process for people."

"Yeah. I just have a weird feeling about it. She hasn't answered my calls or texts either."

"Do you share locations with each other? I'd be happy to go with you to check on her." Jocelyn nods, shifting to the edge of her seat to share her screen with him.

⁜

She's so cute when she sleeps, he thinks as he peers into the living room from his kitchen. The comforting aroma of bacon drifts through the apartment, tantalizing her sleeping senses. She stirs uncomfortably, urging consciousness to prevail. The pounding of her head drowns out the sizzling on the griddle and smooth music emanating from the next room.

Everly winces, shifting against the cool leather beneath her. The world filters through her squinting eyes in a blurry haze as she fights to open them. Looking around, she sees the familiar blue rug and array of sneakers stacked by the doorway. Her brain whirls as contorted puzzle pieces align themselves into a grim picture.

Fighting another rush of nausea, she pushes herself upright on the couch, her head hanging just above her knees. The room moves in gentle waves across her vision, her stomach following the current's unsettling wake.

A slow shiver works from the base of her skull down her spine. Reaching up slowly, she fingers through her hair until a darting pain shocks her body. Pulling her hand back she watches the deep red liquid drip down her fingers and into her palm. The smell of copper floods her nose before her consciousness fades again.

⁎

"And you really think something is wrong?" David asks again.

"I *know* something is wrong. She would never go there by herself, especially now."

"Okay. Hop in," he says, opening the passenger door to his cruiser.

⁎

"Good morning, sunshine!" he calls, walking over with two full plates. She flinches at his booming voice. "Oh, right. Sorry, love. I'll be quieter," he whispers, placing the plates on the coffee table. "How are you feeling?"

Fighting every urge to remain glued to the cool leather cushions, she strains against the heavy weight of her crusted eyes and pushes herself into a seated position.

"I made you some bacon and eggs and toast." He smiles.

"What—" Her voice is hoarse, like her tongue's been coated in sand.

"Here, Ev. Have some water." She grabs it with her shaky hands, downing it in greedy gulps, only stopping when it's drained. Her vision still pulsating with the heartbeat in her head, she tries to keep a neutral face as she stares into Liam's piercingly blue eyes. The eyes she's seen in grocery stores or classrooms or most recently at the funeral of one of her dearest people.

"What is it, Ev?" His voice is soft and attentive.

"What time is it?" she manages.

Glancing at his phone, he reads off the late hour. "Here." He slides the plate of food in front of her. "Breakfast for dinner. Your favorite."

Everly's stomach lurches, but not from the food. "I have to go." She stands up on painfully weak legs, then Liam's hands grapple around her waist before she can fall.

"Ev," he says, seeing the blood trickling down her neck and back. "You need to lie down. Let me take care of you."

"No!" She pulls away, stumbling back from him towards the door.

"Ev, I'm just trying to help you. Please, let me help you." He grabs her wrist, and she wrenches away, collapsing to the floor, her head relentlessly pounding now. A whimper escapes her as more warm blood coats her hair and neck now, lulling her back into the warm embrace of blackness.

Collecting her limp body from the floor, he carries her into the bedroom, resting her gently on the bed. Liam shifts her hair to one side as he lays a wet washcloth on her wound and sets her head back on the pillow. "Sleep tight, my love."

Pressing his lips against her damp, cool temple, he brushes her hair back, admiring her smooth skin dusted with freckles and fine creases before pulling her arm out to the side. Softly guiding her hand above her head, he wraps a thin rope around her wrist, anchoring it to the center of the headboard. After tethering her second arm, he moves to her legs.

She shifts fractionally as he runs his fingers the length of her leg over the light sprinkling of blonde hairs growing in. He looks up to see her furrowed brows shift in panic. "Ev, you're okay." She pulls against the rope digging into her wrists and kicks out, connecting with his jaw. Biting down on a curse, he lunges forward to pin her legs to the bed. "I'm trying to help you, Ev. Just let me help you."

Fighting against the agonizing fire raging in her head, she takes a deep breath to scream when she's smothered with a pillow, the fabric cutting off her cries. "Stop!" Liam's voice threatens. Her legs fight and thrash against him relentlessly until they slowly settle and she's rendered unconscious once again.

Liam lifts the pillow from her face, checking her pulse with two fingers at the base of her neck. "Thank God," he breathes out, reaching for her ankles to fasten them to the bed frame. A loud knock on the door jolts him back from his task.

"Police! Open up!"

"Fuck…" Liam curses under his breath. Tying down her left ankle he covers her with the comforter and sets a pillow behind her head to hide her tightly bound hands. Shutting the bedroom door behind him, he walks towards the front door, kicking her shoes under the couch and sliding her phone into his back pocket. Unlatching the deadbolt, Liam pulls the door open to see a tall police officer with cropped black hair and a razor-sharp jawline staring into his eyes. "Hi, officer, how can I help you?"

"I'm looking for a young woman by the name of Everly. Is she here?"

Pretending to crack his neck, he looks away from the officer. "I haven't seen her."

"Okay. Can you tell me the last time you saw her?"

"Yeah." He runs his fingers through his disheveled hair. "I, uh… I saw her at our good friend's funeral." He clears his throat.

"All right." David takes notes in his jotter. "What was your friend's name?" He looks up to see Liam's face redden in panic.

"Miss Amy," he finally says.

"And her last name?"

Silence.

"You're a lying bastard, and you know it!" Jocelyn storms around the corner from where she'd been out of sight. Pushing past David, she shoves Liam's chest, pushing him a few steps back into the apartment. "See!" Jocelyn points. "Two plates. Someone else is here, and I bet I know who it is," she accuses.

"She doesn't want to see you, Joce."

"Don't try that bullshit with me, Liam. I know she's here. Ev! Everly!" she screams into the apartment. Jocelyn whips out her phone, dialing her third emergency contact after her parents. Liam's back pocket rings in time with Jocelyn's call, and he moves to slam the door shut.

David's hand braces the door, creating enough space for Jocelyn to run through the gap. "Everly!" Stopping mere feet into the living room she runs her eyes over the leather cushions and the dried blood that's crusted along the side of the sofa. Liam lunges for her as she rushes for the bedroom, grabbing a steak knife off the countertop and pressing it to her throat as her hand touches the doorknob.

Releasing the knob, she puts both hands up, quivering against Liam's broad chest behind her. David stares down the barrel of his Glock at the only portion of Liam not blocked by Jocelyn's body, his head.

"Put the knife down. Now!"

"Joce, please," he pleads, "you know how much I love her."

Holding onto his thick forearm, she attempts to pull it away from her throat before speaking, afraid it might cut off her words. “This isn’t love, Liam.”

“I won’t tell you again. Put the knife down,” David demands, his weapon steady.

Wailing sirens grow louder, and Jocelyn can feel Liam’s heartbeat thundering in his chest, his grip on the knife at her throat still firm. “You’re out of time, Liam.” Jocelyn whispers. “You’re out of time.” She can feel him shaking his head behind her.

“No! I refuse to live without her.” His voice quivers. He shifts slightly towards the door, Jocelyn still in his grasp. “I won’t.” Cars screech on the pavement outside, drawing David’s attention for a single second that Liam uses to shove Jocelyn to the ground and charge into the bedroom, knife raised over Everly’s barely conscious body.

Jocelyn shrieks as three deafening shots ring out.

Chapter 44

"Welcome, everyone. My name is Elaine, and I will be leading tonight's meeting. We are all individuals who have struggled with trauma or post-traumatic stress. Fear, anger, guilt, and shame are symptoms we all have in common, and we have found they can take over our lives in unhealthy ways.

"Each of us has a story to tell, but we don't always have someone to tell our stories to. You can tell your story here. There is nothing you could say that we haven't heard, experienced, or felt. You are safe among friends here.

"I see we have a few new members tonight. Welcome to all of you who are trusting us to help you on your journey, and thank you to all our current members for continuing to show up for your own recovery and to offer support to others."

The hinges on the door in the back of the room groan, and all heads turn to face the latecomer.

Grace?

She rushes in, her cheeks a coppery red as she makes eye contact with Everly and settles into a folding chair towards the front.

"Welcome, Grace," Elaine says from the podium. "It's good to see you." She simply nods, her eyes fighting to avoid looking back at Everly's confused expression.

"Would anyone like to start?" An uncomfortable shift moves through the group as people look around, hoping someone else will volunteer. Finally, without raising her hand, Grace walks straight up to the podium, her eyes low.

"Hi," she says into the battered microphone. "My name's Grace."

"Hi, Grace," the room responds.

"We were just driving home," she continues. "Calian was driving, and his best friend was in the passenger seat. Everything was perfect." She smiles blankly. "Listening to our favorite music and dancing in our car, completely lost in our happiness." She pauses, standing up straighter and placing her hands on either side of the podium. "The other car just came out of nowhere."

Rain sprinkles the empty road, reflecting the fireworks and headlights on the pavement. Bursts of red and yellow ignite the sky as the car flies towards their destination. The chill of December's final day stings their cheeks through the open windows, and Grace leans forward to crank the volume up until the car shakes with each bass note.

Calian turns the knob counterclockwise to start counting down. "Ten... nine...eight..." The other two join in, screaming out the numbers.

"Pull over, pull over!" Grace shakes her brother's shoulders.

"Three...two...one...Happy New Year!" The sky erupts as light explodes in streaks of every color imaginable. Grace climbs out of the car that's now parked on the side of the highway and claws her way onto the roof. "Come on!" she urges the others.

Sitting atop the roof, feeling the excitement of the new year unfolding, they relax on the chilled metal, lying back, staring up, and perfectly happy to be in this moment with each other.

After a few minutes, they hop down from the roof to pile back into the car. Grace twists the volume all the way up before settling into the back seat and fastening her seatbelt. "Let's go!" she cries merrily out the window, the breeze blowing her thick black hair in sporadic tornados.

The rain held off long enough for the fireworks to highlight the clouds, but now it pours in vicious sheets. Calian speeds along towards the intersection's green light, chanting out the lyrics reverberating through their bones. He sees the headlights a moment too late to turn.

The world slows around them, the rain falling in blinding curtains, and he can smell the tires burning as he slams on the brakes. Yells and shrieks ring out as the oncoming car slams into the driver side door. Glass shatters, airbags deploy, and

Calian turns the wheel despite hearing the bones in his nose crack and break, but it's no use. The car flips over and over until it lands in a deep ditch on its roof.

The roof where they had just lain together and celebrated the new year.

Red light from the intersection illuminates the glass shards on the road like fireflies beaten down by the furious rain. Only the unrelenting downpour bears witness to the horrible scene.

Agonizing screams shock the night. Footsteps crunch on the glass and slide across the damp foliage as they descend into the ditch. Cradled on either side by walls of earth, the car grips three figures tight against its frame. The blood-curdling screams of a girl ring out as she regains consciousness.

The shattered back windshield offers a way in. A hand reaches in from the darkness for the girl, pulling against the resistance of the crushed metal. Her shrieks peak until shock wins out and silences her voice. Hands drag her limp body along the slick grass and onto the pavement, then the footsteps stumble back into the ditch for the others.

There's just enough space to crawl in through the back windshield. The petrichor scent of rain-soaked earth surrounds them as the rain comes down harder. Two unconscious bodies dangle upside down and bloodied in the front seats. The stranger maneuvers between them, cradling the passenger's body while grappling with the seatbelt's broken mechanism.

Finally released from the seat belt, the passenger still hangs from the seat. Shifting around his body, the stranger sees a stream of blood pouring from his lower leg where it's been lacerated by the warped metal. Biting down on a curse, the stranger gives an immense heave and drags the unconscious body up the steep ditch wall.

The clouds and chilling breeze carry away the rain until it's a light sprinkle again. The passenger is laid on the pavement next to Grace's unmoving but still breathing body.

The final passenger. Panting hard, the stranger crawls through the shattered glass once more to the front of the inverted car. The driver dangles from his seat belt, unmoving. Navigating towards the buckle, the stranger stops, fingers moving to press against the base of the driver's throat.

Nothing.

No, no, no. *Shouts. Slaps. Curses. Cries ring out.*

Grabbing a nearly useless cell phone, the stranger activates the SOS beacon to contact 911. Scrambling up the hill, nearly every inch covered with mud, the survivor climbs into the nearly totaled car and drives off. Leaving the ringing phone in the ditch and two bleeding bodies in the changing light of the intersection.

"Thank you so much for sharing with us, Grace," says Elaine. "It's been a long time coming, hasn't it?" Grace nods mutely. Elaine claps along with the rest of the room. All except for Everly, who sits stupefied in her seat.

When the meeting ends, many people stay to mingle, drink muddy coffee, and pick at stale snacks, but Grace shoots out of her seat.

"Grace!" Everly calls after her.

Grace's limping gait slows, and she finally stops at the base of the stairs. She turns to her friend, wiping the tears from her eyes. "We had my brother's funeral once I was out of the hospital. His friend was so badly injured in the wreck, he might never walk again." She pauses, taking a deep breath. "It's just been a hard recovery," she says, her voice cracking. "I'll probably have this limp for the rest of my life."

PART III

Chapter 45

"Ev, come down for breakfast!" The aroma of fresh pancakes wafts through the house. Everly groans, turning over to hide from the morning sunlight streaming in through her bedroom windows. The world of uncertainty holds her down like a weighted blanket.

A light knock on her door drags her mind from its sleepy fog. She can sense his presence beside her. "Good morning," he says, sitting on the edge of her bed. Her sluggish fingers drag the comforter up over her face against the painfully bright sun. "Come on, Ev," he laughs at her. "Let's eat some breakfast and go for a drive. Sound good?"

Everly groans in agreement. As her eyes flutter shut once more, she's jerked awake by hands shaking her shoulders. "I'm up! I'm up!" she yells, her heart now beating aggressively in her chest.

⁕

The warm sun kisses her cheeks, but the chilling breeze traces goosebumps along her skin as they drive. For years Everly and her dad have allowed themselves to get lost on back roads and in conversation. An easy way to escape life and roam blissfully without a plan. Their drives always start the same way. With a simple yet frustratingly complex question.

"How's life, kiddo?"

Expecting the same question every time doesn't make the response come any easier. Thinking to herself, she sifts through the past few months for an answer. *Well, I graduated college months ago and have no job prospects. I'm living at home with my parents again while my friends are moving all over the country for their dream jobs. And I feel utterly lost in life and have no idea what I'm doing.*

"Life's good." His eyes shift from the road to find hers. She glances up to meet his identically blue eyes. Her heart lurches, knowing she can't hide from him. "I'm lost," she whispers.

The wind through open windows, the chirping of morning birds, and the grinding of dirt under their tires fill the silence between them until he speaks. "We all feel lost sometimes. You just need to take a single step in the right direction."

"I don't even know which direction is the right one," she breathes in agitation.

"Well, you won't know until you try one," he smiles. "And if that one doesn't work out, then you try a different one." Everly fiddles with a lock of her hair, frustrated with his simplification of the situation. "You know, God can only help guide you on your path if you are willing to take the first step."

Her fingers tighten around the strands of hair, pulling rhythmically. "Well, God hasn't done much for me the past couple years," she exhales through her teeth.

"Everything happens *for* you, Ev. There's a reason for everything, you just don't have the perspective to see it."

"Did being kidnapped by a raging psychopath work *for me,* Dad? How about the cancer that ate at Miss Amy for over a year until it killed her? Did that work *for me*? Did God have some grand plan to rip my life to shreds so I can piece it back together in my childhood room while everyone else goes off and enjoys their life?" she yells with tears in her eyes.

The silence is deafening as they turn to drive home.

*

October 4th

I'm stuck in this endless cycle of depression and self-pity that keeps me paralyzed in bed. Stella wrote me a prescription for some antidepressants. What a fucking joke of a human I must be to need some little "happy pills" to keep me from going insane.

October something

I don't even know the date. I think it's been nearly a week since I've left the house. Everything is hard. Even the effort it takes to write this is draining me. When did everything become so hard?

College was hard, but not like this. I thought getting good grades and a degree would set me up for a fulfilling and happy life. That's some bullshit they brainwash you into thinking. Or maybe it's just me. Maybe I'm the failure.

Joce and David both found jobs out west and decided to move out there together. New jobs, new place, happy relationship. What a fucking thought. Guess that's just not in the cards for me.

⁜

"Stella, I can't do this today. It took every ounce of willpower to even show up today. And I know what that look means." Stella looks over the glasses perched on the bridge of her nose, her eyes analyzing the perfect moment for her to speak the information she has to share. "That look means you're about to make my life so much harder somehow." Everly shakes her head. "I can't do it today, okay? Don't do it," she nearly pleads.

"Everly," Stella pulls her glasses off and crosses her legs. "You're drowning yourself."

"What?"

"You are drowning yourself, and you refuse to grab onto any of the hands that are reaching out to help you." She watches as Everly's eyes avoid hers. "With all you've been through, it is understandable to sink into the darkness, but there are ways to avoid having it fully consume you." Inhaling the scent of her new candle that smells of fall rain, she waits for Everly's eyes to connect with her own. "Why haven't you filled your prescription yet?"

"I don't want it."

"You don't want what, exactly?"

Red-rimmed eyes stare blankly at the wall behind Stella. “I don’t want to be fake happy. I want to actually enjoy life and feel excited when I wake up. If I start taking these pills I’ll never *actually* be happy.”

“Okay, I understand your concerns, but you’re looking at this all wrong. Medications don’t create a new reality for you, Everly. Medications help with the chemical imbalance in a person’s brain that has led to their depression or anxiety or whatever they happen to struggle with.

“I also know that the idea of taking medication feels like admitting weakness to you. I need you to know that that is not true. Medication is a helpful tool in creating a more sustainable level of mental health. It is not a weakness to utilize therapy or medication—it is a responsible and healthy means of working through and dealing with hard times.

“And as far as I can tell from what I’ve learned about you, this is a situational need that will help you to balance yourself and regulate your mood for the time being.” Stella waits, watching Everly absorb the words and nod. “Okay?”

“Okay.”

Chapter 46

December 6th

It's been almost two months since I started working with Grace at the marketing firm. And since I started taking my antidepressants. I hate to admit it but I feel good. I feel like I'm making progress in my work and I genuinely feel mentally stable for the first time in a while. Who knew a little white pill and a good friend could make all the difference?

December 12th

I had my big presentation today in front of my boss and some account managers and it went so well! I woke up this morning feeling like I might puke, but I knew the information inside and out, and once I was up there I took a deep breath and delivered one hell of a marketing strategy for our client.

I'm just really proud of myself today.

December 15th

I love working with Grace. The open floor plan of our office makes it easy to throw notes at her and play bumper chairs. But I really love being able to talk to someone at work who really knows me. We usually eat lunch together, with Caleb of course. They've been dating for almost two years now. Sometimes I feel like I'm third-wheeling but they always assure me I'm not.

Caleb works in an office building two blocks down so he always walks over and we eat on the roof or meet up at a coffee shop between us. I wish I could find a guy like Caleb. Someone to prioritize time with me or write me silly little notes to find in my purse or sing horrible karaoke with on the weekends. He really is an awful singer—he only does it to make Grace smile.

Where are all the men like that?

Not that it matters. A man is the last thing I need right now. The first thing on my 'Get my shit together' list is to find an apartment and get the hell out of my parents' house.

⁕

"Everly," her boss calls, motioning for her to come into his office. She stands up, smoothing down her blouse before walking into his office with a mixture of anxiety and confidence.

"Yes, sir?"

"Please, take a seat." *Oh shit.* Anxiety is winning out. "I'd like to talk to you about your recent performance." *Oh shit, oh shit.* Her pulse quickens, thinking back to her recent assignments. He can sense her panic and smiles to ease her tension. "I've been speaking with your team members, and they've all agreed that you have great leadership potential." She exhales audibly, eliciting a chuckle from him. The confidence surges in her chest as she remains quiet, waiting for him to finish. "I'd like to offer you the lead role on our next account. How would you feel about that?"

Everly's eyes widen, her mouth slightly open, waiting for her brain and voice to connect. Finally she collects herself, responding calmly, "I'd be honored. I won't let you down, sir." She rises to shake his hand and smiles. "Thank you for this opportunity."

"Be here first thing Monday morning ready to collaborate with the company's representative." She nods at each of his words.

"Yes, sir. Absolutely."

"That's all." Everly nods again, then turns to leave, doing a not-so-subtle happy dance as she exits.

Bright and early Monday morning Everly has everything in the conference room organized and ready for the meeting. The frosted panes of glass show only her distorted figure pacing the long room. There's a knock on the door, and Everly stands up straight, ready to make a perfect first impression. She exhales in exaggerated disappointment as Grace enters the room.

"You look professional as hell, Ev." Grace smiles, looking from the neatly arranged materials to Everly's put-together outfit.

Everly walks over and embraces her friend. "Wouldn't be here without you." She squeezes her tight.

"And I wouldn't be *here* without you." Everly pulls back, confused. Grace holds out her left hand, and Everly's eyes reflect the shining rock on her finger.

"Oh my god!" she shrieks, jumping up and down, squeezing Grace in a crushing hug. "Ahhhh, that's amazing! I can't believe Caleb didn't tell me he was going to propose, that asshole!" The squeals of the girls reverberate against the glass walls and manage to startle the whole office.

The door opens, and Everly turns to apologize for her animated performance, but her eyes rest on a face that leaves her speechless.

"Sorry, am I interrupting?" His voice lingers in her ears.

Grace looks at Everly's stunned face, then to the man standing in the doorway. "No, not at all. I was just leaving," she smiles. He lowers his gaze as she passes by. Behind him in the doorway, Grace stares back at Everly mouthing the words *he's cute* before slinking off.

Collecting herself, Everly takes purposeful steps towards him with an outstretched hand. "Hi, I'm so sorry about that." Immediate heat advances across her skin as they touch. "Please, come in." She gestures for him to take a seat.

His smile creases at one side as he follows her to the end of the table. They settle into their seats, and he watches her intently as she pulls up the presentation on her computer.

Everly feels the weight of his gaze and struggles to maintain her steady breathing. She looks up, the blue radiance of her eyes melting into the amber glow of his. That same crooked smile appears on his face. "Been a while, Lele."

"Yes, it has," she breathes. "How you been, Jax?"

⁂

Her heart flitters with relief or anger, she can't tell. He looks exactly the same and completely different. He's grown out his hair so it falls in subtle waves against his temples, and there's stubble on his face where it used to be youthful and smooth. His frame still towers over her, but lean muscles now visibly contour his body, even in his button-down.

He smiles the same smile she always loved. She feels nothing but the energy between them, the marketing presentation a mere distraction. She sees nothing but the faint freckles across his nose and his dark lashes as he stares into her eyes, her soul, her entire being.

"How long has it been now? Like ten years?" he offers, bringing her back to reality.

"I'm not sure." She tries to act disinterested. "So," she continues. "I've put together a marketing plan that has the potential to increase your company's revenue by—"

"Lele," he interrupts.

"*Don't* call me that," she snaps back.

"I'm sorry."

"It's fine." She busies herself with the computer.

"No." He leans forward. "I'm *sorry.*"

"It was a long time ago, Jax. It's fine." She cues up the first slide of her presentation.

"Sounds like a great marketing strategy. I'll talk to my team, and we'll be in contact," he says, standing up. Everly reaches out a hand, and he takes it in both of his. Her breath catches as his thumb plays gently across her knuckles. He leans in slightly so she can feel the heat of his body next to hers. Heat prickles across her neck where he hovers. His lips linger a breath away from her ear, and he whispers, "It's good to see you again."

She exhales the tension. Her hand wilts slowly to her side as he releases it. She steps back, taking a deep breath, and forces a smile. "I'll walk you out."

After escorting Jackson to the elevator, Everly rushes for the stairs, her blonde hair flowing in her wake. Grace catches the golden blur and follows. Climbing the final steps to the rooftop, Grace notices Everly's rosy cheeks and damp eyes staring out over the street below.

"Ev," she says quietly, trying not to startle her. "Who was that?"

Everly gazes down at the street, her eyes tracking him as he storms across the busy road and collapses against an alleyway wall, breathless. Grace stands beside her, following her gaze. "Jackson..." Her whisper is carried away on the chilling breeze that tousles her fine golden hair.

"*The* Jackson?" Grace gawks. Everly simply nods. "Ev, I'm so sorry. I had no idea."

⁂

"Where were you?" she screams. "All those times you promised to be there for me. All the times I needed you. *At your own mother's funeral!* Where the hell were you!"

A malicious smile works across his lips, that crooked smile now unrecognizable. "I never loved you, and I never needed you. She didn't either. I bet she'd be disgusted if she knew you even showed up. You never cared about her. Not when she was alive anyway."

⁂

"Where have you been? Her face softens against the impending tears. "I needed you."

Jackson rakes his fingers through his tawny hair, pacing in front of her. "You deserved so much better, Lele. I couldn't face you again and have you hate me. I'd rather go my whole life hoping you missed me than knowing you hated me."

⁂

"Jax," she reaches out, her fingers catching at his.

Whirling around he looks at her, his eyes blank. "I'm sorry… Do I know you?" Everly pulls away, her fingers burning without his touch.

"I—" Her panicked eyes meet the warm honey of his. He stares at her without recognition, and she lets out a whimper before rushing past him, her legs carrying her as fast as they can go.

⁂

"Where have you been?" she scowls, her nose scrunching like he's a disgusting piece of trash that's been dropped beside her.

"I'm so sorry, Lele." His voice is but a whisper.

"It's too late." She stands up to leave when he catches at her wrist.

"Please," he begs.

Turning on her heel, she stares straight into his shit-colored eyes, a devilish sneer on her face. "Fuck. You. Jax."

⁂

"Where were you, Jax? I needed you."

"Lele, please believe me. Every waking moment we've spent apart I've been dreaming of the moment I'd see you again. To admire how you've grown. To stare into those eyes that have never left my mind. To kiss those lips that I've dreamed of every night since the first time they met mine. I needed you too, Lele. And I need you now. Right now."

His hand grasps the back of her neck while the other traces the smooth skin under her dress. His weight pushes her against the door, and a moan escapes her throat. Her hands tangle aggressively in his hair, exploring its length. His lips caress her neck, and shivers run down her spine as he breathes in her ear. Her hands claw at his back, aching to remove the fabric. With a strong grip he clasps her hand in his, pushing it above her to the door. She gasps, smiling seductively up at him. Her eyes linger in the honey of his, as his other hand guides the zipper down her back. The fabric lingers only on one shoulder. His warm fingertips move slowly from her neck down to her shoulder, inviting the strap to fall away. The dress pools at her feet, revealing the paler skin even the sun's never kissed.

He lifts her from her feet, her legs lacing around his torso, and carries her towards the bed. The cool satin welcomes her. The warm light of a single lamp casts shadows across his olive skin. The ripples of lean muscle and his chiseled features make him almost angelic. Her mind captures him in this moment, hoping to hold onto it forever.

She moves restlessly on the sheets as he waits, holding himself just above her. His smile grows with her yearning. A single finger traces around her lips, down her jaw and neck, each collarbone and over the fading tan lines on her breasts. He can see her pulse thrum at the base of her throat. He leans in, placing his soft lips there, feeling the beats quicken.

Her impatience takes over, and she pulls him to her, rolling over, now straddling him. Her hands push the thin fabric up over his chest, and in a swift motion his hand tears the shirt over his head. Her body presses against his bare chest, his hands grasp at her hair, pulling her to his lips. Her tongue dances across his, moving to his lips and across his jaw. A low growl lingers in his throat as her teeth nibble his ear, her lips now pressing to the smooth skin of his body. Her hands trace the muscles of his torso, each kiss led by her tongue's tantalizing touch. She looks up and catches him staring breathlessly at her. Smiling, her lips continue down his body.

His hands grip the satin sheets, his nerves burning with each touch. Suddenly he leans forward, pulling her face to his and lifting her onto him in one swift movement. His strong grip curls around her as they roll once again, his body now above hers.

Their eyes lock, reflecting each other's hungry desire. She watches in surprise as he raises his hand—*slap!*

Everly jolts upright in her bed, glaring around the sunlit room. Her cat scurries away at the sudden movement. "You little shit!" she yells, rubbing her tired eyes. "Stop smacking me while I'm sleeping, or you're going back on the streets!" She groans, wishing to go back and finish her dream—or to have her dream finish her.

Meow! Athena leaps up onto the bed again and saunters towards her, demanding to be fed. "Hang on," Everly complains, rolling off the edge.

Everly had found the malnourished kitten outside her apartment by the dumpsters a couple of weeks before and decided to take her in. She's aptly named *Athena,* goddess of war, for her cleverness and aggressive demands for love and food. Everly groans as she fills Athena's food bowl.

"Really, you couldn't have waited like five more minutes?"

Chapter 47

"The same dream? That's like a week straight of the same thing."

"Well…" Everly's cheeks redden as she thinks about it. "Last night's was a little different," she giggles.

"How so?" Grace asks. Everly chuckles a little louder, holding the phone away from her ear. "Was it spicy?" Grace exclaims more than asks. "Tell. Me. Everything."

Everly recounts the steamy details as she and her friend cackle over the phone together.

"Okay, okay!" Grace pleads. "You have to stop before I pee myself." Wiping the tears from her eyes and sitting up in her chair, she returns to the reason she called in the first place. "So, tonight."

"Right." Everly shifts into the new topic of conversation.

"The gala starts in two hours. Do you want us to pick you up, or will you just meet us there?"

"I'll meet you there. I have to start getting ready," Everly responds. "How fancy do we dress for this party, anyway? I have three dresses that I'm debating between."

"Oh, people at the company go all out. When I interned here in college, I showed up in a casual dress and immediately drove home to change. I was so embarrassed," she laughs.

"Oh god, okay." Everly looks over her choices doubtfully.

"Ev, don't worry. You look good in everything anyway. We'll meet you there, okay?"

"Okay, sounds good."

Ugh. Which dress says, "Yes, I absolutely know how to be an adult"?

Okay, which dress would my mom pick? She scans each option laid out on the bed, finally settling on the long blue dress with lace detailing along the sleeves and neckline. *It's elegant, conservative, and professional. My mom would definitely pick this one,* she thinks, tossing the dress to the floor.

"Okay, Athena, now we have two real options. Which do you like more?" Athena occupies herself by swatting at the hanging fringe of Everly's bookmark on her nightstand. Her claw catches, sending a pile of books to the floor and her scurrying under the bed. "You're no help at all."

As she kneels down to collect the books, she cradles one she's looked at a million times, holding it but never scanning a single word between the covers. The worn leather and rough parchment pages smell of roses and thyme. *Señora Morales,* she smiles to herself.

Everly settles onto the floor, the book resting gently on her legs as she inhales the distantly familiar smell and opens the cover. Señora Morales' penmanship looks the way fairy tales feel—wistful and magical.

My dearest Everly,

Hope in a hopeless world can change your life forever. So, have hope and know that there is always potential in the hardest of times. There is always potential in heartbreak.

El amor lo conquista todo.

Con cariño,

Lucía Morales

Everly sits beside her bed translating the words in her head. *Love conquers all—well, that hasn't worked out for me so far.* Her hands rake through her hair as she takes a deep breath thinking about Jax. *No.* She stops herself.

Standing up, she stretches and speaks aloud to the empty room. "Thanks, Señora Morales, but I don't think true love exists," she scoffs, tossing the book onto her desk.

"Shit, shit, shit! Is that the time?" she exclaims looking at the clock in a panic. Hysterically shoving aside piles of clothes on her bed, she recovers her phone. It rings once, twice, three times…

"Ev!" Jocelyn's smiling face shows up on her screen.

"Joce, I need your help or I'm gonna be late," she blurts out.

"Okay, okay. Let me see what you got." She concentrates on her screen. Everly sets her phone down on her bedside table. "Ow! Ow!" Jocelyn cheers, seeing Everly in only her black bra and thong. "Damn, Ev. You look hot! Just go in that," she teases. Everly smirks and rolls her eyes.

"Shut up. Which one do you like?" She holds up the first dress. "Simple, strapless black dress. It's a classic, goes with everything, and it can be dressed up or down. Thoughts?"

"I've always loved that dress, but let me see the other one." Everly holds up her second option, but before she can get a word out Jocelyn shrieks. "Holy shit, Ev! A million times, yes. Put that on right now."

Everly giggles, her cheeks reddening to match the vibrant color of her dress. "Okay, give me a minute," she says, slipping out of view to change.

A moment later Everly moves into view, and for the first time in memory, Jocelyn is speechless.

*

The blustery wind whips her hair across her face as she walks towards the building. One hand focuses on holding the hem of her dress above the wet pavement, while the other grips her clutch and tries to fight the wind for control of her hair.

In the elevator her heart thrums anxiously in her chest as she watches each floor number illuminate. Everly releases the lengthy hem and settles into a confident posture before the doors slide open.

In the ballroom, Grace and Caleb look dapper in their matching emerald green attire. Her thick black hair hangs in a long braid, a spray of winterberries contrasting with its darkness.

"Ev just texted me. She's on her way up," she calls to Caleb over the din of conversations and music. He's oblivious, occupied by the hors d'oeuvres and string quartet. She pokes him aggressively in the side.

He jumps and squeals at her touch, looking around hoping no one heard the noise that just came out of him. "What?" He smiles, bending lower to hear her.

"Ev is coming up. Let's find her." He nods, guiding her through the crowd. She stops abruptly to grab two champagne flutes, clinking them together and taking a generous gulp before continuing on.

"...And so my wife said to me, 'Don't be too charming or smart. Just be yourself.'" The group erupts in laughter. Jackson smiles at his boss, knowing that joke could quite possibly be true. He scans the room, taking in the extravagant decor and the vaulted ceiling and searching for one pair of blue eyes he can't seem to forget.

"Excuse me," he says, shifting away from the group. Straightening the lapels of dark suit jacket, he wanders aimlessly through the crowded scene. His long fingers comb back the golden brown hair from his eyes, one strand lingering over his dark brow.

Ding. The elevator comes to a stop, and he looks over just as the doors open.

His brows rise and his cheek creases with a broad smile. "Wow," he says aloud.

"Stunning, isn't she?"

He pulls his gaze away to see Grace standing beside him, Caleb lingering just behind. "Yes." He clears his throat. "Stunning." His gaze settles on Everly for a moment more before turning fully to Grace. He shifts uncomfortably in front of her.

"I know who you are." He stiffens, frozen in place. "Jax, right?"

He breathes out on a smile. She must be close with Everly because there's no one else in the world who calls him by that name.

"Jackson." He reaches out his hand to her.

"Grace." She takes his hand. "And this is my fiancé, Caleb." Caleb reaches over to shake his hand firmly.

"Nice to meet you both." Jackson grins politely.

"You should tell her." Grace's dark eyes stare intently into his. Again, his heart ceases to beat in his chest for a moment. "Tell her she looks stunning. And tell her all the things she deserves to hear. You owe her that much."

Jackson straightens up and smooths the expensive fabric of his jacket before accepting a champagne flute and walking towards the elevator.

Everly stands beneath a festive arbor in the entryway, her hands kneading her clutch anxiously. Her eyes scan the large room for Grace and Caleb.

Wow. She takes in the ballroom. Crystal chandeliers hang from the lofted ceilings, perfect centerpieces of winter foliage grace the tables, and every person is dressed to the nines, dancing to the string quartet's exquisite melodies.

A knot starts to form in Everly's stomach as people begin to notice her presence. The unfamiliar eyes stare at the red satin that hugs her slim figure and pools at her heels. She's a radiant burst of color in a sea of deep blues, blacks, and greens.

Everly smiles at no one in particular, casting her eyes down as she turns to hurry away from the entrance, and crashes into a solid figure in front of her. "I'm so sorry," she gasps, looking up to find the smooth lapel of a black tux, a sharp jawline freshly shaven, a crooked smile, a freckled nose and two eyes that reflect her soul. "Hi, Lele."

The breath leaves her body as she struggles to speak. "Hi, Jax."

"You look stunning." His eyes roam over her admiringly, and she looks away as her cheeks redden, from embarrassment or anger, she can't yet discern. Looking anywhere but in his eyes, she counters, saying, "I didn't think you'd be here." Jackson takes a step back like he's been punched in the stomach, hurt written all over his face. Everly stands her ground, white-knuckling her clutch.

"Ev!" Grace calls out, breaking the unbearable silence as she collides into her sideways. Luckily Caleb's long arms are prepared to stabilize them both. Everly's nerves dissipate as she embraces her friend. They've been friends for years, yet still greet each other with joyful hugs. "Holy hell, you look incredible!" Grace blares.

"Oh, hush, you literally look like you hopped out of a fairytale. Are those real winterberries in your hair?"

Grace lifts her emerald skirt, twirling in an exaggerated circle, "Why, yes. Yes, they are." She winks at Everly. "I told you people go all out for these things." Everly nods, looking past her to the elegantly dressed crowd. Grace snaps her fingers in front of Everly's face. "Well, don't just stand there. Come dance with me," she insists, dragging her by the wrist. Everly snatches the champagne flute out of Jackson's hand before allowing Grace to haul her to the dance floor.

"Mind if I cut in?" Grace yields Everly's hands and winks as she moves to find Caleb. Jackson's hand envelops hers, while the other rests lightly on her waist. His fingers graze the skin exposed by her open-backed gown, sending hot shivers down her spine. They glide in synchronous movement, long swaying locks, vibrant satin, and elegant power.

As the music rests on its final notes, women curtsy and men bow to their partners before deciding whether to keep dancing or rest. "I can't believe you actually let me lead for once," Jackson smirks as he guides Everly through the crowd.

"For once?" she questions, her silver-lined eyes narrowing.

He stops at the edge of the dance floor to remind her. "Don't tell me you've forgotten about all those talent shows we put on for our families growing up." A staticky image of two innocent souls holding hands and flailing about starts to form before her eyes. The memory of youthful squeals and endless joy seeps into her body like she's experiencing it all again. His voice breaks through the image. "You *never* let me lead."

Everly's lips tremble slightly as she looks up at the man she's tried so hard to forget. *Where have you been?* The question claws at her throat, hoping to escape. Those four unrelenting words that have tortured her for years.

Jackson leans forward to brush a gentle finger along her cheek to clear it of the fallen tear, but Everly grabs the hem of her dress, darts into the crowd, and vanishes in the sea of people.

Chapter 48

"Lele, are you up here?" On the rooftop, the gusting wind whips his hair across his eyes and brow in the same disheveled yet charming way it had when they were kids. "Lele," he calls out again, "please just talk to me."

"And say what?" She rounds the corner, her dress reflecting the warm tones of Edison bulbs strung about. Jackson stands still, stunned.

"Anything," he manages to say.

Everly storms towards him, coming so close she nearly collides into him. "I've played this over in my mind a million times," her voice rages like wildfire. "Where have you been? Why didn't you ever call me? What happened to you all those years? How could you not show up to your own mother's funeral? Did you ever even care about me? I have a million fucking questions for you, but I don't want the answers because I *want* to hate you." She pants breathlessly, watching his unreadable expression. "I need to hate you, Jax."

He stands there motionless, staring out over the rooftops at the stars that have gathered to shine across the dark sky. "I…" His voice breaks, and he screws his eyes shut for a beat. Staring past her still, he clears his throat, his lips quivering ever so slightly. "I deserve your hate. I deserve every hateful word, every bit of blame, every ounce of resentment you have for me. Because you're right. I wasn't there. And I could spend the rest of my life explaining to you why, but it wouldn't change a damn thing. So," he smirks, with that infuriatingly beautiful crooked smile, "Everly Dianne, I hope."

Everly gapes at him, her heart pumping so fast she's worried she might faint.

"I hope. That in a world so cruel and unrelenting there is a place where love and forgiveness win out. And maybe it's not in this lifetime that you'll forgive me, but I'll wait for the next one. Or the next one after that. Because every day of my life *you* have been my guiding light. My purpose. My heart. My reason to stay when I didn't think it was possible." Tears well up in his dark eyes as he smiles down at Everly, pulling her hands into his.

Jackson leans in as the wind blows her hair back from her neck to cascade down her bare back. His lips just barely graze her ear as he whispers, "I will spend the rest of my life fighting like hell to be the man you've always deserved. I swear it." His breath sends hot waves through her as he presses a light kiss to her cheek, releases her hands, and walks through the dark doorway, leaving Everly standing on the rooftop completely alone with the chaos of her thoughts.

Taking each step with dazed concentration, she makes her way back to the ballroom where she spots Caleb easing Grace off the dance floor, her steps more unsteady than usual. As Everly approaches, Grace drapes her arm over Everly's shoulder and sways off beat to the music. She reaches toward a passing tray of champagne flutes only to be thwarted by Caleb grabbing her wrist and planting a kiss on it.

"No more, my love. We have to get you home," he says, untangling her limbs from Everly.

"Oh yeah?" she says friskily. Her fingers run along the trim of his tux.

"To bed, you horny monster," Everly laughs, loading the rest of Grace's weight onto Caleb.

"Thanks, Ev." She plants a big, wet kiss on Everly's lips. She staggers back, stunned, then lets out a loud cackle.

"Hey, at least buy me dinner first," Everly manages between laughs.

Caleb shakes his head, smiling. "All right, let's head home before you grope anyone else."

Everly grins up at Caleb as he shifts closer to Grace. "Do you need help?" she offers.

"No, I have this down to a science now," he smiles, lifting Grace off the ground and into his arms. He looks into her dark eyes adoringly as he walks towards the elevator. A true knight in shining armor appreciating the princess he longs to love for the rest of his existence. *A perfect match, if such a thing were to exist,* Everly thinks.

⁕

Hope in a hopeless world can change your life forever. The words replay in her mind as she slumps against the wall of the elevator. Exiting, she pads across the smooth marble floor and spots a figure seated in the grand foyer. A familiar figure with his head in his hands.

Everly saunters over to the array of lounge furniture in front of the magnificent flaming hearth and sits across from the disheartened boy she once knew. His hands wipe at his eyes as he gazes up to see Everly seated before him, her legs crossed under the brilliant scarlet of her dress and her bare feet tapping at the air.

"Hope, eh?" Everly swings her stilettos gently back and forth on her finger, allowing a small smirk to shift her pink lips.

Jackson looks up, his eyes lingering on the exposed skin of her neck and the freckles that lead up to her face. Encircle her lips. "It's all I have left," he shrugs, smiling.

"Well," she starts, rising from her seat to stand only inches taller than his seated body. "I guess that'll work for now." She grabs his cuff, then his hand, and leads him out into the street.

The streets quiet as the darkness deepens, and the stars shine brighter over the dimming city lights. Jackson combs his fingers through his hair, inhaling the crisp air deeply. "I'm sorry," he starts, breaking the long silence between them.

"Don't." She cuts him off. "Can we just walk? Please."

And so they walk in silence, taking in the night as traffic dwindles and apartment lights wink out. Everly watches each of her steps carefully, maneuvering her shoeless feet around broken glass and unidentifiable puddles. "Okay." She looks up at him for a moment. "Let's play a game." Jackson's smile glimmers under the streetlamps as he awaits further instruction. "The question game. We go back and forth asking each other questions about ourselves to see if we've changed or if we even remember. Does that make sense?"

He moves a step closer to her, his nearness warming her skin. "I think so. You start."

"All right. What was my first dog's name?"

"Cocoa, easy. What pair of shoes did I wear every day of third grade?"

"Your Spiderman Converse. What's my favorite color?"

"Trick question, you could never pick just one. You like them all for different things. You love the orange of sunsets and the blues of the ocean and the purple of hyacinths that you'd smell by sticking your whole face into them."

"They smell amazing," she defends, knocking into his side playfully. "I can't believe you remember that."

"Of course I do." He stops for a moment, reaching out for her hand.

Everly quickens her steps as she skips up the front stoop to her apartment building. Jackson waits on the sidewalk, unsure. Street lamps illuminate the red satin clinging to her body, a beautiful rose in a sea of darkness.

Banging on the frosted pane of the thick wooden door with closed fists, she lets out a loud, frustrated sigh. Jackson takes the steps quickly, jumping to her side and grabbing both her wrists before she can split her knuckles.

"Hey, hey," He pulls her away from the door, searching her eyes for answers. "What's wrong?"

A sob escapes her burning throat. "I forgot my clutch. It has my keys in it." She pulls back from his grasp, a painful memory flashing in her mind. "Don't you dare grab me like that again."

"I'm sorry." He backs down a step. "I'm sorry, Lele." He watches as she settles down onto the top step, resting her shoes beside her. "I can head back to get it for you," he offers.

"It's past midnight, they've probably locked up," she counters.

"You're welcome to spend the night at my place. I can call a cab."

Everly shakes her head. *This is some shitty déjà vu.* "I have to get in to feed my cat." She drops her head into her hands. "God, she's going to be pissed." She releases a sardonic laugh. "She's actually going to kill me." A real, genuine laugh builds as she imagines the various ways Athena has probably plotted her demise already.

Jackson settles onto the stoop beside her, wrapping his jacket over her goosebump-covered shoulders. She flinches away, then accepts its warmth. "What floor are you on?" She looks up at him curiously. He descends the few steps, holding his hand out to her. Her stomach twirls in anxious butterflies as she looks at the outstretched hand, white scars she's never seen littered across its surface. As her eyes trace along his wrist to his muscled forearm under the white dress shirt, she can't help but see the young boy with olive skin and crooked teeth she once knew. The boy she loved and trusted with every fiber of her being. *Once upon a time.*

A few long moments pass before she accepts his outstretched hand, allowing him to guide her down the alleyway towards the back of the building. Squinting in the dark, Everly skips over broken bottles and discarded garbage while holding her shoes and the hem of her dress and clutching the comforting fabric of Jackson's oversized jacket.

The neighboring building reflects the moonlight enough for them to distinguish the fire escape above. Jackson starts rolling up his sleeves as he walks over to the rusted structure, analyzing its height. "It's too high," Everly protests. He looks back at her with the smile of the adventure-seeking boy, who more than once busted his lip trying to run up trees. "You're going to do something stupid, aren't you?" She mirrors the smile growing on his face.

He winks his dark lashes at her before taking a running start at the wall, propelling himself upward with one foot against the brick and clamping his long fingers around a rusted rung. He hangs for a moment until the ladder gives way with screeching protest. Landing with a thud, he looks back at her, his white shirt now ripped down the front. Everly bursts out with a cackle at the sight of him, his hair splayed in wild directions, the tattered fabric of his shirt shifting in the midnight wind, and his boyish smile twitching with slight embarrassment.

Before he can speak she looks at him, really looks at him.

Those eyes pierce into her. His lips, quirked into that beautiful smile. Those new muscles, contouring the slight torso she used to know. Her brain fogs as she looks at him, scrambling to think of a word perfect enough to describe him in this moment.

Angelic.

"Ladies first." He disrupts her thoughts, holding his hand out to her once again.

Ascending the rusted fire escape proves more difficult than they expected as many steps have significant corrosion and even gaping holes. Climbing each stair with calculated precision, Everly chances a glance upward to see Athena pacing on her windowsill, complaining to the empty room. Jackson keeps pace behind her, monitoring her steps as she goes. "Wait!" he shouts just as the red satin plunges through the crumbling landing and her terrified shriek rings out.

Jackson lunges forward, crashing down on the jagged metal, grasping for her flailing arms. Suspended ten feet above another corroded landing, Everly looks through the sharp-edged hole above her to see Jackson's face, his grip digging into her wrist. He watches as her shoes drop forty feet into the dirty puddles below. "You're okay, Lele," he breathes. Sweat starts to bead on his brow beneath his disheveled hair. "Give me your other hand. I'll pull you up," he urges. Her dress flutters in the now-freezing wind, and her body shakes with cold and adrenaline.

"Jax," she pleads.

"I've got you." That crooked smile makes her believe it. Swaying in the wind, she stretches out her other hand to reach him, only inches away, when his feet slip, sending him forward with a sudden jerk.

Everly screams, "Jax!"

His muscles strain against the weight and his legs shake, trying to find a stable position. Locking his feet between two metal posts, he stretches farther, their fingertips touching. "Grab my hand, Lele." His voice tightens as he fights to seize her hand. She secures her hand around his wrist over a faded loop of braided thread. Inhaling deeply, he wrenches her up with every ounce of strength he can muster until her arms grapple against the metal to get leverage. Finally, Jackson pulls her through, and they collapse breathlessly.

His torso is crosshatched with cuts, the blood blending seamlessly over the torn scarlet fabric of her dress. Their chests rise and fall together, each breath producing a warm cloud in the freezing air. Everly nestles into Jackson's neck, shaking. His arms wrap around her. "I've got you." Resting his lips against her hair, he repeats it until her trembling eases. "I've got you."

Carefully holding on to one another, they ascend the last few steps to rest on her broad windowsill. Everly exhales a shaky breath, sliding open the kitchen window with ease. Athena's complaints and a comforting blanket of warm air welcome them as they climb in. Settling onto the wooden floor, Everly welcomes Athena's incessant nudges of love. Jackson closes the window, sinking down next to her. Without looking at him, she rests her head on his shoulder. He flinches in pain. "How'd you know?" she nearly whispers.

"Know what?" He shifts to watch her fingers intertwine with Athena's tail.

"That it'd be open." She lifts her head to look at his face, wanting desperately to wipe away the sweat on his brow but controlling the urge. "The window, I mean. How'd you know it would be unlocked?"

Jackson rests his head back on the sill, that crooked smile appearing as he recalls a memory. "You told me it would be." Everly's brow furrows as she looks at him. "Before I left." Adjusting himself to look into those beautiful blue pools he's wished for, longed for, dreamt of, he continues. "You said, and I quote," he chuckles, "'for the rest of my life, I'll leave my windows open, hoping that one day you'll come back to me.'"

He remembered. Her eyes search his face, and her fingers shift the cuff of his shirt to see the faded string tied around his wrist. Without hesitation she presses into him, their lips colliding in perfect sync. The nerves, doubts, fears, all of it dissolves with their kiss.

Before she can catch her breath he's lifting her up, his hands cupping her smooth curves as he carries her to the couch, setting her down gently. Her tongue traces the muscles of his neck, savoring the salty flavor and smell of pine. He suppresses a deep growl as Everly gnaws on his ear, her breath sending infuriating chills throughout his body. Pressing her lips to his cheek, she leans in to whisper. *Meow!*

They both shoot up to find Athena sauntering along the back of the couch. Everly throws her head back into the cushion. "For the love of God! You're going back on the streets." She rolls her eyes as she shifts out from under Jackson's body to fill the small food and water bowls in the kitchen. Athena meows a thanks, food already coating her whiskers.

Turning back to the living room, she stills, watching the muscles of Jackson's back shift as he lifts a picture from the mantle. He's removed his shirt, the tattered material in a pile on the floor. The moonlight paints the living room into a monochrome movie scene, highlighting and contouring the features of his body. He turns, sensing her presence as she moves quietly towards him. The words catch in his throat as he gazes upon her, the silver light catching in her eyes and the sheen of her dress. He clears his throat. "Do you have a shirt I could borrow?"

Her eyes rake over his lips as they part into a smile. "Hmm…" She speaks slowly. "I'd also like to slip into something more comfortable. Let me see what I can find."

Everly returns moments later with an oversized t-shirt that will likely fit snugly around Jackson's muscled torso, but it's the best she can find. "Thank you." He opens his hands to receive it, but she pulls it out of reach.

"Could you," she pauses, turning around, "unzip me, please. I can't reach it." A lie.

Jackson's cheeks burn as he guides her golden hair over one shoulder, exposing her bare back and the zipper starting near her waist. She closes her eyes, feeling his breath on the side of her neck. Her body shivers as he gently grasps the fabric at the base of her spine, undoing the fastener and guiding the zipper down. Admiring his work, his fingers move up, tracing the thin straps of the gown and gently leading one off her shoulder. The gown shifts slightly as she turns to face him, only one strap remaining. Their eyes reflect their longing.

Everly raises her chin to him, the moonlight bathing her features in silver and shadows. Standing so close, she breathes in his scent, snow and pine and comfort. Heat flows between them as Jackson traces his fingers slowly along her arm. They both hold their breath as the red satin pools on the floor, burning bright in the darkness.

Her body pulses quietly in front of him, her eyes admiring the places her hands yearn to feel. Jackson's hand grazes up the smooth plane of her arm, igniting every nerve in a prickling frenzy as his fingers trace delicate patterns along her skin.

Her hands shift restlessly, eager to reach for him. Finally reaching her neck, his fingers brush back a few loose strands of hair silvered by the radiant moon. His breath is warm, comforting, and invigorating as he whispers in a low growl, "I've missed you, Lele." His lips graze her ear, and her knees threaten to buckle.

The waves of his hair hide his face, but the muscles in his arms and torso visibly tense as he awaits a response. Everly reaches out to caress his face, the stubble on his chin stimulating her fingertips. A wash of calm and happiness flows through him at her touch.

Looking up at his shadowed figure, her eyes glistening in the light, she whispers, "I've missed you too, Jax."

Chapter 49

Buzz... Buzz... Buzz.... Everly groans, shifting her comforter aside as she reaches for her phone.

"Hello?" She drags out the word.

"Did I just wake you up?" The voice sounds stunned.

"Yes," she responds bluntly.

The voice on the other line snickers. "Never thought there'd be a day where I woke up before you, Ev."

"Ta da," she mocks. Looking around, she sees no sign of Athena, who would never have let her sleep in this late. "Everything okay, Joce?"

Lazily pushing the covers aside, she pads into the kitchen to see Jackson seated by the window with a steaming cup of coffee and Athena curled up in a little orange ball on his lap. "Good morning," he smiles as she approaches.

"Everything's great, but who was *that?"* Jocelyn shrieks on the other end of the phone.

A giddy smile plasters itself on her face and her unoccupied hand comes up to cover her rosy cheek. "I'll tell you later," is all she can manage to say.

"Ooooo," Jocelyn coos excitedly. "You better tell me everything!"

"Bye, Joce," she laughs into the phone.

"Have fuuuuun," she drags out the words teasingly. "I love you."

"Love you more." Everly hangs up the phone, immediately flings it across the room, and flops into the chair across from Jackson, basking in the morning light.

"How'd you sleep?" he asks, passing a steaming mug of coffee across the table to her.

"I slept great." Gripping the mug in both hands, she holds it just below her nose, blowing lightly, then inhales the revitalizing aroma before taking a sip. Gazing up from her mug, she watches as Athena stretches out on his lap, her white and orange fur disheveled from sleep. "I see you stole my snuggle buddy."

"What can I say? She and I enjoyed the couch very much."

"I'm so glad," Everly smirks, taking another sip of coffee.

"Except she kept trying to nurse from me."

Everly nearly spits her coffee across the table. "No she did not!" She coughs on the liquid in her throat.

Jackson chuckles at her. "No, she didn't."

"I knew it! Liar," she laughs, shaking her head.

"But she did make plenty of biscuits for us." His smile lights up the room more than the sunshine somehow, and Everly gets lost in it for a moment before speaking.

"Yes, she's a very good baker. Did you save any for me?"

"Absolutely not. We worked hard on those biscuits. They were all for us."

Everly gasps sarcastically. "Rude."

Warm winter sun leaks through the frost-edged windows and bathes them in its yellow glow. Gazing over at her, his eyes trace along every beautiful detail. The way her hair is teased and tousled on one side showing which side she sleeps on. Perfectly rosy cheeks that glow with the warmth of rest. How her eyes have yet to fully open with the weight of sleep still lingering upon them. Every inch. Every detail. As beautiful as before. Somehow even more so.

⁕

Propping the door open, Everly enters the conference room with her perfectly organized materials. The frosted panes of glass obscure the figures walking past as she sets a folder at each seat and connects her laptop to the large screen at the end of the long table. A knock on the door draws her attention from the screen. "Am I interrupting?" Jackson stands half in the doorway smiling at her. Everly shakes her head and busies herself with the remote. Flipping up the doorstop with his foot, he walks towards her as the door gradually shuts behind him.

"You're early," she says without looking up.

"Yeah, I thought I'd see if you needed any help." He reaches around her to take the remote, setting it down on the table and taking her hands in his.

"Jax…" She pulls away. "This was a mistake." Walking around the other side of the table, she straightens the folders in front of each seat labeled with each investor's name and title.

"Lele," he starts.

"We'll be working together for the next six months, at least. So it's a conflict of interest and just unprofessional."

He stares at her, though her eyes avoid him. "That's not why." She looks up at that. "Have dinner with me this weekend. I'll answer any questions you have. Anything you want to know."

"Jax," she sighs, "I have to get ready for this meeting."

"Just think about it. Okay?" She nods, and he straightens the rest of the folders as he walks out, propping the door open as he leaves.

⁕

"Delivery for Everly—"

"I'll take that. Thank you," Grace grabs the large bouquet of flowers from the delivery person, inhaling their aroma as she waltzes them over to Everly's desk.

Clasping her hair back in her favorite claw clip, Everly pauses when she sees the flowers and note on her desk, her hands still in her hair.

"So?" Grace scutters across the space between their desks in her rolly chair.

"So, what?" Everly asks without looking at her.

"Are you going to go tonight?" She bumps the back of her chair into Everly's legs. She whirls around with a grimace.

"I don't know." The note feels like a weight in her hand.

"Ev, this could be your chance to answer the questions that have been eating at you for years. Even if he's not the person you once knew, maybe he's someone much better."

Flipping open the card, she reads the words silently. One sentence. One sentence that convinces her to hope for the best but expect the worst.

⁕

Shooting up from his seat, Jackson stands tall as the hostess escorts Everly to his table. He pulls out the chair for her and eases her close to the table. "I'm so glad you came," he smiles, moving around to take his seat.

"Jax, this place is so fancy." Her eyes shift around, taking in all the elegantly dressed diners, then back to her jeans and sneakers. Even Jackson looks nice in a button-down and dress pants.

"It's not *that* fancy," he argues.

"The waiters look like butlers," she whispers aggressively across the table, and he snickers. "There's a pizza shop a block over. Can we just go there?" Jackson can sense her discomfort and insecurity growing as people start to look in their direction. "Please?" she urges.

"Yeah, of course." They make their way towards the exit, Everly keeping her gaze low, away from judgmental stares. Jackson pauses behind her, glancing at all the critical onlookers. Selecting one particularly judgy-looking man in a suit and tie, Jackson makes direct eye contact with him as he rips his shirt wide open, sending buttons flying across the room. The witnesses gasp as he walks towards the exit, his torso completely exposed. Everly turns to see the wait staff rush over to usher him out the door.

The surprisingly temperate evening air still brushes goosebumps along his bare skin as he straightens up, his abs aching from their relentless laughter. "What was that?" She chokes on her laughter, leaning against the brick wall.

Jackson simply smiles at her joy as he attempts to close his shirtfront with little success. "You know," he smirks at her, still trying to catch her breath between laughs. "I need to start wearing cheaper clothes when we hang out."

"True," she agrees. "I'll buy the pizza." Turning on her heel, she starts off down the street, Jackson taking a few running steps to catch up.

Resting back on the cracked maroon cushion of the narrow booth, Everly grapples with her drooping slice of pizza. Cheese stretches out from the slice as she moves to put it on her plate until Jackson frees her of the tether. Using her tongue, she scoops up each inch of cheese until it's all stuffed in her mouth. Jackson takes a bite of his own piece, mimicking her exactly. Swallowing hard, he looks at her intently. "Okay, Lele. Ask me anything."

Her mouth dries, and her brain empties. Ten years of unanswered questions lost in a second. "I don't know where to start."

"Then start at the beginning."

And so she does. From the moment he left, the unanswered texts and phone calls, to the day he found out his mom was sick and when he'd first called her again.

"The day of the funeral…" The words catch in her throat. "Where were you?"

Jackson drops his eyes from her gaze and looks at his fingers as he folds his napkin over and over. Pushing his plate forward, he finally looks her in the eyes. "Rehab." Everly's breath catches, and her chest ceases to expand as he continues. "I didn't even know she had died." He pauses, clearing his throat. "Right before she got sick, she kicked my dad out. Things had been bad for a while, and one day she finally had enough. She packed up our things, and we moved back east. That's when I first reached out," he added. Everly's heart stops beating altogether as she gawks in disbelief.

"I'm so sorry."

"Don't be, Lele. You have nothing to be sorry for. There was no reason for you to have wanted to speak to me after what I did to you." Their labored breathing is the only sound between them until the waitress comes over to refill their water glasses.

"Okay," he exhales. "After we moved, my mom and I were constantly fighting. I guess I took after my dad in that regard. I stopped coming home and spent weeks and weeks on peoples' couches getting wasted or high. But when I finally did come home again, she tried to tell me. That she was sick. But I slammed the door in her face before she could say anything." A quiet sob escapes his throat as he sits up and crosses his arms over his chest. "I left. It was another month before I came home, and when I did I saw what was happening to her. She was so weak. Her hair was falling out. The house was a mess. She could barely walk up the stairs. And yet she still welcomed me home with open arms." Everly's tears flow down her cheeks and sprinkle her jeans as she moves to sit beside him, her hands reaching to soothe and comfort him as he continues.

"Her doctor called. She said the treatment wasn't working. I lost it. I left that night to drown myself in whatever booze I could find and… and I tried to find you."

Everly's hands freeze for a moment as she processes his words.

"After that," he presses on, "I just… I just really messed up, Lele." He collapses into her, shaking and sobbing.

"Jax, it's okay." She rubs his back in wide circles. "You don't have to tell me."

"I…" he breathes, "I need to." Wiping at his eyes and nose, he reclines into Everly's open arms. "I need you to know."

She nods, still rubbing him comfortingly. "Okay." Looking around at the wait staff and other patrons, Everly says, "Let's get out of here." He nods, and they walk into the night, allowing the cool air to cleanse their lungs and dry their tears.

⁂

Collapsing onto the long sectional in his impressive lofted living room, he watches the ceiling fan spin before starting again. "That was the worst night of my life. I drove home completely obliterated, covered in blood and paranoid, and despite all of that, she wanted to help *me.*

"But she told me she needed to go to the hospital, so she drove us. I wasn't in any state to question it, and when we got there I ran in yelling for anyone to help her." He pauses. "She just shook her head at me with a sad smile.

"I wish I could take back everything from that day." His voice shakes. "I've never said such vile things to anyone in my life. I just remember looking around and realizing where we were and what was happening. I turned and shoved her so hard into the pavement that it broke her arm. I heard the snap of her fragile bone." Jackson hunches forward, sobs escaping him in painful gasps. "Before they sedated me and dragged me away, she said something I'll never forget." His breath catches raggedly.

"What did she say, Jax?"

Exhaling a deep sigh, he speaks quietly, "She said, 'I love you, my boy. Endlessly and above all else, I love you. Be good for me and have hope.'

"Those were the last words she ever said to me. They took her in to set her arm… and she never left the hospital."

"My dad picked me up when I was discharged. I hadn't seen him since we left and hadn't seen anyone else I knew since I got in. We drove to my mom's house in silence. When I walked in the house everything was the same. Nothing had changed. Not a single thing.

"I remember walking in and calling for my mom. I walked through all the rooms looking for her. Her car was in the driveway, her shoes were by the door. My dad just stared at me, and for the first time in my entire life, I saw my dad cry.

"We sat on the front steps and cried as he told me everything. They had a funeral for her, the way she would have liked, with bright colors and happy music. She begged my dad not to tell me because she was afraid I'd relapse. I almost did when I went upstairs to pack a bag and found a leftover stash, but I just heard her voice in my head saying, 'Be good for me and have hope.' And now, everything I do is for her."

Chapter 50

"Jax, where are we going?" Everly calls out over the blustery wind coming through the windows of his car.

"You suck at surprises," he teases.

"What's that supposed to mean?" She grapples with her wild hair as it flies around her in vicious swirls of ash-blonde and gold. The wind dies down as he puts on his flashers and pulls off to the side of the road, only expansive fields of flowers as far as the eye can see. "What are you doing?" Everly asks as she ties her hair up in a messy knot atop her head.

"Wait here." He smiles before hopping out of the car and jogging into the field of wildflowers.

She watches as he meticulously collects flowers, arranging them into a perfectly disorganized bouquet just for her. Leaning out the window, she inclines her head to look him in the eyes as he holds the flowers in front of her. Lost in those honey-hued eyes, she barely pays attention to the flowers in his hand. "Close your eyes."

"Why?" she protests.

He rolls his eyes at her. "Just do it."

"Fine." She sits still, crossed arms resting on the passenger side door, waiting impatiently for whatever it is Jax has in mind.

Holding the flowers up to her with one hand, he uses the other to support himself against the hood of the car. "Now, smell the flowers."

She smiles and takes a deep inhale. Then another one.

He watches as her nose scrunches with each sniff and licks his full lips before lowering the flowers and pressing his warm smile to hers. Everly pulls back, startled, then leans into the newly familiar comfort of his mouth. Her hands move through his hair and pull him closer.

Finally leaning back, he stares down at her, into those clear blue eyes stunningly bright in the spring sunlight, and revels in the joy on her face.

The water mirrors the orange clouds and blooming trees as they perch on the big rock, hand in hand. Birds glide on the cool air and dance among the treetops in search of a place to settle. At the lake house on the hill above them, the wall of windows reflects the deepening sunset colors.

"I never thought we'd be here again." She rests her head gently against his shoulder, nudging her nose intimately against his smooth skin.

"I did."

She straightens up. He continues to gaze out over the water, that perfect dimple and crooked smile lingering after his words.

"Really?" she asks.

"Really." He turns to her, and she sees that the orange clouds accentuate the honeyed gold of his eyes. Those eyes trace delicately along her face, admiring each freckle, each smile line and scar, every single inch of the girl he's loved his whole life.

"What?" Her nose scrunches as she watches his eyes admire her.

Peeling his gaze away, he looks back over the water. "Do you think that still holds weight?" He points up to the battered rope swing that sways lazily in the evening breeze.

Golden waves shake back and forth as she starts to laugh. "No one's touched that since the last time our families were here. I bet it snaps the moment you pull on it," she teases.

"I'll take that bet," Jackson counters, standing up and dusting off his pants. "What do I get when I win?"

"Well, I know I'm right."

"Then you won't mind betting something big." A devious smile spreads across his face.

"Like what?"

"Hmm," he strokes his chin as he ponders. "I'll decide after I win."

"Well, I know exactly what I want when *I* win." She laughs before she can get it out. "You get to give Athena a bath."

Jackson rakes through his hair. "Oh god. That's a hefty bet."

"Better hope that thing holds up." She looks past him with a wide grin at the tattered rope fibers.

Jumping from one rock to the next, he lands on the lofty boulder. Taking the rope in his hand he pulls at it, assessing the likelihood of having to bathe a feisty cat. He looks back at Everly, her arms wrapped around her knees, watching. Without hesitation, he takes a running leap out over the water. The tree above creaks its protest but holds strong as he swings out and back, his feet scuttering to a triumphant stop on the boulder.

"Ha!" he exclaims. Everly gapes at the rope, astounded by its stubborn strength. Taking hold of the rope again, he springs off the boulder higher than before. Everly watches as he reaches peak height then hears the snap. Jackson yelps as he plummets into the frigid water. Coming up for air, he whips his hair out of his eyes and hears Everly's sweet breathless laughter. His favorite sound.

The water ripples the sky's vibrant reflection across the lake as he swims to shore. "I win," Everly roars.

"No way!" Jackson protests. "It did not break the first time."

Everly springs to her feet. "But it did break!"

"You weren't specific when you made the bet," he counters.

"Neither were you!" Everly crosses her arms over her chest as she looks him up and down, his soaked clothes clinging to his toned body. "All right, fine. Maybe we both lose then."

"Or maybe we both win," he offers.

She nods at him, "Yeah. I like that."

He looks at her, admiring how the setting sun casts its orange glow on her freckled skin and blonde hair. His crooked smile appears as he looks down at his soggy clothes and then back to her. "Well, you're going to hate this." He lunges for her at full speed, but she dodges him and sprints up the hill towards the house.

"Jax!" she squeals. He catches up with ease and wraps his dripping arms around her. Pulling her into him, he kisses her smile then her cheeks and neck and forehead. Everly returns his kisses as the sun drops beyond the horizon. A brisk breeze raises goosebumps across their damp skin as they gaze into each other's eyes.

Smiling up at him, staring into those dark eyes, she sees the boy she grew up with, the boy who was always there for her, the one who helped her when she struggled with homework, the one who was her trusted ear and shoulder to cry on, her first kiss. Her first love.

"What?" he asks, meeting her adoring gaze.

"I love you."

⁂

"Jax," Everly whisper-shouts as he pulls her into the hallway, his lips eager to taste hers. "Jax, we can't do this here." Despite her best efforts, a gleeful giggle escapes her as his hands grip her waist, and she scans the hall for any coworkers.

Pressing his cheek against her, he growls into her ear. "Shh, or we'll get caught."

Grabbing his torso, she swings them around, pressing his back to the wall. Standing on her tiptoes, her mouth grazes his neck and moves towards his ear. "Then don't make a sound…"

⁂

Just like those warm summer nights when they were young, he races over and greets her with three knocks. Three knocks for their past, present, and future.

The door swings open and Jackson storms through, pulling Everly up into his arms, her legs locking around his torso and her lips finding his smile. Jackson kicks the door shut with his foot, moving into the kitchen to rest her on the countertop. "How are you more beautiful?" he ponders, tucking her hair behind her ear.

"More beautiful than what?" Everly asks, nuzzling into his hand.

"More beautiful than all the days before. More beautiful than the sunrises over the mountains and the sunsets over the seas."

Everly gazes at him utterly stunned, her cheeks threatening to seize from smiling so wide. "Jax," she breathes out.

"Lele," he begins, pressing his smile to her cheek. "Move in with me." Her eyes widen at the demand that's actually a plea, and somehow her smile broadens even more. Before she can answer, he interjects. "You kind of have to say yes. This was my end of the bargain."

Her brows crinkle. "What bargain?"

"Our bet. I held up my end. I'm pretty sure Athena gave me some new scars after tubby time." He grins at the fuzz ball curled up by the sofa. "Now it's your turn to hold up your end."

Everly loosens her legs around his waist. "That was months ago. You knew then?"

"Lele, I've always known. It's always been you. It will always be you." Her legs and arms wrap tightly around him, and she breathes him in as she nestles into his neck. "So, is that a yes?" he asks through the veil of her hair.

"Of course."

⁕

"What are you looking at, weirdo?" Her eyes shoot up to catch him staring.

"Everything." He smiles as she stretches out her stiff muscles, Athena doing the same.

Her squinting eyes fight against the morning light seeping in through their large industrial windows. "We need curtains in here!" She protests against the brightness by pulling the covers over her head.

"I made breakfast," he offers, hoping to entice her.

"Is there coffee?" she asks, her voice muffled under the sheets.

"Of course."

She throws off the comforter, her hair staticky and disheveled, to find him holding out a steaming mug of the revitalizing brew.

⁕

"Can you feed Athena before you leave?" Everly calls as she grabs her coffee mug and purse by the door.

Jackson stumbles out of the bedroom trying to pull his pants the rest of the way up. "Yeah, I will. Do you still need me to bring those documents into our meeting later?"

Everly watches as he feeds his belt through the loops and fumbles with the buckle. "No, I grabbed them. Okay, I have to run, or I'll be late."

"And whose fault is that?" He watches as she pauses, turns on her heel, and saunters towards him.

Coming in close enough for him to smell her perfume, she whispers in his ear, "You didn't seem to mind." She grabs hold of his belt buckle, tightening it the rest of the way, presses a kiss to his cheek, and strides out the door.

⁕

"It's been great working with you, Everly. I hope to do business with you in the future."

"I do as well, sir." Everly shakes his hand firmly, then shakes the hand of each of his associates as they file out of the conference room. Jackson is the last at the table, collecting his paperwork and stuffing it into his briefcase.

Everly walks over to his chair as the frosted glass door slowly closes behind the last associate. "It's been a pleasure working with you," she says, holding out her hand to him and leaning against the table's edge.

"The pleasure is all mine." He pulls her hand to his lips and gazes up at her. "Now, if I may be so forward." He stands and clears his throat. "I have been admiring you for some time now, and it would be an absolute honor to take you out sometime." She smiles, her chin now lifted to look up at his honey-hued eyes. "Say, this evening? Our place? For exquisitely crafted Italian?"

"Oh, how romantic." Everly beams and waves an imaginary fan near her face. "I'd be delighted."

Jackson slaps his knee. "Hot damn!" His shout rings through the enclosed room, no doubt escaping it as well to startle her coworkers.

"Keep it down, weirdo!" He smirks at her reddening cheeks and presses a cooling kiss to her skin. "So, spaghetti and frozen meatballs then?"

"Yup," he says before kissing her mouth and pulling her into his arms. "You did a great job with this account, Lele. I'm really proud of you."

"Thanks, Jax. I'm really proud of me too."

"Okay, I'll see you at home." He kisses her forehead before straightening his shirt and walking towards the door. Turning with his hand on the door, he looks back to her with that perfectly crooked smile. "I love you."

"I love you, too."

Chapter 51

September

"...And then you'll both recite your vows. You'll repeat after me and exchange rings. Everything's perfect, and then *ta-da* you may kiss your bride." Grace squeals as Caleb reaches around and pulls her up into his arms, their sweet smiles pressing against one another's.

"Save it for tomorrow, you animals," Everly teases.

Grace turns to her wedding party, beaming. "Thank you, everyone, for being a part of this. I wish I had better words to express how much you all mean to me and what it means to have you be part of our special day." Her voice breaks as tears begin to well in her eyes. Caleb's long fingers comfort hers. Looking into her eyes he smiles, then surveys the room full of their friends and family and finishes her thought for her. "We love you all dearly. Now, let's get some food! I'm starving," he laughs.

*

"That was such a nice rehearsal dinner." Everly's voice carries into the kitchen from the bedroom as she undresses. "Don't you think?"

Jackson sits at the counter, unconsciously wringing his fingers. He's done this since he was a kid, an indication that he's anxious about something. The steady beat of his heart thrums loudly in his ears, drowning out her voice. Athena rubs her whiskers affectionately against his legs, bringing the present moment into focus.

Everly's bare feet pad across the chilly tile floor. From behind she drapes her arms over his shoulders, her chin resting against the base of his neck. "What's wrong?"

"Sorry." He swivels around in the barstool to face her, the thrifted seat squeaking in protest. "Just not feeling that great."

"Can I do anything for you?" Her fingers intertwine behind his neck as her legs straddle him. A warm flush washes over his body as she settles onto his lap. Her seductive smile presses against his neck, breathing him in, and she trails her lips against his skin. A low moan escapes his throat as she nibbles on his ear. She squeals as he propels himself forward, hugging her against him, and strides towards the bedroom.

⁕

"Jax, we gotta get ready," Everly calls out to him.

He snickers as he pours his cup of coffee. "*You* need to get ready, Lele. It'll take me all of five minutes to change."

"Oh, shut up," she giggles as she sits atop her vanity, feet in the sink, leaning into the mirror to perfect her makeup. The first time he walked in on her in this ridiculous position, he ended up on the floor laughing like a hyena. She was a sight to behold—hunchbacked on the countertop with wild hair half falling from her bun and mouth gaping open as she applied her mascara. He loves to recount that memory to friends whenever he can, which usually results in a nice firm punch in the arm from Everly.

Jackson settles onto the sun-warmed cushions of the sofa in the living room and gazes out the industrial windows. Little swirls of steam dance along the rim of his coffee cup.

Athena lies lazily in a patch of sunshine on the rug, stretching out her body in an attempt to wake up. Her eyes squint open for a moment looking at Jackson, then close blissfully as she curls back into a sleepy ball of fur.

Everly hurriedly walks out into the kitchen, attempting to put her earrings in as she goes. "Okay, do I have everything I need?" Jackson knows it's a rhetorical question she's asking herself. His smile creases his cheeks as he presses the warm mug to his lips.

The knots in his stomach ease slightly as the hot liquid settles. "Lele," he calls out to her. "Lele," he calls again, hoping his voice can be heard over her own racing thoughts.

"Yeah, hi, what's up?" she sputters. She's pouring a cup of coffee in the kitchen wearing only her bra, thong, makeup and glasses. She's a beautiful mess. Her hair is tied up in a disheveled messy bun, and her glasses fog up as she takes a sip of her drink. His words catch in his throat and retreat before he can say them. "I, uh…" he shakes his head, shifting thoughts. "You look beautiful."

Her cheeks lift into a beaming smile as the fog on her glasses dissipates. "I feel like a mess," she giggles.

"Oh, you are," he teases. She scoffs and strides over to punch him in the arm. He flinches defensively, laughing. "A hot mess though!"

"All right, I think I'm almost ready. We still have an hour until I have to meet Grace, but we can always leave early and then I can make sure everything is going according to plan and on time and—"

"Everything is going to be fine. Just sit down and relax for a little bit. Okay?"

Exhaling deeply, she sinks into the comfort of her favorite armchair. "Okay," she breathes.

Sitting in blissful silence, they soak up the morning sunshine, recharging their social batteries for the day. Jackson leans forward, setting his mug on the rustic coffee table. Everly notices his nervous tics of wringing his fingers and tapping his foot. "What's wrong, Jax?"

Tap. Tap. Tap.

He inhales deeply, filling his lungs. "I need to tell you something," he exhales.

Everly's stomach turns over. A burning sensation of dread creeps along her skin. *Nothing good ever comes from that sentence.* She sits, waiting.

He doesn't speak. Her eyes search for his but they're burning holes into the floor.

"I could tell something's wrong. For weeks, you've been quieter. Secretive." She looks at Athena to calm herself. "Just tell me, Jax. Whatever it is. No more secrets."

"No more secrets," he repeats, his eyes finally finding hers. "I can't go to this wedding."

Everly cocks her head, confused. "Why not?"

"I don't feel good—" he starts. "I don't feel good about being there."

"What do you mean? What are you not telling me, Jax?"

He looks away again, his head hanging down. "Lele, I can't hide this from you anymore."

That sense of dread washes over her again, "Okay."

"But I need to say all of this without you interrupting me. Otherwise I won't get through it. Okay?"

"...okay."

There's a long, torturous pause before he begins to recount the story that will shatter her heart all over again.

Alcohol-fueled panic quickens each step as he moves about the room in search of her. The one person who might know how to comfort him, who might know just what to say.

I need to see you. *He sends the message as he shoves past a group in the kitchen creating some giant cocktail he'll likely come back for.*

Who is this? *the phone reads.*

There. Looking up he sees a long-limbed brunette drag her across the room. He'd recognize that face anywhere. He'd know it by touch if he were blind. Each step brings him closer to her, her headstrong voice protesting against the game.

"Plus, I don't have a partner," she calls to her friend across the table. Jackson pushes past another group when he *steps in front of him. Everly doesn't turn immediately when he volunteers but waits. Jackson steps back from the human wall in front of him, retreating and hiding among the other partygoers before she can identify him.*

Stupid, stupid! She probably wouldn't even recognize me. She probably hates me. I wouldn't blame her if she punched me the moment she saw me. Fuck this. *Jackson storms into the kitchen, where a group of guys is doing keg stands and funnels. "My turn," he says, grabbing a funnel and allowing them to pour beers down the tube as they chant like barbarians in the Colosseum.*

Music blares through the house and the colorful lights spin, moving in uncoordinated arcs. Everly. Where is she? He stumbles through the kitchen doorway towards the ping pong table. "It's almost midnight!" someone yells, and he's cut off by a stampede of people rushing over to watch the ball drop on TV. Squinting hard, Jackson caroms off a body and collides into a bystander, trying to reorient himself.

"My bad," he slurs.

"Hey, fuck off, dude." The guy shoves him, sending him to his knees on the sticky floor.

No, *he tells himself,* I gotta find her. *Jackson snarls a curse at the guy before continuing towards the table. Just in time to watch Everly lead that tall asshole down the hall, handcuffed together.* What the fuck.

Resting against the door jamb next to a hole kicked in the drywall, he grabs a bottle of water, downing it but spilling most of it on his shirt. Lele, *he thinks again, urging himself down the hall.*

The dark hallway is full of kissing strangers and secretive dealers. Jackson staggers to the door, preparing to face her after years of silence. He trips forward, knocking on the door and awaiting an answer. Silence. Seconds pass like lifetimes as he sways on his feet waiting for her to open the door.

"I should have known," he spits. Shuffling further down the dark hallway, he nods at the guys loitering in the corner. "You got anything good?"

Flying down the street, windows open, he's invincible. His hair whips in dark spirals as he stretches both hands out the sunroof, hollering into the night as fireworks erupt above the barren highway. The colors explode in dazzling displays across the horizon until the looming clouds lower and extinguish them with sudden sheets of vicious rain.

Jackson curses, rolling up his windows and closing the sunroof but not before getting generously soaked. The empty highway blurs beyond his useless headlights as the car hurtles forward, and the euphoria of his high battles against the rage in his heart. The speedometer needle climbs as he skids and slides through the pouring rain, pounding against the wheel in frustration, racing towards the changing light.

The world slows before him as his foot hesitates a moment too long to hit the brake. The acrid smoke of burning rubber fills the air, and the cars collide violently. Shrieks drown out the blaring music as glass shatters, airbags deploy, and metal twists, and the t-boned car spins out across the pavement, disappearing off the road into a deep ditch.

Blood thrums through his veins and from a shallow cut above his eyebrow, and adrenaline overpowers the drugs in his system. "Oh god." He sits in his car, too stunned to move, the reality of what just happened settling in. The rain pelts the earth more forcefully than he's ever seen before. "Fuck!" he screams, beating against the steering wheel.

Sitting for interminable, dread-filled moments, he contemplates driving away. How could anyone have survived that? But something nags at him, won't let him start the car. Looking at himself in the mirror, he wipes away the blood from his brow and takes a deep breath before racing out into the storm and sliding down into the treacherously slippery ditch.

The vicious downpour is nothing compared to the outpouring of blood-curdling screams coming from the mangled car. Alive, good. *He exhales sharply, wiping his sopping hair from his eyes.*

The doors are pinned on either side by the steep dirt banks and kicking in the front windshield could do more harm than good. Crawling carefully along the trench, he reaches the back of the car, the shrieks filling his ears.

Reaching through the shattered rear window, he feels a desperate hand grab hold of his wrist, and he pulls with every ounce of will he can muster until the girl shifts towards him, her screams suddenly silenced. Dragging her limp body through the freezing rain, he rests her on the pavement, noticing the long gash down her calf before stumbling back to help the others.

Diving into the car through the rear window scores his hands and forearms with cuts as he reaches in to untangle the passenger from his seatbelt. It takes more strength than he knows he has to yank him out of the overturned car, his leg severely mangled.

The two passengers lie unconscious and bleeding on the pavement as Jackson races back for the driver. The rain lightens to a sprinkle as he crawls into the car again, glass crunching under him. Blindly searching for the seat belt buckle, he comes face to face with the man. The young man. Probably only a few years older than him. His black hair and light brown skin drip red. His eyes are slightly open with a fixed gaze, and no pulse moves below his sharp jawline.

Jackson reaches over to check, his fingers searching anywhere for a pulse. Nothing.

"No, no, no!" he shouts. He slaps the unmoving man across the face, bruising his hand on the high cheekbone. Once. Twice. Deep, guttural sobs erupt from him as he collapses on his back onto the bloody shards of glass, the seats of the car above him. Wiping the tears and rain from his face, he looks at the stranger once more, his hair dripping blood, before crawling out into the night.

Skittering up the embankment, Jackson holds a shattered cell phone in his hands. He looks at the overturned car and the bleeding bodies on the road. He looks to his car, then back at them. His mind whirls in nauseating loops of intoxicated reasoning as he dials 911, throws the phone into the ditch, and speeds away.

"That was the night my mom took me to rehab." He stops talking, unable to look her in the eyes.

Everly sits stoically, tears streaming down her cheeks. "So… Grace?" He nods. "And her brother?" He lowers his head further but nods.

"Lele—"

"Don't!" she barks. "Don't you fucking dare." She storms out of the room and slams their bedroom door. Athena jumps at the noise and sprints behind the long curtains.

Trying to catch his breath, Jackson inhales sporadically as his throat and eyes burn against his body's urge to sob. He rakes his fingers through his hair in frustration.

A few minutes later Everly pounds into the kitchen, her makeup newly perfected and her things ready to go. Jackson jumps up from the couch. He can't manage a single step before she holds up a hand. "Don't you fucking come near me." She breathes deeply, trying to compose herself. "Don't even think about coming to this wedding, or I'll kill you myself." She suppresses the urge to cry again. "Don't be here when I get back." She turns on her heel and slams the door with such force that the framed photo of them falls off the wall and shatters.

Chapter 52

The doors swing open, and the guests erupt into cheers, their sparklers crackling on either side of Grace and Caleb as they beam at one another. The ambient light casts a beautiful golden glow on her bronze skin and reflects in her dark eyes, perfectly contrasted by her elegant white dress. Caleb's light freckled skin warms in the glowing light, and his long pale fingers disappear in Grace's silky black hair as he dips her back, kissing her deeply.

The world around them recedes as they cherish this moment. Music fades, sparklers dim, and they are lost in each other's eyes. It's not a happy ending but a magical beginning neither of them had ever imagined.

MISSED CALL
MISSED CALL
MISSED CALL

Everly's skin burns where her white knuckles grip the phone. Antonne approaches from behind her, grabbing both of her shoulders. "Shit, Antonne! I almost peed myself," Everly shrieks louder than intended. Tossing the phone back into her purse, she allows him to pull her onto the dance floor. Sadie, Raven, and Jocelyn lead a conga line serpentining around the pillars of the venue.

"Typical, right?" Antonne turns to Everly.

"Ridiculous." She rolls her eyes, smiling, before they both hop in to join the shenanigans.

Ring. Ring. Ring. "Lele, please pick up."

"Hi, you've reached Everly. Please leave your name and number, and I'll get back to you as soon as I can. Thanks. At the tone, please record your message, then hang up, or dial one for more options." *BEEP.*

"Lele. I love you. Every day of my life I have loved you. I want a chance to talk this out. I hope—"

*

"In case you don't know me, I'm the reason all of you are here tonight," she giggles into the microphone. "My name is Everly, and I set up these two adorable lovebirds."

"Liar," Grace calls from her table.

"All right, all right! But I heavily influenced them getting together by inviting them to the same game night. Anyway, the first time Grace and I met, she threw coffee in my face—"

"Also a lie!" she giggles from her seat.

"This is *my* speech, Grace. Shhh!" The crowd laughs at their banter. "Caleb and I met in college. He's always been kind and caring and really bad at beer pong."

"You know I have a bad wrist!" he calls out.

Everly gestures towards them, "See, neither of them can stand to be wrong." The crowd roars. "Once I got to know Grace a little more, I tried to set her up on a date—with someone else." *Booooo!* "I know! I know! But she said she'd already met someone. It took forever for her to finally tell me it was Caleb. But when she did, it all made sense. I've never met two people who connected so easily. From the first moment they met, it seemed special, and as I thought about it more, I realized that Caleb was the only person who could give Grace the kind of love she deserved, and she was the only one capable of gifting him that same kind of deep, meaningful love in return.

"And I kid you not when I say I screamed so *everyone* on campus could hear when I found out they were officially together. I can still remember Grace's face turning bright red. From then on they've been inseparable.

"Now, I could end my speech here and say, 'then they lived happily ever after,' but I want to share with you how I knew these two were meant for each other.

"First of all, anyone who can deal with living with Grace deserves an award," she laughs. "But really, watching them grow and learn and care about each other has been incredible. Grace and I have been working for the same company for almost a year now, and Caleb comes every single day, without fail, on his lunch break to eat with her.

"And Grace is just as caring for Caleb. It's been interesting to watch because they've really taken the time to talk and learn about how each other receives love. Caleb has figured out that acts of service and quality time are what Grace enjoys most. But Caleb appreciates words of affirmation and gifts. Now, when I tell you there are hundreds of disgustingly cute notes all over their apartment, I am not kidding. But what really gets me is the fact that every single morning Grace writes a little note to him and leaves it by the coffee pot for him to read after she's left.

"Now don't get me started on how much they both love physical touch…" The crowd erupts, and Grace hides her face in Caleb's shoulder.

"I'm just kidding," Everly calls over the noisy crowd. "I'm kidding." She pauses. "Kind of," she smirks and giggles as they blush.

"Anyway," she projects, "they've been building this strong foundation of love and admiration for each other that has led to this day, and I am so grateful to be a part of it.

"I know these two deserve unconditional love that grows as their life together moves forward. This is the type of love and mutual appreciation I hope for all people to find one day.

"I love you both so much. So let us raise a glass to the bride and groom. May their love and appreciation for one another flourish with each passing day. Cheers!" *CHEERS!*

MISSED CALL
MISSED CALL
MISSED CALL

Everly's phone rattles the silverware on the table. Jocelyn leans over to silence it, then notices the multiple notifications. *Why does Jackson keep calling?*

She picks up the phone just as an unrecognized number calls. Something inside her tells her she should answer it, so she does.

Jocelyn shoves her way through the crowd, pushing people out of the way. "Ev!" she yells above the music. "Everly!" She finally spots her twirling around the dance floor with Sadie.

Their eyes meet, and Everly stills.

Chapter 53

"Can someone please tell me what happened!" she cries shrilly as the nurses rush her down the endless hallways.

The cold draft and artificial light seep into her bones as they make their way around a corner. Room 247. The nurses block the entryway before Everly can push past them. Tears swim in her eyes waiting for the right moment to fall. She looks at them, confused and shaking.

"You should prepare yourself," the blonde nurse says sympathetically as she lowers her arm from the doorway. Everly rushes past her, throwing back the curtain.

The breath leaves her body and her knees buckle. Crumbling forward, she grapples for the bedside rail to support herself. The tears fall unchecked now, each one chased by another. "Jax," she whispers. She moves to his side, the one without the swollen black eye and the wound bleeding through the bandages. His chest rises and falls with the machine's rhythmic artificial breath.

The wavy hair that she'd often brush out of his eyes has been shaved and his head wrapped in bandages. Two white casts encase his legs in stiff misery. And his skin. His beautiful olive skin is blighted with deepening purple bruises and oozing lacerations.

One of the nurses lingers off to the side before stepping forward to check his vitals. Everly looks up with swollen eyes. "What happened?" she begs.

The nurse turns to her, that same sympathetic look on her face. "He was in a car wreck, honey." Everly's look urges more details. "The police are doing everything they can to find who did this. He'll get what he deserves when they catch him though. Don't you worry now."

Everly's hand rests gently atop his motionless fingers, her breath eerily matching his new automated one. "Is he going to be okay?" Her voice is barely audible. Her eyes gaze unfocused at the blankets, avoiding his face for fear of breaking down again.

"We had to put him in an induced coma to allow his body to recover. We just have to wait and see for now. I wish I had a better answer for you, sweetheart."

Everly rests her head on the blankets, her fingers gently holding his as she sobs inconsolably into the night.

Chapter 54

Jocelyn walks down the hall with Stella, matching her stride. "Do you know when she last slept?" Stella asks as they take the elevator to the second floor.

"She's been here all day, every day since the accident. Security comes in each night to escort her out and call her a cab. And when she's home, she just lies on the couch staring into space."

"And the accident was five days ago?"

"Six, now. And I fly out tomorrow. I just need to know someone will take care of her when I leave."

"She'll be okay, Jocelyn. Don't forget that you have to care for yourself too. I know you carry the weight of these things for other people, but Everly cannot overcome this if you carry her pain for her." She pauses before they round the corner, putting her hand on Jocelyn's shoulder.

"We all have to face what comes knowing that it's always possible for good to come from the bad." Jocelyn nods in acknowledgment, then turns the corner.

"Hey, Ev." Jocelyn eases into the room quietly. Everly rests in the same chair beside his bed that she's sat, slept, and eaten in for six days now. Her hair falls in ratty knots behind her, and the dark bags beneath her eyes make her look like she's recovering from a fight. Turning dazedly towards them, Everly flashes an emotionless smile. "Stella is here with me. I think you should talk to her."

Stella shifts a chair from the corner to sit by the window, sliding it open. "Everly," she starts, "I'd like you to come sit over here with me." Everly stirs slightly but remains by Jackson's side, her fingers tracing anxious circles on his hand.

A chilling breeze wafts through the window, blowing the curtains and sending goosebumps up Everly's arms. She stands abruptly, striding towards the window and slamming it shut. The force shakes the monitors in the room. "Do you want the cold to kill him?" she snaps.

Stella looks at her, unfazed. "Please. Sit." She gestures to the chair across from her. Jocelyn and Stella nod at each other, and Jocelyn slips quietly out of the room. Everly looks to the door, watching Jocelyn's shadow disappear into the hall, then refocuses on Jackson's chest rising and falling in sickening robotic movements. Her eyes finally drift back to Stella's. "Now, let's talk about Jackson." Everly is crying before she can even cradle her face in her hands. Her wrenching sobs ease only long enough for her to cough out the words.

"I killed him."

Chapter 55

"Everly, there are some very important things I need you to understand and acknowledge. Okay?" Everly nods. "You are not responsible for this tragedy. You cannot change your past, Jackson's past, or Grace's past. But you *are* responsible for how this moment affects you and what you take away from it." Everly sits curled up in the chair across from Stella, hugging her knees into her chest as she nods. "I've asked Grace to come in today." She gestures towards the door. Everly whips around to see Grace lingering silently in the entryway.

Before Grace can say a word, Everly rushes into her arms, sobbing. Breathless cries claw at her lungs. Finally, she pulls back, looking at her friend with dazzling blue and bloodshot eyes. "I'm so sorry, Grace," she whimpers.

Grace cups her friend's face in her hand, her fingers guiding the tears aside. Smiling gently, she says, "You have nothing to be sorry about, Ev." The warmth and comfort of her energy fills the room. "What's over is over. My grandfather taught me this. He said that when something happens, it was meant to be. Everything happens for a reason and serves our development in this life. He always told me that it's better to let go, move forward, and forgive, to embrace the experiences that we've now gained."

Everly shakes her head. "I don't know if I can forgive him for what he did to you."

Grace takes Everly's hand, guiding her to sit on one side of the bed while she moves to sit on the opposite side. Jackson's systematic breathing is the only sound between them for a long moment. "Ev, I want you to talk to him."

"I can't. I can't do it." She looks away from them both, new tears falling.

Grace shifts in her seat, taking Jackson's limp hand in hers as she gazes at his battered face. "I loved my brother. He was my best friend and biggest role model." Everly's stomach tenses, and her body stiffens as she listens. "His life was not cut short by what happened. He lived exactly as long as he was meant to live in this world. What happens is the only thing that can happen. I'm sorry you've lived with this guilt all by yourself. I believe that if you had not been driving that car, someone else would have. So…I forgive you." She holds his hand to her forehead and breathes in deeply. "I forgive you, Jackson." Finally, she lays his hand back on the bed and looks to Everly encouragingly.

Everly takes his hand in hers, trembling at his cold touch. "I'm so mad at you," she breathes out. "I'm so mad that you didn't kiss me sooner. That you left me alone when you moved. That despite everything we shared, you still abandoned me. And that you struggled and suffered alone, knowing that I would have given up anything to help you. That I would have been there in a heartbeat when your mom was sick if you had just asked." Her breath catches in her throat. "I hate that you got in that car. That you were so lost that you risked your life and ruined others in one stupid moment. But I hate you most for making me sit here holding your hand…" Sobbing, she chokes out, "...when you're about to take my heart and leave again."

Grace leans forward, her palms resting over Everly and Jackson's intertwined fingers. "Now," she says, searching for Everly's eyes. When their eyes finally meet, Grace continues. "Forgive him."

Everly looks at Jackson's face for the first time. Newly changed bandages cover his head and the severe cuts on his arms. She studies his face beneath the yellowing bruises and livid healing cuts. "I—" she inhales deeply, sitting up straight in the chair. "You are part of me. Since we were kids holding hands in secret and playing in the tree house, you've been part of me, and I have loved you.

"I love the way you care for others, the way you look at me like I'm the only person in the world, and the way you've inspired me to be the best version of myself I can be.

"I've loved you my whole life, and I will continue to love you. Deeply. Painfully. Hopefully. And…" she stumbles over the words. "And I forgive you. For everything." She takes a deep breath in and holds it for a moment before releasing it, feeling the ever-present weight in her chest finally begin to dissipate. “I forgive you,” she smiles, looking down at him. “And I love you.”

Chapter 56

November 12th

Today was Jackson's funeral. Those are words I never thought I'd say until I was old and gray. Maybe we'd have kids and grandkids next to us to celebrate his life. But here I am, young and lost, burying the love of my life.

November 14th

My boss sent me home from work today. I hate feeling his pity, but I really didn't want to be there anyway.

Athena kept me company while I put on his favorite sweatshirt and cried. It's losing his scent...

November 24th

This morning I was lying on the sofa and Athena walked into the living room with one of Jackson's socks in her mouth. I took it from her and laughed and sobbed for an hour.

December 2nd

I haven't left the apartment in over two weeks. I can't move. I can't eat. I feel like I can't breathe without him here. Grace stopped by the other day. At least I think it was her. I didn't answer the door. I think whatever she left at the door has gone bad by now.

December 7th

Stella called. She left another voicemail. I'm too exhausted to talk to her. All I've managed to do is get lost in the fantasy worlds my bookshelf provides and feed the cat.

December 12th

My dad stopped by today. I forgot I'd given my parents a key to our apartment so he barged right in. He came in the way he always does—with good intentions that falter and result in us both getting upset. He acts like I should be better by now. That I should somehow be able to be happy in a world where my person doesn't exist anymore. But I know he'd collapse and shatter if my mom died. Hypocrite.

Everly hears the door knob jiggle in its socket, a key coaxing the deadbolt that's been locked for weeks. The still air finally moves with the opening swing of the door. "You here, Ev?" her dad calls into the silent apartment.

"Yeah." She raises her arm from the couch. He walks over, straightening things up as he goes, and looks at her over the back of the sectional before settling into her favorite armchair. "I love what you've done with the place," he jokes.

"Dad. I'm not in the mood."

"I know, I'm sorry. How are you, my sweet girl? We haven't heard from you in a while. Haven't seen you for longer."

"I'm fine, Dad."

"Ev—" He shifts forward, leaning on his knees. "You gotta get out of this apartment. You still have his shoes by the door and his coffee mug by the pot. How are you going to get over this while you're holed up here with all of his things?" Everly's eyes shoot up to stare directly into his, mirroring their color.

"Don't you dare barge in here and tell me how to grieve. What do you want from me, Dad? I just buried the love of my life in the fucking ground! How do you just move on from something like that?" She looks around, noticing that she's now standing.

"I just came here to help you get out of this funk, Ev. I'm sorry I don't know how to be helpful to you right now."

Everly rakes her hands through her hair as she paces around the couch. Leaning her palms against the back, she faces her father, furious. "Get out! You have no right to come in here and make me feel bad for grieving. Get the fuck out!"

His blue eyes narrow, locked onto hers. He walks stiffly towards the door. "You'd better think of a good apology before coming home next." The door clicks closed, and the overwhelming silence weighs on her once again.

December 25th

I almost didn't go but I swallowed my pride and apologized to my parents. There were a few times today it almost felt normal. Like I could actually be okay. But then I saw the gift I made for him months ago and I realized that it'll just sit there forever until I have to throw it away.

How do you even begin to do that? To throw away the things that made him smile or the clothes that I'd steal from him or the photos of us together. How do you get rid of those things without getting rid of that person too?

January 2nd

I quit my job today. Being there reminds me of him. Of sneaking around like horny teenagers to make out in a supply closet. He was so spontaneous.

Was. *That hurts to say.*

January 11th

My parents found out I quit and want me to move home for a while. I told them no. We fought about it until I agreed to start seeing Stella again.

But how am I supposed to move past my grief when all Stella will do is poke and prod at it more? It's all I can do to survive each day at this point.

February 4th

I almost couldn't pay rent last month. This apartment is too big for just me and Athena.

February 22nd

I've canceled on Stella three weeks in a row now. Nothing she says or the "homework" she gives me helps. I'm stuck in this cycle of endless despair that crushes me from the moment I wake up to the moment I fall asleep. It's unrelenting. I don't know how much longer I can take this.

March 15th

I keep replaying that argument in my head. If I had just listened and talked to him about it, maybe he never would have gotten in that car. None of this would've happened. It's my fault.

June 26th

I'm being evicted from our apartment. Apparently they don't care if you've been emotionally incapacitated for months on end by the loss of love.

Caleb and Grace said I could stay with them for as long as I need, so today is the first day of touching all of his things. His toothbrush, the book he was so close to finishing, the antique typewriter he found to write love letters with, his goofy little coffee mug with two frogs holding hands on it.

"I can't do it," she whispers to herself in the open room. Athena nudges her lovingly then leaps into the empty box beside her. The wall of windows glows bright with afternoon light, dust particles floating on the stale air like little fairies. Athena bats at the sleeve of his hanging dress shirt and skitters across the floor when she sees her own shadow. "Chill out, you weirdo." She smiles at the cat. The first genuine smile she can remember in months.

Weirdo. That was her nickname for him when they were kids. They'd grown into more adult nicknames like *love*, or *babe*, but *weirdo* always made her happiest because he'd look at her and scrunch his nose and his perfectly crooked smile would appear. He lit up her soul with that smile. It was effortless.

Taking a deep breath, Everly surveys the apartment with its lofted ceiling and open floor plan. Each area littered with their belongings and the memories attached to them. A knock on the door jolts her from the overwhelming thoughts.

Pushing off the ground with significant effort of her stiff muscles, she looks through the peephole.

Everly's heart mends just a little as she opens the door to find all of her friends and family standing with boxes, food, tissues, and smiles. "We're here to help."

And so she spends the rest of the day with her favorite people, minus one, sifting through all their belongings and the remnants of their short time together.

Chapter 57

November 10th

One year. It's been a full year without him here pretending to lose at Scrabble or hold me during the scary parts in movies or tickle me until I was ready to punch him. I just want to talk to him one last time. I don't even know what I'd say. I just want him to know that I'm sorry and that I love him.

⁜

My beloved Jax,

It has been 365 days since you've left me and I've thought about you every single day. You consume each thought and feeling I have.

I wish you knew that I forgive you. That Grace forgives you. I wish I had told you that you are the person I wanted to grow old with. I wanted to sit beside you, all wrinkly and gray, and watch the sunset over the hills from our porch.

I want so desperately for my last words to you to have been kind or loving or hopeful. I have so many regrets in my life, but the biggest will always be giving up too soon. You deserved all my love, unconditionally.

I'll love you till the day I die. So, for now I'll just hope. I'll hope that there is another place, another life where you are existing happily and know that I love and miss you desperately.

Love always,

Lele

⁜

Jamming the final pieces of furniture into the storage unit, Everly steps back to look at the perfectly organized masterpiece of everything she owns. "Thanks for helping, you guys. It means a lot."

"Of course, Ev." Caleb sighs, wiping the sweat from his brow.

"I mean for everything. All these months you've dealt with me at your place. I'll never be able to thank you enough."

Reaching out to pat her arm, Grace tilts her head and smiles at her. "It's been wonderful having you, Ev. But I'm excited for this next chapter of your life."

Everly nods, then pulls on the rope to shut the storage unit door. The sound bounces off the metal walls like captured thunder.

"So, what's the plan?" Caleb asks.

Everly smiles up at him, and the light he'd thought was extinguished sparks to life in her eyes once again.

PART IV

Chapter 58

"A one-way ticket to Spain, please." Everly smiles over the counter at the ticket agent. His name tag reads *Earl.*

"One-way, huh? You headed out for something special?" His deep voice booms as his aged fingers slowly type one letter at a time.

"I hope so," she smiles. A wedding band and modest engagement ring dangle from the chain around his neck.

Earl catches her eye, and his whole face brightens. "My wife." He looks back at the computer screen. "She made it home before I did." Taking up Everly's passport, he scans it and searches through flights.

"I'm sorry for your loss."

"Don't be. I'll see her again, and I'll have plenty to talk to her about." He smiles, and his eyes crinkle at the corners. "What city are you looking to fly into, dear?"

"Whichever has the earliest flight."

"All right then. Looks like you're headed out on the first flight to San Sebastián, Spain."

"Great." Her nerves start to kick in as she hands him her credit card. *Am I really doing this?*

Earl prints out her ticket and double-checks all the information before handing it over to her. His hands reach out to cup hers as she accepts the ticket. His smile somehow eases the growing tension in her chest. "Now, Everly," he says kindly. "Go find what you're looking for, and be fearless in the pursuit of what you deserve." He releases her hands. "Safe travels."

Tears well in her eyes as she hikes up her backpack. "Thank you, Earl."

"God bless you, dear."

⁂

May 16th

I've missed this. The mellow way of life, the culture, and oh god the coffee! I landed around lunchtime so now everything is closed for siesta. I thought walking around the coastal city with my backpack would make me stick out like a sore thumb, but I've seen plenty of people walking past with hiking poles and backpacks. Also, I just found out that they speak the Basque language here more than Spanish. I've never heard of Euskara before but apparently it's unlike any other language in the world. It's fascinating.

Tonight I'll be staying at a cheap hostel by the beach. I have no idea what I'm doing tomorrow. Or the next day. Or the day after that.

I just know that I need to move forward. One step at a time and this is where my heart told me to go.

May 19th

I've met such wonderful people at the hostel I've been staying at. We've spent meals together, I taught them how to surf (the best I could), we even went out in the old town–Parte Vieja–for pintxos and dancing.

It's been ages since I've enjoyed myself that much.

And yet the guilt still eats at me sometimes for having fun without him. Just over a year and a half now. When will I allow myself to be happy again? Will it ever truly be possible?

"It's a five-hundred-mile pilgrimage to Santiago de Compostela that thousands of people trek each year."

"And people do that on purpose?" Everly asks, flabbergasted.

"Absolutely!" Jonas interjects. "This will be my fourth Camino."

"What on earth makes you come back to do it over and over again?"

Combing through his lengthy graying beard, he looks off into the mountainscape looming above the coastal town. "It's an inner journey," he says as he rifles through his bag. Pulling out a thick, leather-bound journal, he continues. "I have taken this book on my treks each time, and I continue to learn about myself. The Camino is more than a trail, it's an experience. It's an opportunity to delve into oneself in search of balance and clarity."

"And you're all doing it? The whole five hundred miles?" Everly glances around the table at the nodding heads of all different ages and colors. "Wow. I admire that."

"You should join us, Everly." Mae encourages, Zahir nodding beside her.

"Oh, I don't know. I'm not prepared for that kind of trek."

"You'd be astounded by the generosity of strangers on your way." Jonas bumps into her shoulder. "I will help you on this journey, my friend. For as far as our paths align."

They all stare at her intently, awaiting a response. She finally caves and exhales an excited, "Fine! Yes, I'll do it." The group erupts in cheers and hollers. *Five hundred miles,* she thinks. *I can do this.*

Day 4:

I can't do this. It's day four, and my legs ache like I've never experienced before. How the hell am I supposed to keep going, especially at this superhuman pace Jonas and Zahir keep setting?

Day 6:

Mae and I said goodbye to our friends this morning. The two of them set out for a different route, but I'm hoping we cross paths again. I only knew them for a short time, but I feel like I've learned more in this past week just talking to them than I've learned in years.

After they left us, Mae and I started on our 18-mile hike for the day. The sunshine made it easier to get up and going. We're taking the northern route, Camino del Norte, which follows the coastline and is exceptionally scenic. The rolling hills seem to go on forever.

Sometimes you go hours or even a whole day without seeing any hikers, and other days the trail is painted with the bright colors of people, each of them seemingly kinder than the last.

Day 10:

Mae and I parted ways today. She's staying in town to visit one of her friends who happens to be in the area. So, today was my first solo trek. I thought I'd feel lonely walking alone, but I enjoy the silence. It's freeing and gives me a chance to reflect. Sometimes I don't even think, I just walk. Each step makes me feel lighter, happier even.

Day 11:

I stopped to have lunch, setting up a little spread along a stone wall next to a field, and I offered some of my snacks to a cute older couple walking by. They were the only people I'd seen all morning.

They took a seat, and we got to talking. Thankfully they spoke some English, and I remembered some of my Spanish, so together we understood each other's broken tongues. Marco and Ana have been married for 52 years this spring and decided to celebrate by hiking a portion of the Camino.

Ana asked me why I was here, and I didn't know what to say to her. As I was trying to think of an answer she took my hands in hers and said, "Life gifts us with hardships to show us the potential good in the darkness." She hugged me tightly before they continued on their trek, hand in hand.

It was a surreal moment for me, and I cried the rest of the hike into town.

Day 17:

The wildflowers cover the rolling hills and brighten up the overcast gloominess. The clouds spat at me all day, but I finally got to warm up by the wood-burning fireplace in this hostel. And I've made a few new friends here.

Morgan is solo backpacking across Europe before heading off to university in England, and Geoff hikes a new portion of the Camino every year.

It's nice not to be alone anymore. The solitude has felt good. Essential, really. But having people to talk to and laugh with is something I've missed. For longer than these past weeks.

They don't know me or my pain, and they probably won't learn much of either. But it's nice to just enjoy each other's company for what it is—simple human connection.

Day 19:

As I walk alongside Morgan I ask myself, "Was I that young and hopeful once? Did I look at the world and see only possibilities?" I wish so badly for her life to live up to those expectations, but at some point the cruel hammer of reality will drop, I'm sure.

Or maybe it doesn't have to. I'm trying to remember what that group of women told me on the beach after I graduated high school. I can't remember their names now. I think it went something like, "When life brings terrible pain or heartache your way, continue to hope that good and healing come from it. Hope can change your life."

Hope. I guess it's all we have in this life.

Day 23:

Morgan and I have been hiking buddies for a while now, but she's heading off for a different trek tomorrow, so we spent the day talking about life, love, and loss and enjoying each other's company. We were about three miles from the next hostel when the sky opened up and started to pour on us. Luckily we were walking through a little village and knocked on a random door hoping to wait it out inside.

The door opened and once the man saw us soaking wet he invited us inside, gave us towels and some warm sweaters, and offered us some tea. He did all this before we even introduced ourselves. Once we were all seated around his kitchen island enjoying our warm drinks, we went around sharing our names.

His name is Antonio, and he may be the nicest person I've ever met. He told us that he's always excited to invite people making the big pilgrimage into his home because they share the most incredible stories. As he was telling us one about a young man with only one leg who passed through just a day ago, the door opened.

Another man entered the house carrying a few bags of groceries and a dripping umbrella. Antonio introduced us to his husband Santiago, who immediately invited us to stay for dinner.

I've never experienced such kindness from strangers. It's been remarkable. Santi is a chef and Antonio owns a bakery down the street. They crafted a dish called bacalao al pil pil with freshly baked bread and wine. I never thought I'd like codfish, but I'd probably eat anything Santi served me.

Now, I'm curled up on their couch by the fireplace where they invited me to spend the night. I let Morgan take the guest bedroom they offered upstairs. The rain is still coming down pretty hard—thank God for the kindness of strangers.

Day 25:

I have walked 350 miles. I cannot believe it.

I feel like it was just yesterday I flew into San Sebastian and met Mae, Jonas, and Zahir at the hostel. I hope they're all doing well on their journeys. I wouldn't be here without them. This has turned into the most amazing adventure I didn't know I needed.

I wish Jax and I had had the chance to explore together. We always talked about saving up enough to fly all over the world. I still feel guilty that I can even enjoy life without him here.

I want so badly to believe that everything happens for a reason, but there could never be a good enough reason to have taken Jax from me so soon.

I burned the letter I wrote to him hoping that somehow that might release this pain from inside of me or maybe the words will reach him somehow. Now they're ash on the earth. Just like him.

Sometimes I hope there isn't a God because if there is, then he's the cruelest being in existence. Taking what we love away from us and watching us suffer. How could he be anything but cruel?

Chapter 59

Day 31:

A broken heart is mended when the soul gives it space to breathe. Everly underlines the words in blue ink. She flips to the inscription on the cover page: *Travel this path with an open mind and grateful heart. You will find meaning along the way. ~Antonio & Santi* Everly's heart swells, and she holds the book tightly against her chest, a token of their time together and their shared love of reading.

She packs up her morning snacks and gear. Looking at the long path ahead, she takes a deep breath and sets out, one step at a time. The persistent aching pain in her feet has lessened to a mild discomfort, and her muscles have now adapted to the weight of her pack. Her knees still crack when she bends too sharply, but Geoff taught her how to use the hiking poles he'd gifted to her.

Blooming wildflowers dance blissfully in the gentle breeze. Everly turns toward the array of bells chiming in the hills, watching cows migrate across the scenic pastures. The cowbells toll in a discordant symphony as the cows gather near an outcropping of trees. "Listen to the cows," Santi had told her. She laughed it off, thinking it was a joke, but seeing the swift-moving clouds, she reconsiders it as advice.

Miles from the nearest town in either direction, Everly ventures off the path, up into the hills where the cows now rest. The higher elevation tests her lungs as she presses onward. The wind picks up, tossing vibrant petals across her path. Fat droplets start to fall slowly around her.

Everly stiffens as she approaches a long-horned cow in her path. The giant creature looks at her with gentle eyes, lowering its head and allowing her to pass without conflict. She moves on, climbing up the steep hill to where a collection of boulders have fused into the mountainside over hundreds of years, creating an ideal shelter to wait out the rain.

The cave-like space winds back into the base of the mountain, providing a safe refuge as the rain begins pelting down. Everly sets her pack against the rough stone wall as she moves to the edge of the opening, just out of reach of the chilling rain. The bells continue to toll as the cows chew contentedly and nod gentle greetings to each other from the cover of the trees. She walks back to her pack to collect one of her empty water bottles when she hears a shuffling noise coming from deeper in the cave. Everly bolts upright, squinting into the darkness.

A shadow appears as she rummages for her headlamp, and she hurls the metal bottle full force, hitting her target. Grappling with her headlamp, she quickly shines the light on it. On *him.*

"Ouch," he says, laughing lightly and pressing a hand to his temple.

"Shit, you scared me!" Everly paces back to the opening to catch her breath before turning to face him. "I thought you were a bear or something." She presses her hand to her chest, calming her breathing.

"I'm impressed you stood your ground then. And you've got one hell of an arm there." He smirks, his hand still pressed to his head as he settles onto the ground.

"Are you okay? Here, let me look at it."

"It's all right. I've been through plenty worse."

"You're bleeding." She shifts his hand away, noticing rough calluses on his palm. Brushing back his dark-gold hair she sees a small leaking cut on the big goose egg that's starting to form just above his temple. "Let me dress this." Digging through her pack, she pulls out a compact first aid kit in search of Band-Aids and a cloth. "I'm sorry," she finally says.

"It's no problem. Just adds color to the story."

She smiles over at him. "I like that." He nods like he should be wearing a cowboy hat. "So, how long have you been up here? You're the first person I've seen all day."

"Only an hour or so. I saw some of the cows moving up this way, so I figured I'd follow them. Someone told me to—"

"Listen to the cows," she finished for him.

"Yes." He looks sidelong at her.

"A friend told me that before I headed out this way."

"No kidding? I met a couple the other day who helped me out with my pack when the strap broke. They invited me right in. Antonio and—"

"Santi." Everly grins at him.

"Looks like we got the same friends." He shifts upward, wincing at the pain.

Everly wets the cloth in the cold rain then drags her backpack over to him, allowing him to rest against it as she puts the cold compress on his head.

She hovers over him, trying not to meet his eyes, but his gaze wanders helplessly over her. Her hair's tied up in a golden mess with pieces sticking out every which way and bouncing in a sudden rush of wind. His eyes trail down her face, where her dark lashes create deep shadows in the blue of her eyes. Her fair, freckled nose and cheeks redden when she catches his eye for a moment. A slight dimple forms only on her left cheek as she tries to conceal a smile. His eyes trace the subtle curve of her pink lips and the smooth line of her neck.

"Okay." She clears her throat and shifts her hands. "That should help a little with the swelling. Here's a Band-Aid for the cut. She holds up two options with a smile. "Dinosaurs or pandas?" They both snicker.

"Let's go with dinosaurs."

"Good choice," she says as she brushes back a strand of hair again, tucking it behind his ear and placing the Band-Aid on the cut. She sits back on her heels, finally looking him in the eyes. Deep blue with fine lines etched by a lifetime of smiles. "I'm sorry," she blurts, holding her hand out. "I'm Everly."

His face expands into a beautiful vision of white teeth and smile lines hidden beneath a dusting of stubble. He reaches out, taking her small hand easily in his. "Hi, Everly. I'm Brooks."

Resting against the cool stone, they stare at the rain pounding against the ground outside. "So, what made you decide to pursue this trek?" Brooks turns to look at her. "It's not really a spur-of-the-moment decision for most sane people," he observes.

"Guess I'm insane then." His face pales, and she laughs at his blank stare. "It's all right." She nudges his shoulder. "Originally, I just wanted to get away from my life back home. I bought a one-way ticket, put everything I own in a storage unit, and flew out on the first flight anywhere in Spain. I didn't have a plan when I got here until I met some people my first night who were planning to make the trek. I'd never even heard of the Camino until a few weeks ago."

"Wow. That's incredible."

"Incredibly irrational, yes. But honestly it's exactly what I've needed." There's something about Brooks that makes her feel at peace, so she opens up more than usual. "The past couple years have been pretty rough, and every day that I'm out here I feel like it sews up old wounds."

Brooks growls an agreement. "I've been in a bad way these past few years, too. Nothing like some immense tragedy, deep depression, and a funeral to put a damper on life for a while."

"Wow."

"Sorry, that was dark."

"No, no. I just meant that it seems like the narrative of my life too." She pauses. "I'm sorry for your loss."

"Thank you. I'm sorry for yours as well." He looks up at her through a curtain of dark gold locks before raking them back from his eyes. He clears his throat and glances past her. "Looks like the storm's gonna pass soon. We should try to get to the next hostel before dark."

"Good idea." Everly pushes off the wall to stand, stretching her arms far above her head. Brooks leans against the wall, using his hiking poles to get himself up. "So, how far is th—" Everly's eyes widen. Brooks stands before her, fixing his prosthetic leg into its proper position.

He catches her glance and smiles. "Sorry, I should've told you earlier that I'm a robot."

Her cheeks burn. "I'm sorry." She turns away, busying her hands with her pack.

"Don't be sorry. I would've mentioned it sooner, but I haven't figured out a casual way of bringing it up, you know?" he chuckles. She nods, avoiding eye contact still, with him and the leg.

Once their packs are organized and ready to go, they set out towards the next town. Dissonant cowbells clang as the cows ramble further into the mountains. Everly takes the lead down the hill towards the trail, her shoes slipping in the slick pasture. "Watch your step," she says just as her feet slide out from under her. Brooks leans forward to grab her pack and brace her fall, but they slip in unison. He holds her pack against his chest as they slide furiously down the hill on his backpack.

A terrific shriek of fear and adrenaline escapes Everly as they blindly careen down the steep foothills of the mountain. Brooks kicks out, trying to catch onto something to slow them down. A final steep drop plops them down mere feet from the trail, and they lie there, laughing breathlessly.

Finally controlling his breath, Brooks manages to say, "Well, that was definitely the quickest way down." Everly shifts off his chest, clutching her aching stomach in a continuing fit of laughter. Brooks exhales a single laugh, enjoying the sweet squeaks that punctuate each laugh she lets out.

Regaining her composure, Everly looks over at Brooks, covered in mud and damp with the residual rain. As he sits amongst the wildflowers, she sees that he managed to keep her mud-free and dry on the ride down, their path clearly visible in the field of flowers above them. She looks up into his eyes as she drags her fingers in the mud. Brooks watches curiously as her smile broadens and she smears the thick mud across her cheeks, giggling as she shrugs at him. "I didn't want to feel left out."

His smile lines appear as he lets out a deep laugh that settles around her like a security blanket. "I'm sure glad you did it, because it was going to take every ounce of self-control not to do it myself." She scoffs at him, flicking mud that lands in the scruff on his jaw.

He gives her a warning glance as she prepares to do it again. But she sends the mud flying anyway, and he's quick to respond, flinging a decent handful at her. Everly collects herself, running towards the trail with another handful of mud as Brooks follows close behind, shielding himself with his pack. Everly lobs her mudpie straight at him, but it splats against the stone wall Brooks now hides behind.

Popping his head up, he slings his own glob of mud at her, and it splatters across her shoulder. Her infectious laughter feels comforting and warm, like home.

Lost for a moment in the joyous noise of her, he fails to duck as more mud splatters across his pack. Missiles fly in the unrelenting battle, inaccurate throws plopping against stones and trees.

"Truce! Truce!" Everly squeals as mud finally splatters across her neck and chin.

"All right, all right," he breathes, his stomach now aching from the incessant laughter. "I totally won that though."

"No way. It was a truce," Everly counters.

"You only called a truce because you were losing." She whips her head around, her ponytail flying around to whack her temple.

"I won't go so easy on you next time then."

"Oh, don't let this leg fool you. I'll still run laps around you." He smiles at her and can't help but notice the way her high cheekbones redden and darken her freckles.

⁂

Settling into a good pace, they follow the Camino's guiding yellow arrows towards the next hostel. "So," he starts. "Who are you?"

Everly stares at him, confused. "That's a pretty broad question."

"Yep." He smiles at her. "Lots of ways to answer. You could tell me your profession, your ancestry, your hopes and dreams, your experience, whatever you want. You are whoever you tell me you are."

"And what if I don't want to tell you who I am?"

"Then this'll be a long, awkward walk." He grins.

Everly rolls her eyes at him. "Fine."

The scenic path meanders over rolling hills, nothing between them and the horizon but the clouds. *Who are you?* The question lingers in the air between them as her mind starts to turn the rusted cogs of her memory. She shares the highlight reel of meeting her best friends and the time she spent working for Lucía in Seville, until she can't dance around the hardships that have plagued her the past few years.

"You know," she says, clearing her throat. "I haven't allowed myself to smile or laugh or even think about enjoying life for a long time." Brooks combs his hair back but remains quiet as his blue eyes lock on her profile. "There has been this unrelenting pain and loss in my life, and I thought I was building up barricades to protect myself, but I'm realizing now I've buried myself alive." She breathes in deeply.

"I feel like this trip, this ridiculous five-hundred-mile hike, has been clawing at the dirt that's suffocating me. Like each day and each person I meet is playing some role in tearing down my defenses." Everly glances up to see his eyes on her, the beginning of a smile resting on his face. "I guess I don't know who I am right now. But I'm trying to find out.

"Anyway…" She shakes off the feeling of vulnerability and returns his gaze. "Who are you, and why are you here?" Brooks smiles down at the ground, watching each of his steps. Everly follows his gaze, seeing the way his prosthetic leg drags slightly on the dirt path.

"Do you want to know what happened?" he offers.

She clears her throat, focusing her eyes down the long trail. "You don't have to tell me."

"I know." He smiles at her.

The wind and rustling flowers, along with the distant clanging of cowbells, are the only sounds between them for a few moments. Brooks inhales the earthy scent of the post-rain air before speaking. "I wish it was a more interesting story like fighting off a shark or saving someone tied to a train track. It was about five years ago." He tells the hazy story of a car wreck he can barely recall and the pain of waking up in the hospital.

"The first thing I remember after waking up was looking around me and seeing my family. But when I looked into my mom's eyes, I knew." Everly knew what he meant before he said it. "I knew my friend didn't make it." Taking a calming breath, he looks at the horizon, its permanence settling him.

"We grew up together. His family was my family, and my family was his. We pretended we were twins even though he's Native American and I'm a southern white boy. Obviously." He gestures to himself, and they both snicker.

He pauses, resting against a long stone wall. "I trust you." Shaking his head and brushing a hand along the scruff on his chin, he looks into her eyes. "There's something about you. I just… I don't know." Everly can feel his gaze settle around her like sunshine.

"Anyway," he continues. "After his funeral I was in a *really* low place. I refused to leave my house for months, not that the leg really helped. I didn't work, barely ate, couldn't sleep. There were times when I wished it had been me instead.

"Then his dad came over one day, and I will remember this for the rest of my life. He dragged me out of my bed. Literally. He threw me over his shoulder and carried me outside to this big oak tree we used to climb as kids.

"He set me down against the tree, looked me in the eyes, and told me that when he named his son, it was for a reason. The name means 'warrior of life.'

"Wow," Everly breathes out, listening intently.

"At first I didn't know why he was telling me all this, but then he explained that he would want me to carry on living for him, to be a warrior of life for him."

Her heart catches, and the tears she didn't know were there finally slide down her cheeks.

"He said that he deserves us to live life to honor him, not refuse to live because of losing him." He huffs a laugh at the memory. "Then he kissed me on the forehead, dropped my prosthesis on the ground next to me, and walked away.

"I sat against that tree for over an hour debating whether or not to just drag myself across the lawn. But I really thought about what he said. That we should be living to honor him. So I grabbed the prosthesis, hauled myself up against the tree, and fought for my first steps since the accident.

"I lost count of how many times I fell. I almost gave up so many times, but I knew that he was looking down on me, cheering me on. So I did it. For him."

Everly shakes her head, the tears scattering. "What was his name?"

"Calian."

Everly collapses into the stranger beside her, her arms wrapping around his strong shoulders and pack as she quietly sobs against him. "Thank you for sharing that." After a moment of shock, Brooks embraces her in a hug that begins to mend the deep wounds that have refused to heal.

⁕

The power of human touch to restore balance and comfort is unmatched by anything else. A hug is simply an immense collection of emotions too powerful to be spoken; it must be felt.

Chapter 60

The sun gently nestles into the mountain's shoulder like the sleepy head of a child, providing just enough light to see the hostel up ahead. They walk the last mile in comfortable silence. Nothing needs to be said—each of them exists in the calm of the present moment.

Brooks finally breaks the silence as they approach the stone structure. "I can't wait for the shower."

"I know, me too," Everly agrees.

Brooks holds the door open for her. "I meant for you. You're gross." She shoves his shoulder as she walks past, hiding her smile. The stone walls retain the warmth of the fireplace, inviting them to relax and warm up. Everly looks around the corner for someone to welcome them. No one's around, but laughter emanates from somewhere down the hall, so she follows the sound.

Stepping into the room she waits shyly for someone to notice her presence when suddenly a booming voice calls out, "¡Hola! Welcome our new friends." The room erupts in cheers of different dialects, and a beautifully genuine smile approaches her. "Hello, my friends. Welcome to our home." He takes her hands in his as he leads her into the room of people. "This is my wife Isabella, and I am Mateo. We are happy your journey has led you here."

Brooks walks in behind them, soaking in the noticeable joy flowing through the room. Everly accepts Isabella's outstretched hand in hers. "Hi, my name's Everly." She turns, trying to make eye contact with Brooks, but he's distracted by the other smiling faces. "This is Brooks. Do you have space for two tonight?"

Mateo's voice booms again, "Of course! Come in, relax…" He looks them up and down. "...shower, then join us this evening for a small fiesta." Everly's cheeks brighten with embarrassment as Isabella leads her and Brooks to their bunks, then directly to the showers.

After a long and badly needed shower, Everly changes into her only dress. The fabric flows gracefully along her curves, the cotton cinching perfectly at her waist. Her sore feet carry her towards the laughter and music down the hall. Peeking through the entryway, she spots Brooks dancing across the open floor with Isabella.

Standing comfortably in the shadows, Everly jumps when a voice whispers in her ear. "May I have this dance?" Mateo grins widely as Everly curls in on herself. Gently pulling her hand into his, he looks deeply into her eyes and her muscles lose their nervous tension. His presence feels like salve on a burn, soothing and healing. "Come." Everly has never met someone who exudes such kindness. If joy were a tangible thing, it would be Mateo's smile.

Cheers ring through the room as new couples join them on the dance floor. The music picks up in quick, rhythmic strums, and they're off. Swinging, clapping, laughing, tripping. Mateo swings Everly around effortlessly; there's no time for her to stiffen up.

The graceful movements grow in intensity until both Brooks and Mateo spin their partners across the dance floor and into the other's arms. Everly falls back into Brooks as he dips her, one hand caressing her golden hair and the other comfortingly strong around her waist. They stay there for a second longer than the beat, captivated by each other's eyes.

Pulled to her feet, Everly stands with her face a breath's distance from his neck. She imagines herself leaning into him, the perfect height for her cheek to rest against that smooth skin, for his chin to rest atop her head, his arms long and strong, safe and secure around her.

The music pools in rich tones, quickening the tempo. Brooks leads her across the floor, her feet moving without thinking until her nerves catch up with her. She stumbles as she steps on his foot, pushing back from him. "I'm so sorry," she blurts out.

"It's okay, I didn't feel a thing," he jokes, lifting up his prosthesis slightly.

Everly pales. "Do you want a drink? I'm gonna grab a drink." Turning on her heel, she pours a generous glass of wine for herself, downing a few gulps before Brooks can accept her offer.

The music serenades them through the night as Everly sits wrapped in a blanket staring up at the stars and nursing a bottle of wine. The sweet melodies drift on the night air like a message in a bottle floating through open water. Stoic mountains watch over the little town as it sleeps, their line of defense unbreakable.

Everly looks up at the sound of the stiff wooden door groaning. Brooks steps out into the night, the glow of the moon reflecting in his eyes. "Hey." He steps towards her. "Can I sit?" Everly scooches over on the bench. He inhales deeply, breathing in the cool night air.

"I—"

"I have to tell you something," she blurts out, cutting him off. He grins at her urgency.

"Okay."

"I… uh…" She leans forward, her hands cupping her face. "I think I know what happened to you." She pauses. "I mean, who did it to you." Turning her face towards him, she sees his smirk hasn't vanished. "Calian." She starts again. "Calian was the name of Grace's older brother." She looks to him for a response, a sign of recognition, anything. "Which means you were the other person in the car when—" She chokes on the words, her hands shaking as they rake through her hair.

"Everly." He places a comforting hand on her knee. "It's okay." The moments of silence linger between them. "It's okay. I know what happened, and it's okay."

Everly's walls crumble as she folds forward sobbing, and without hesitation Brooks embraces her trembling body. "Shh, it's okay." He comforts her, his hand rubbing circles along her back and tucking the loose strands of hair behind her ears. "Grace told me what happened when she found out. That's why I'm here." Everly looks up at him through teary eyes. "I'm here to forgive him," he says finally.

"Me too," she cries out.

Chapter 61

Sitting back against the exterior wall of the hostel, Everly wipes away the last lingering tear on her cheek. She looks up at Brooks, the moonlight silvering his features. Sensing her gaze, he looks down at her.

"Did you know who I was this entire time?" she asks.

"No. At first I just thought you were a beautiful whack-job who was going to beat me to death with a water bottle." They laugh in sync, and Everly glances at his still-swollen temple.

"Yeah, sorry about that."

"All good. Definitely broke the ice," he chuckles. "I started to piece it together on our walk. I'd never met anyone named Everly before, so I thought it was just a coincidence until you mentioned your time with Lucía Morales." Everly looks at him, confused.

A small dimple appears in the stubble on his cheek as he smiles and hands her something. Her fingers close over the aged leather as she delicately traces the etched lettering of the familiar title. Brooks gazes at her as she lifts the front cover, reading the inscription on the flyleaf.

My dearest Everly,

Hope in a hopeless world can change your life forever. So, have hope and know that there is always potential in the hardest of times. There is always potential in heartbreak.

El amor lo conquista todo.

Con cariño,

Lucía Morales

"*Love conquers all,*" she translates aloud. Tears brim over her lashes. "How—" she starts, choking on a sad laugh.

"I found it in a stack of donated books," he starts. "It kind of spoke to me, you know." He watches her finger move over the inscription. Clearing his throat, he continues. "I'm sorry I marked it up a little. There were just some things in it that I needed to remember."

She thumbs through the thick pages of words she's never read. Blue ink underlines poetic phrases of wisdom and grace, and her heart aches with regret.

"I never read a single word of this," she says almost to herself.

"Why not?" he asks.

She smiles sadly, looking up at the moon that shines its silver light across the pages. "I never wanted to be heartbroken, I guess. I mean, *The Potential of Heartbreak* really just means that whenever you choose to love someone or something there's a chance of getting your heart broken." She pauses. "Who wants to think about that?"

"I don't think that's what it means at all," he counters. She looks up at him. "Once you read the book you realize that, yes, to love and be loved by someone has the potential of hurting you, but more than that, each heartbreak or painful experience has the potential to push you towards the person you're meant to be with." He leans over, flipping to the flyleaf again. "She even wrote it in her message to you. 'There is always potential in heartbreak.'"

Everly snickers at herself. "Wow," she laughs aloud. "I love that crazy woman."

"Yeah, she's an amazing writer."

Everly sits up straight. "What do you mean?"

Brooks looks at her, confused, before taking the book and flipping the cover closed. He runs his fingers over the faded letters of the author's name: *Lucy Reeds.*

"Lucía Morales. That's her pseudonym, her writing name. It's pretty clever actually," he chuckles, handing it back to her.

Everly smiles, looking up into the cloudless sky, and laughs.

Chapter 62

Everly groans, turning away from the morning light streaming in through the frosted window. "Ugh." She shifts, pulling the covers over her face when a soft chuckle startles her.

Flinging the covers back, she looks down from the top bunk to see Brooks smirking over the rim of his coffee mug, the steam dancing in the morning light. "Morning, sunshine," he teases. "How'd you sleep?"

She collapses back dramatically. "Fabulous. You?"

"Like a brick. Mateo and Isabella set up a whole breakfast spread in the main house and brewed fresh coffee for everyone. I brought you a mug." He holds the steaming liquid out to her. Everly shoots up, seizing the mug, and holds it against her lips to warm up her body and breathe in the aromatic comfort.

"You're a godsend," she says in between sips.

"I figured you could use it after last night." His cheek dimples with a grin. "Lots of emotions and information and wine."

Her fingers massage her temple gently. "Yes. Lots of each of those."

"We should grab some breakfast before heading out. No rush though." He smiles at her. His wild hair glows like a halo, illuminated by the brightening sun as he walks away.

"Good morning, Everly." A heavy French accent greets her as she steps into the dining room. Louis leans in to kiss her on both cheeks as he pours more coffee into her cup. His salt and pepper scruff grazes her skin lightly.

"Bonjour, Louis," she smiles up at him. His hooded eyes squint and his face contours with the permanent smile lines he proudly displays. "As-tu bien dormi?"

Everly glances around her, looking for anyone who might know what he just said to her. "Uhhh…"

His smile broadens as he senses her panic. "Zat is okay. Our lessons were short last night. How did you sleep?"

"Oh, I slept well. Thank you." Everly looks past him to the elaborate spread on the table. Louis guides her into the room, inviting her to grab a plate.

Before digging in, Everly greets each person, trying her best to respectfully emulate their native tongue. "Guten morgen, Lena. God morgon, Anders. Sabba elkhir, Hajar. Ohayo, Tomoyo." Each of them greets her with a reassuring hug, like they've been friends for years. The incredible bond of travelers collapses an average social timeline.

"Mateo, Isabella." Everly reaches out to embrace each of them. "This has been so lovely. Thank you for making us feel at home."

"My girl, you make this house feel like home." Isabella presses her lips to Everly's cheek, leaving a red lipstick print behind.

Mateo reaches out to grab her hand before she turns away. "Allow this journey to change your life, my dear. You deserve the happiness it will provide you." He releases her hand and watches with a smile as she and Brooks walk out into the sunshine of the new day.

⁕

"There it is," Brooks calls to her from the hilltop. "We're almost there."

Everly pushes her hiking poles hard against the worn path as she makes her way the last few yards up the hill, panting steadily. "It's beautiful," she manages to say between breaths.

"Yes, it is." Brooks stares out at the towering cathedral before setting his gaze back on Everly.

"What are you waiting for, lazy? Let's go!" She smacks her backpack into his shoulder before taking off down the trail.

"Making fun of the cripple, I see," he calls after her, a giant grin across his face.

"Excuses, excuses," she teases.

⁂

The sound of eager voices and hundreds of feet shuffling along the cobblestones tells them they're close. Everly looks through the busy press of pilgrims and residents. "Is that…" Brooks follows her gaze. "Morgan!" she calls out over the animated voices around her. The girl turns, searching the crowd until her green eyes land on Everly, and she sets out in a full sprint.

Everly opens her arms and rushes only a few feet before they collide together with gleeful squeals. "I thought you'd be off on another adventure already." She pulls back, looking into the girl's teary eyes. "Oh, what's wrong?" She cups Morgan's face in her palms.

"I'm just really happy to see you again." She pulls Everly back into her arms. Looking over her shoulder she sees Brooks standing a few feet away, giving them space to talk. "Oh!" She shifts in Everly's arms. "Who's the handsome cowboy?"

Everly turns to see Brooks looking off into the distance, trying to pretend he didn't hear her words and hiding his smile. "Morgan, this is Brooks. Brooks, this is Morgan. She was my hiking buddy for a good chunk of this trip. She's incredible."

"Hi, Brooks, it's nice to meet you."

He takes her hand in his for a comforting handshake. "The pleasure's mine, Morgan."

"Wow, a gentleman." Morgan bumps into Everly with her hip. "Oh!" she blurts out suddenly. "Geoff said he made it here two days ago. We should see if he's still in town." Everly nods her agreement.

"Everly?" someone calls behind them. Brooks sees the lanky Viking and smiling Indian walking towards them.

"Jonas! Zahir!" She rushes to give them each hugs. "How did I beat you here?"

"Hey, hey," Zahir protests. "We took the longer route and still made it here the same day as you," he teases. "It's great to see you, Everly."

"You too, Z." Morgan comes to stand by her right side, Brooks on her left. "Jonas, Zahir, this is Morgan and this is Brooks."

"Great to meet you both," Jonas says. They exchange handshakes and pleasantries, then Everly cuts into their conversation.

"Shall we?"

"We shall," Morgan replies, linking her arm in Everly's and skipping towards the cathedral that towers over them.

Santiago de Compostela. The end of their journey.

⁜

Before stepping into the cathedral, I stopped and watched the rest of my friends enter in silent awe. The last few steps into this place would mark the end of my journey.

I was frozen in place, consumed by the thoughts of what comes next. What does life look like after I finish this journey that's guided me to exceptional places, to remarkable people, and through the all-consuming guilt that has festered within me?

It wasn't until I felt Brooks intertwining his fingers in mine, his demeanor utterly patient and calming, that I took a step into that cathedral. A step towards my new life of accepting my past and living every day knowing that hope in a hopeless world can change your life forever and that love really does conquer all.

Chapter 63

The charms sing the same tune as they had so many years before, and the heavy wooden door still seals in the sweet smell of aged flowers and herbs. Valencia red roses cinched with thyme. Dried bundles still decorate the ceiling, illuminated by streaks of sunlight.

Walking into the bookshop feels like no time has passed at all. It almost feels as though life could be as simple as it once was.

Everly walks in, taking in the scent, the familiarity, the memories of this place. She settles into her favorite armchair, inviting Brooks to settle into the soft cushions of the green vintage couch she and Jocelyn had found all those years ago. But he sets his pack down beside the sofa, taking up his book and favorite blue pen before meandering through the narrow aisles, feeling guided by a knowing breeze.

The door chimes as Lucía pushes against its rusting hinges. Her eyes shift from her feet to the beautifully grown woman sitting in her armchair. "Mi amor!" She shuffles hurriedly towards Everly, embracing her and resting her cheek against her neck. "My sweet girl, how I've missed you." Everly's heart aches with happiness, Lucía's voice like an ancient lullaby she's longed to hear again.

"I've missed you so much." She squeezes tighter before releasing her.

They look deeply into one another as they hold hands, seeing how life has changed them over the years. Each deep line on Lucía's face shares the story of a happy life. Her eyes glossy and lightening with age. Her beautiful white hair tied back in a long braid with a single red rose intertwined.

Lucía scans over Everly, seeing a strong woman where there once stood a beautifully naive girl. She has settled into herself, grown into her curves, and embraced her strength. She exudes the power of Athena and the beautiful grace of

Aphrodite. "*Bella.* My beautiful girl!" She squeezes her fingers before releasing them. "Come in," she says as she waddles back into the stacks. "I have something for you." The aging floorboards creak as she shuffles across them towards her favorite hidden room.

A soft noise escapes her as she sees the young man studying the spines of her books. He turns to her, dropping the book in his hand. "I'm so sorry." He bends to pick up the book. "I didn't mean to intrude."

Everly races over. "Lucía, this is Brooks," she states.

"I've heard great things about you." He offers a hand as she wobbles down the few steps into the room. Her light eyes scroll over him, her face unreadable. Finally, she brings her frail fingers to rest along his jaw, her eyes creasing as she smiles. Brooks smiles back, something urging him to lean into her gentle touch.

Looking down, he watches as she lifts the book from his palms, her hand moving from his face to glide along the etched letters and loved pages.

His bright eyes move from Lucía's to Everly's before he smiles at each of them and moves toward the arched doorway to give them the room. Everly steps into the room with her, staring at the titles stacked against the walls from floor to ceiling. Lucía holds out the book with shaky hands and rests it in Everly's open palms, her eyes reading Everly's face before squinting shut with a knowing smile. "You never read my book, did you?" she chuckles.

Everly's fingers trace the title of the book she's pushed around for years, the distressed edges and faded lettering painting a picture of neglect. "No." She breathes out. "I didn't."

"But now you've found it." Lucía's eyes rest happily on Everly's face, admiring her growth.

"Found what?"

"The potential of heartbreak." She shakes her head, trying to clarify her thoughts. "The potential in being heartbroken. The good that comes after." She smiles. "You found it. You found *him*."

Chapter 64

A summer breeze kisses the freckled skin of Everly's exposed shoulders and carries the sweet smell of roses with it. She rests on her front steps beside Grace looking out over the yard. Caleb walks through the grass with Kai balanced on his shoulders, his little giggle fueling their endless love for him.

A car rumbles down the long driveway. "Auntie Joce!" Kai squeals, fighting to get down from his dad's shoulders.

"Kai, don't run near the car," Grace calls out to him. "They'll be right out, stinker." Grace shakes her head at Everly.

Another youthful squeal sounds as a little girl toddles across the lawn. "Get over here," he calls out as he picks her up over his head and brings her down in an ambush of kisses. Brooks cuddles his little girl in his arms, carrying her towards the car that's just parked.

Everly's heart soars at the sight of her little family. Grace squeezes her hand lightly, and she helps pull her to her feet. Arm in arm they walk down the stone pathway to greet their friends.

Joyful screams ring out as Kai flies into Jocelyn's arms. "Oh my goodness! You gotta stop feeding this chunker, he's too grown up! Feel how heavy," she says, passing him over to her husband.

Kai squeals, "Nooo!" He giggles uncontrollably as David tickles his round belly. "Not the tickle monster!"

"I'm the tickle monster!" David growls before setting him back down.

"Now, where's my sweet girl?" Jocelyn moves around the car to see Brooks carrying his daughter. She squirms and breathes excitedly when she sees Jocelyn, holding out her arms to embrace her.

Her round rosy cheeks nuzzle against Jocelyn's neck, hiding under her long dark hair. "Oh, my sweet girl. You are too cute!" Her voice squeaks the way everyone's does when they talk to babies. "Where's your mama?" She sways back and forth, kissing her soft cheeks.

"Hey, stranger!" Everly calls out.

Jocelyn hands off the baby to Brooks before skipping over to the pair and embracing them. She crouches down, holding the sides of Grace's distended belly. "Hey, sweet boy, Auntie Joce here. I can't wait to meet you in a couple of weeks. We're gonna have so much fun, I promise." She looks up at Grace and Everly snickering down at her. "And you'll have a new friend to play with in a couple months, too." She looks up at Grace and Everly who stand gaping at her.

"Are you serious?" Everly whispers.

She nods, joyful tears pooling in her eyes as she stands up to hug them.

"I'm so happy for you, Joce," she sobs blissfully against her neck. "David, get your butt over here!" Everly yells, collecting him in their hug.

The joy is overwhelming as everyone hugs and laughs and cries together. Jocelyn settles into David's arms, looking around her circle of friends. "When did we grow up?" She wonders with a chuckle.

⁂

Everly looks up at Brooks as she nestles beside him. A lock of golden hair falls over his dark brow and lashes. Their sleepy miracle curls up against her daddy's neck. Her light blue eyes flutter with promises of sleep as she sucks her thumb. A perfect mix of all the strength and beauty in both Brooks and Everly.

He is everything she's ever wanted and everything she never knew she needed. An acknowledgement that all you seek and all you deserve exist somewhere.

In a world of heartache, pain, devastation, and loss, remember to hope. Because hope in a hopeless world can change your life forever. So, have hope and know that there is always potential in heartbreak.

My heartbreak has led me to him. To the man I never thought existed. And to the family I never imagined I'd have. To her. To my baby girl. *Lucy.*

⁂

Dear Lucy,

This morning I woke up to you and daddy dancing around the kitchen. I can't believe how much you've grown. You turned 4 this week. Standing on his feet you giggled and squealed your little head off. We spent the morning singing along to your favorite songs and making pancakes.

You are such a gift to me.

I've been thinking about when you were just a concept in my mind. A dream. But then I fell in love with your daddy and we shared our dream of you together.

You make me believe in magic, my sweet girl.

I'm writing this letter to give to you on your 18th birthday, when you're all grown up and eager to live your own life.

This is a story of love and tragedy and hope. This is The Potential of Heartbreak.

THE END

Dear Reader,

I never really intended to write this book. It started as journal entries about real-life events, but then I started adding different names and writing out what I wished had happened, or more interesting outcomes, and poof, *it started to turn into a book.*

As you read this book I hope you see that the title has so many interpretations. The one I want to really resonate with you is that with each heartbreak, hardship, or misfortune, there is something positive that can come out of it. You may not be able to see it at first, or after the first year, or even a decade, but life has a funny way of putting things in your path you didn't realize you needed.

A friend said to me once, "Not everything happens for a reason, but you can find reason in everything."

I hope this book has made you laugh and smile and cry. I hope it broke your heart but showed you how to put it back together. I hope that you go purposefully seek out who you are and surround yourself with people who truly love and deserve you.

As a kind stranger once told Everly, "It's not what you do that matters. It's what you believe. It may be the hardest thing you do in life, but when life brings terrible challenges or heartache your way, know that there is potential for good and healing on the other side of that pain. That little bit of hope will change your life."

I love you all. Thank you for reading.

Emma

About the Book

To learn more about the writing process, the real-life inspirations and events that were included, and the dream that sparked the main idea for *The Potential of Heartbreak,* go to **LiveBetterForYourself.com** to view related blog posts.

Or follow on social media:

- Book Instagram: **@the_potential_of_heartbreak**
- Personal Instagram: **@17ewagner**

Mental Health Resources

You deserve to feel safe and supported in whatever you are dealing with. Here are some resources to utilize if you need help.* Please reach out to a medical professional, as these are only suggested resources.

The website below addresses mental health topics such as:

- Anxiety Disorders
- Autism Spectrum Disorder
- Borderline PErsonality Disorder
- Eating Disorders
- Post-Traumatic Stress Disorder
- Suicide Prevention
- Attention-Deficit/Hyperactivity Disorder
- Bipolar Disorder
- Depression
- And more

https://www.nimh.nih.gov/

*Based within the United States.

Made in the USA
Middletown, DE
06 November 2023

42088765R00172